Books by Sheldon Siegel

FELONY MURDER RULE

FELONY MURDER RULE

Sheldon Siegel

Sheldon M. Siegel, Inc.
www.sheldonsiegel.com

ISBN: 978-0-9913912-9-5
Ebook ISBN: 978-0-9913912-8-8

In loving memory of Charlotte Siegel
July 16, 1928 – March 9, 2016

1
"I NEED YOUR HELP"

The waif-thin woman eyed me nervously from the creaky swivel chair opposite my gunmetal gray desk. Melinda Nguyen tugged at her shoulder-length black hair flecked with silver and spoke to me in a tense whisper. "I need your help, Mr. Daley."

When you're the co-head of the Felony Division of the San Francisco Public Defender's Office, *everybody* needs your help.

I took a sip of room-temperature Diet Dr Pepper from a can I'd bought on my own dime. The Great Recession had nearly wiped out the rest of the U.S. economy, but business was still brisk at the P.D.'s Office. Our caseloads were heavier than ever, but our overextended budget left little room for even modest amenities like free sodas. Or, for that matter, air conditioning. The latter was especially unfortunate because summer weather had arrived in San Francisco right on schedule—on the first day of fall. At eight a.m. on Thursday, September twenty-first, the sunshine was fighting a losing battle to find its way through my dirt-encrusted window, and it was almost ninety degrees inside my ten-by-twelve-foot office. I'd been at my desk for almost two hours, and I was late for a staff meeting. Life at the P.D.'s Office in the new millennium was strikingly similar to the old one.

"Ms. Nguyen—,"

"It's Melinda, Mr. Daley."

Fine. "And I'm Mike."

"Okay."

She was dressed in a plain white blouse from the racks at Target. She wore no makeup. Her delicate features suggested that she could have been in her twenties, but the worry lines on her forehead and the tic at the corner of her mouth indicated that she was older. Her eyes were as pale blue as the San Francisco sky, hinting that someone in her ancestral chain may have come from somewhere other than her native Vietnam.

She took a deep breath and spoke to me in a hushed tone. "My son needs a lawyer."

My lungs filled with stale air as I looked around at the sagging bookcases and mismatched file cabinets in the office where I'd worked for eighteen months. My digs were an upgrade from my first stint at the P.D.'s Office two decades earlier, when we were still housed at the old Hall of Justice in a musty bullpen with leaky windows, spotty plumbing, and inadequate ventilation. During the heady economic times of the late nineties, we moved a block south into a remodeled cement bunker on Seventh Street with a labyrinth of narrow hallways and the ambiance of an auto repair shop. A decade and a half of deferred maintenance later, it, too, had leaky windows, spotty plumbing, and inadequate ventilation. And I was lucky—I had a window and I didn't have to share my office with a Deputy P.D.

"What's your son's name?" I asked.

"Thomas Nguyen."

Got it. He was about to go on trial for first degree murder in connection with a botched armed robbery at a liquor store in the Tenderloin. The case was generating more buzz than usual because Thomas hadn't entered the store or fired a shot. The victim was his accomplice, a small-time drug dealer named Duc Tho, who had gone inside and allegedly flashed a Saturday Night Special. The shopkeeper pulled out a Bushmaster AR-15 semiautomatic assault rifle—purchased legally in Nevada—and filled Tho's chest with bullets—right in front of the cash register in view of the security camera. He calmly called the cops, who arrested Nguyen without incident as he was sitting in the car. Nguyen claimed he didn't know that Tho had a gun.

You might think the owner of the store would have been charged with a crime, but SFPD decided he'd acted in self-defense—not an entirely unreasonable conclusion in the circumstances—and he walked away scot-free. My respected colleagues at the D.A.'s Office figured they had to charge somebody with something. After all, Duc Tho was still quite dead. Instead of accusing Nguyen of conspiracy or attempted robbery, they charged him with first degree murder under California's so-called "felony murder rule," which says you can be convicted of murder if someone—even a fellow perpetrator—is killed during the course of a felony. Ordinarily, the rule doesn't apply if the fatal shots are fired by somebody other than one of the perps—like, say, a shopkeeper who is being robbed. Then again, it isn't a newsflash that the hardworking professionals at the D.A.'s Office occasionally overcharge and negotiate deals for lesser offenses. Coincidentally, this seems to happen more frequently during election years. In any event, that's how a senior at Galileo High who was sitting in a beat-up Honda and listening to Kanye West on his iPhone ended up facing twenty-five to life. The workings of the criminal justice system in the new millennium were also strikingly similar to the old one.

"I thought Sandra Tran was representing your son," I said.

"Not anymore."

Sandy Tran had started at the P.D.'s Office shortly before I'd left. She went into private practice after a decade as a Deputy Public Defender. She was a savvy legal tactician and a gifted trial lawyer who represented members of San Francisco's Vietnamese gangs. "She couldn't have quit four days before trial. That would have violated the California Rules of Professional Conduct." And it would have been a *really* crappy thing to do.

"Thomas fired her last night. She wanted him to accept a plea bargain."

"That's between your son and Ms. Tran." It wasn't the first time that a client had disagreed with his attorney on the eve of trial. It was also conceivable that Sandy had gotten herself fired for tactical reasons. Maybe she thought the case was a loser or she was trying to buy time. Over the course of my long and occasionally illustrious career, I'd invoked a similar strategy from time to time. It rarely changed the ultimate outcome of the case, but it gummed up the wheels of justice for a few months. Sometimes, that's the best you can do. "Ms. Tran will arrange for a new attorney for your son."

"She's talking to the judge right now."

"They'll work it out." They had no choice, and it wasn't my problem—yet. I glanced at my watch. "I'm due in a meeting. Why did you want to see me?"

"Thomas needs a new lawyer."

Here we go. "Putting aside the question of whether it was a good idea for your son to fire his attorney on the eve of trial, our office isn't allowed to take his case just because he was unhappy with his lawyer. We only represent defendants with demonstrated financial need."

After a year and a half back in the saddle at the P.D.'s Office, bureaucrat-speak was flowing naturally again.

"I have no money, Mr. Daley. I paid everything I had to Ms. Tran. For the last two months, she hasn't charged us."

"If you want to request our services, you'll need to complete some paperwork, talk to one of my colleagues, and provide financial information. Are you employed?"

"I clean apartments when I can. I have a bad back."

"Any money in the bank?" I didn't enjoy asking strangers about their finances, but it was my job.

"About four hundred dollars."

It would have paid for a couple of hours with a private

lawyer. I didn't ask how she managed to pay her rent—*if* she had an apartment. "I'll set up a meeting with one of our attorneys. If you meet our requirements, we'll petition the judge to let us represent your son. It'll take a day or two."

"Thomas's trial starts on Monday."

"I'm sure that Ms. Tran has already requested a delay."

"What if the judge says no?"

Your kid is screwed. "If we're appointed, we'll ask for a continuance."

"I was hoping you might be willing to handle Thomas's case yourself."

I used to be a pretty soft touch when I was in private practice. Nowadays, it was easier to say no. I wasn't unsympathetic, but my plate was overflowing with the mundane—and essential—administrative tasks of my job. "Until the judge authorizes our office to represent your son, I'm not allowed to give you legal advice. In fact, I'm not supposed to talk to you. Even if we're appointed, I don't have time to do trial work."

"I was hoping you'd make an exception. I've read about you. The *State Bar Journal* said you were one of the best Public Defenders in California."

That was almost a quarter of a century ago. Since then, I'd gotten a few high-profile acquittals between countless convictions and plea bargains. A losing record comes with the territory when you represent criminals for a living. I went to law school after a brief and undistinguished career as a priest. I joined the P.D.'s Office hoping to change the world—or at least help a few people like Thomas Nguyen. Things didn't work out exactly as I'd planned, although I did meet my then future- and now ex-wife, Rosita Fernandez, who was the co-head of the Felony Division. She was sitting two doors down the hall.

I reverted to old habits and invoked my confession voice.

"If your son qualifies for our services, I'll assign one of our best attorneys to his case."

"Would you be willing to meet him?"

"It would be more productive to spend time with his new lawyer."

Her tic became more pronounced. "Thomas was going to graduate near the top of his class at Galileo. He was working part-time and saving money to go to State. He didn't even go inside the liquor store."

"I'm sure Ms. Tran explained that you can be charged with murder if someone is killed during a felony—even if you don't fire a shot."

"It isn't right."

"It's still the law."

Her voice filled with desperation. "I'm begging you to make an exception, Mr. Daley."

"I can't."

"Yes, you can. And you should."

"Why?"

"It's personal." Her eyes darted. "Would you mind if I close your door?"

"Why don't you leave it open and tell me what this is about."

"I knew your brother."

My younger brother was a former cop who now worked as a private investigator. "How do you know Pete?"

"I knew your *older* brother."

What the hell? "Tommy died in a plane crash in Vietnam almost forty years ago."

"He died in Vietnam, but *not* in a plane crash."

2
"WHEN WAS THIS TAKEN?"

My door was now closed. "My brother's plane went down in 1974," I said. "The U.S. Army found the wreckage in the North China Sea. They told us that there were no survivors."

Melinda shook her head. "They were wrong. He ejected."

"They sent a search party."

"They didn't know where to look. Our village had one dirt road. My mother found him in a tree. He had a broken leg and two broken arms. We didn't have a doctor. The nearest hospital was fifty miles away."

"Why didn't she turn him over to the police?"

"There weren't any."

"What about the North Vietnamese Army?"

"They would have killed him. It was a miracle that he survived. My grandmother was a midwife. She and my mother helped him recover. They weren't savages, Mr. Daley. They wanted the war to end, too."

The grainy memories came rushing back. Tommy's chiseled shoulders and charismatic smile. Playing catch behind our house at 23rd and Kirkham in the foggy Sunset District. Tommy heaving the ball into the stands after scoring the winning touchdown in his last game at Cal. His determined expression as he boarded the plane taking him eight thousand miles from home to fight a war that most Americans— including me—no longer supported. The knock on our door when the uniforms came to inform us that his plane had gone down. My father's depression. My mother's despair. The futile bureaucratic wrangling to find out what had happened. And now—almost four decades later—the stranger sitting in front of me purported to know.

"When did he die?"

"1978. Jungle fever."

I fought to get my bearings. My parents had gone to their graves without answers. I'd been waiting almost forty years for closure. I thought I would have felt a sense of relief, but there were too many unanswered questions, and I didn't know if the stranger sitting in my office was telling the truth. "Why didn't he contact us after the war?"

"There were no cell phones. We had very little communication with the outside world."

"I want to talk to your mother."

"She died when I was a baby."

I drummed my fingers on my desk. "When were you born?"

"1976."

"You weren't alive when my brother's plane went down, and you were only two when he died—if your story is true. How do you know about this?"

"My uncle told me everything. He took care of me after my mother died. We came here in 1984 when I was eight. He died of lung cancer when I was sixteen."

"Who looked after you when he died?"

"I did."

Fair enough. "How did you get here?"

"We went to Thailand on a fishing boat. My uncle got us onto a tanker to Guam. We ended up on a cargo ship to the U.S. It was a miracle that we made it." She said she had no relatives in Vietnam. "Thomas is my only family. I don't want to lose him."

It was going to be difficult—if not impossible—to corroborate her story. I e-mailed my secretary to cancel our staff meeting. I leaned forward. "You've been in the U.S. for almost thirty years. Why didn't you contact me?"

"I was afraid you would think I was looking for money or attention. I'm sorry."

"Not as sorry as I am. My parents died without knowing what happened to Tommy."

She clenched her fists. "I came here illegally. I was scared of being deported."

"I can have your immigration file re-opened."

"I had to take a chance. My son needs a lawyer. I didn't know where else to turn."

"How did you know that I'm Tommy's brother?"

"My uncle knew your name. Your brother told him that if he made it to the U.S. and got into trouble, he should try to find you."

"I became a lawyer after Tommy died."

"He said that you're really smart."

Not *that* smart. "Are you a U.S. citizen?"

"Yes. I became a citizen after I married Thomas's father."

"How old were you when you got married?"

"Seventeen. My husband was a Vietnamese-American named Danny Nguyen. He was born here. Danny died in a motorcycle accident when Thomas was a baby."

We could verify that part of her story. "I'm going to ask you some questions. If any of your answers are wrong, your son isn't the only one who will need a lawyer." I started with an easy one. "What was my brother's full name?"

"Thomas James Charles Daley, Jr."

Correct. "When was he born?"

"November 25, 1953, at St. Francis Hospital."

Two for two. "Where did he go to school?"

"Grammar school at St. Peter's. High school at St. Ignatius. College at Cal. He was the starting quarterback before he joined the Marines."

"What number did he wear at Cal?"

"Nine."

She'd done some homework. "What were my parents' names?"

"Thomas James Charles Daley, Sr. and Margaret Murphy Daley. Your father was a police officer. Your mother was a homemaker. You have a younger brother named Peter and a younger sister named Mary. Pete used to be a cop. Now he's a private investigator. Mary is a teacher in L.A."

She could have gotten that much from Google or a PI, although it seemed unlikely that she could have afforded one. I upped the ante. "My brother had some distinctive physical features."

"He had birthmarks on his right knee in the shape of a square. He had a scar below his left ear where he accidentally hit himself with a hammer when he was a kid. The pinky on his left hand popped in and out from a football injury."

All correct. "He had a tattoo."

"He had the letters "S" and "I" on his left ankle. They were the initials of his high school, St. Ignatius. He was afraid to tell your parents."

All true. In 1970, it was unthinkable for the altar-boy son of a San Francisco cop to have a tattoo. Tommy did it on a dare when he'd pounded a six-pack of Buds after S.I. had won the city football championship. He showed it to Pete and me, then swore us to secrecy. As far as I knew, my mom and dad never found out—or they never mentioned it. "My brother was an all-city quarterback at S.I. and the starter at Cal. A lot was written about him."

"I knew him."

"Prove it."

She reached inside her soiled backpack and took out a scuffed leather box. She set it on my desk, opened it, and removed a gray medallion about the size of a quarter. "My uncle gave this to me when I turned fifteen."

I recognized the Vietnam-era dog tag. The first two lines

read, "Daley, Thomas J.C." The third line had his social security number. The fourth said he had Type A+ blood. The fifth confirmed that he was Catholic. The information was accurate.

I eyed her suspiciously. "You can get replicas on the Internet."

"Show it to an expert." She took out a manila envelope from her backpack and handed it to me. Inside I found a faded black-and-white photo. "It's the only picture I have. I made copies. You can borrow this one and have it tested, but I want it back."

Tommy looked more like our father than the athletic twenty-year-old whose memory was frozen in my mind. His hair was thinner, eyes hollow, face drawn. His body was emaciated, and his right arm—his golden throwing arm—hung limply at his side. His smile hadn't changed. He was standing next to a woman who looked like a younger version of Melinda. Tommy's shirt was off. He was holding a baby in his left arm.

"Where did you get this?" I asked.

"My uncle found a Polaroid camera in an abandoned American base."

I was sweating. "When was this taken?"

"A few weeks after I was born." She pointed at the woman in the picture. "That's my mother." Her finger moved over to the baby. "And that's me."

"You're saying—,"

"Tommy Daley was my father."

3
"I NEED TO SEE YOU IN MY OFFICE"

The co-head of the Felony Division stood in my doorway, arms folded. Rosita Carmela Fernandez's cobalt eyes lit up as her full lips formed the inquisitive half smile that I still found so seductive two decades after we'd met in the old P.D.'s Office and eighteen years since we'd divorced. Her straight black hair used to cascade halfway down her back. A couple of months earlier, she'd had it shortened into a softer look.

She was fluent in Spanish, but the Mission District native spoke English without an accent. "I'm due in a meeting in ten minutes. You need to talk?"

"I do." I introduced Melinda and explained that she was Thomas Nguyen's mother. "Her son fired Sandy Tran last night. He wants a P.D."

"Happens all the time. Sandy knows the drill. She'll file papers to ensure an orderly transition. In the meantime, you know our procedures."

Rosie started backing out the door, but I stopped her. "There are extenuating circumstances."

"There always are." She pushed out the impatient sigh that I'd heard the first time when I was a rookie P.D. and she was a rising star who had just been promoted to the Felony Division. She was spinning out of a bad marriage, and I was flattered that she noticed me. She mentored me on the Byzantine workings of the San Francisco criminal justice system. In her spare time, she provided remedial training on subjects that weren't addressed at the seminary. We'd covered a lot of territory since then: marriage, birth of our daughter, divorce, formation of our own law firm, her battle with breast cancer, birth of our son, and our return to the P.D.'s Office. Another potential change was in the air. A couple of months earlier, our boss had announced his retirement, and Rosie decided to run for P.D. The election was six weeks away. If you believed the polls, she was favored to become San Francisco's first Latina Public Defender.

She took a seat in the swivel chair opposite my desk and spoke to Melinda. "Mr. Daley will set up an appointment with one of our attorneys to discuss intake. Assuming your son qualifies, that lawyer will probably handle your son's case. Given the timing, we'll put this on a fast track."

"I want Mr. Daley to handle Thomas's case."

"He doesn't do trial work anymore." Rosie adjusted the sleeve of her Armani Collezioni jacket. She'd upgraded her wardrobe for the campaign. "If I were inclined to give your son some free legal advice—which I'm not—I would tell him to reconsider. Sandy Tran is an excellent attorney. It's a bad idea to switch lawyers a few days before trial."

"Mr. Daley told me the same thing."

"Mr. Daley is also a very good lawyer."

Melinda turned to me, eyes pleading.

I spoke to Rosie. "Melinda just informed me that she's Tommy's daughter."

Her eyes narrowed. "Your brother?"

"Yes."

"Is he . . . alive?"

"No. She says he died in Vietnam in 1978."

"He survived the plane crash?"

"Melinda says he ejected and landed near the village where she was born. Her mother and grandmother helped him recover."

"Why didn't he contact you after the war?"

"He couldn't."

Rosie took a moment to process the information. She

pointed a finger at Melinda. "You're saying that you're Mike's niece and your son is Tommy's grandson?"

"Yes."

"Prove it."

Melinda handed her the photo and the dog tag.

Rosie studied them for a moment before she turned to me. "You're sure it's Tommy?"

"Yes."

She turned to Melinda and put on her lawyer face. "How do we know these are real?"

"I'll do whatever it takes to prove it."

"Are you willing to take a lie detector test and give us a DNA sample?"

"Yes."

"Let's start with your birth certificate."

"I don't have one. I was born in 1976 in a village called Cib Tran Quang." Melinda said it was fifty miles southeast of Haiphong near the Gulf of Tonkin. "There aren't any records." She repeated her story that her uncle had smuggled her into the U.S. in 1984.

"That was a long time ago. Why didn't you contact Mike?"

"I came here illegally. I was afraid of being deported."

"Seems you aren't afraid anymore."

"My son needs help. I've been a U.S. citizen since 1995."

"And it's just a coincidence that you're claiming to be the niece of the co-head of the Felony Division of the Public Defender's Office four days before your son is going on trial?"

"Yes." Melinda turned to me. "I understand why you won't help me, but I was hoping you'd help your brother's grandson."

"I don't know for sure that he is."

"I expect you to verify everything I've told you."

I exchanged a glance with Rosie, who was fingering the yellowed Polaroid. She grabbed a legal pad and took out a Bic pen. She rolled up her sleeves and spoke to Melinda in the tone that she reserved for hostile witnesses, unprepared judges, lazy cops, obnoxious reporters, and me. "What's your legal name?"

"Melinda Nguyen."

"Date of birth?"

"1976. My uncle said it was July 14, but I don't know for sure."

"Social security number?"

Nguyen recited it.

"Address?"

"497 Ellis."

"Your name wasn't Melinda Nguyen when you were born."

"My birth name was Xuan Ho. I became Melinda Nguyen when I got married." She filled in the gaps in her biography. Married at seventeen. A mother at eighteen. A widow at nineteen. Tried to make ends meet as a single parent in the Tenderloin. Fought depression, alcohol, drugs, and a debilitating back injury. A stint at a massage parlor ended badly after her boss raped her—a crime she hadn't reported.

Rosie listened attentively, interrupting occasionally. "What was your mother's name?"

"Lily Ho. She died when I was a baby. My uncle was Lu Ho."

"Brothers or sisters?"

"None. No children besides Thomas."

Rosie glanced at me.

"Melinda, what do you remember about my brother?"

"Little things. He was tall. And handsome. And kind. He spoke a little Vietnamese. He had a big smile. He had trouble walking. He could barely lift his right arm. He smelled like cigarettes." There were tears in her eyes. "Will you represent your great-nephew? Please?"

"We need to make some calls."

Her voice cracked. "I know where my father and mother are buried. I don't know if there are markers, but I can tell you where to look."

"You were only two when Tommy died. How can you possibly remember?"

"My uncle and I visited their graves every Sunday."

"Tell me now."

"Not unless you handle Thomas's case."

"We don't trade legal services for information."

The stuffy office filled with an intense silence. Finally, my ex-wife, former law partner, and soon-to-be Public Defender of San Francisco spoke to the woman purporting to be my niece in her best closing-argument voice. "Here's how we're going to proceed. We need to confirm every detail that you just told us. If anything is untrue, we'll have you arrested. Understood?"

"Yes."

"You're going to write down the exact location where Mike's brother is buried right now." Rosie's lips turned down. "Last chance. Do you want to change your story?"

"No."

"Good. *If* it checks out, and *if* we determine that your son is eligible, and *if* a judge orders us to represent him, then we'll talk about staffing."

"I want Mr. Daley to handle Thomas's trial."

"This isn't a negotiation." Rosie turned to me. "Please take Ms. Nguyen to see an attorney about intake. Then I need to see you in my office."

4

"YOU CAN'T BE SERIOUS"

Rosie took a sip of coffee and set the white mug on her desk. "You can't be serious."

I tried not to sound defensive. "I'm just doing my job."

"We have procedures."

"Which I'm following. Melinda is talking to one of our attorneys. If her son qualifies and the judge approves—which appears likely—we'll assign somebody to handle it."

"Our procedures provide that the intake attorney handles the case."

It was true. Our office operated on a system of "vertical representation," which meant that the same lawyer usually handled intake, arraignment, preliminary hearing, trial, and research. "Not in all cases," I said. "The circumstances are unusual because of the timing."

"You want to do it yourself."

Yes, I do. "We'll see."

"Yeah, right."

She knew me better than anybody on Planet Earth. I sat down on the armchair opposite her desk. Rosie's office was the same size as mine, but it felt more spacious. She was a better housekeeper and she'd bought her own furniture. Her files were stacked neatly on the credenza next to her laptop. A campaign poster was propped against the wall.

I pointed at the framed Little League picture of our ten-year-old son, Tommy, who looked like his namesake uncle. "All good in fifth grade?"

"Status quo. He's still spending a little too much time playing video games, but he likes his teacher and his grades are solid."

"He has a game on Saturday." Tommy had inherited his uncle's throwing arm. He was making me the smartest Little League coach in Marin County. "Can you make it?"

"I have a fundraiser."

"Another time." Her schedule had been packed before she'd decided to run for P.D. Nowadays, her evenings and weekends were crammed with political events. I understood the necessity, and I tried not to be resentful. It wasn't as if we were married. I pointed at the high school graduation photo of our eighteen-year-old daughter, Grace, a freshman at USC, who was a dead ringer in appearance and temperament for her mother. "Heard anything?"

"Not much. I check her Facebook page every day, but I don't post. I can't deal with the humiliation of being unfriended again. You?"

"She responds to texts occasionally. You still good to go to Parents' Weekend?"

"For now. Do we have to go to the football game? Cal is going to get killed."

"Part of the program for an Old Blue like me."

Rosie was an alum of San Francisco State and Hastings Law School. I went to Cal for undergrad and law school. We were still trying to wrap our heads around the fact that our daughter had turned down my beloved Golden Bears to go to USC. The mighty Trojans had cushioned the blow by awarding Grace a President's Scholarship—in essence, a four-year free ride. It wasn't quite Reggie Bush money, but it helped. As a token of my gratitude, I no longer referred to USC as "The School of the Devil."

Rosie returned to the matters at hand. "You really think Melinda is your niece?"

"She knew stuff about Tommy." I told her about the birthmarks and the tattoo.

"If she's telling the truth, he died when she was two. Somebody fed her the information."

"It must have been her uncle."

"We still have to go through the process. We can't give special treatment to a family member."

"It wouldn't be the first time."

"Appearances are important when you're running for office. How are you planning to verify her story?"

I held up a sealed evidence bag containing two strands of Melinda's hair. "We'll start by doing a DNA test to see if she's Tommy's daughter."

"You have *her* DNA."

"We have Tommy's, too. My mother kept a couple of his baby teeth."

"The county lab is backed up for weeks."

"Pete plays softball with a guy at UCSF who'll do it today. It isn't official, but he's always right. We got a DNA sample from Thomas when he was arrested. I want to make sure he's Melinda's son."

"And if he is?"

"I plan to welcome my niece and great-nephew into the family. I will also respectfully request that you appoint me to handle this case."

"I need you to run the office. The campaign is sucking up every spare minute."

"I'll do everything I can to help you."

"It's a bad idea to represent family members."

"This is no different from the time we represented Angel."

Ten years earlier, Rosie's niece had been accused of bludgeoning her husband to death during a drug- and alcohol-induced rage. The conventional wisdom says you shouldn't represent relatives. In that case, Fernandez family loyalty trumped the conventional wisdom.

Rosie wasn't buying. "We were still in private practice. We

got to choose our clients."

"We're going to be appointed to represent Thomas. It's our job to decide on staffing."

"There was no question that Angel was my niece."

"I won't handle this case unless we can prove that Thomas is my great-nephew."

"His trial starts on Monday."

"We'll get an extension."

"Don't be so sure."

"Then we still have four days to prepare. We used to do it all the time."

"Not for a murder case. We aren't as young as we used to be."

"Sleep is overrated. And we aren't *that* old, Rosie."

"A girl with purple hair and a nose ring offered me her seat on a Muni bus last week."

"It doesn't mean you're old. The kid had good manners."

"We have a policy against representing family members."

"We'll make an exception. At the very least, I'm going to talk to Thomas. There's no rule against conducting a preliminary interview with a potential client."

"It violates our protocol."

"For God's sake, Rosie. You sound like a bureaucrat."

"I *am* a bureaucrat, Mike." She grinned. "It's only going to get worse if I win the election."

"*When* you win." I returned her smile. "And you'll never be one of *them.*"

"I hope you're right. Are you going to see Thomas now?"

"I want to talk to Pete first."

5

"HE LOOKED JUST LIKE YOUR FATHER"

The heavyset bartender's pale blue eyes twinkled as he tossed a soiled dishtowel over his shoulder. "What'll it be, lad?"

"Just coffee, Big John. Heard from Pete?"

"On his way, Mikey."

My uncle, John Dunleavy, was born eighty-two years earlier at St. Francis Hospital. According to family lore, he was dubbed "Big John" when he weighed in at eleven pounds.

"You okay, Mikey?" He'd never been outside the U.S., but he could summon an Irish brogue at will.

"I'm fine."

"You look like you saw a ghost." He arched a bushy gray eyebrow. "Never lie to a barkeep—especially your favorite uncle."

"I'm fine," I repeated, "and you're my *only* uncle."

His jowls shook as his face transformed into a whimsical smile. He grabbed a chipped mug from the shelf behind the weathered Monterey pine bar that my dad had helped him build more than a half century earlier. Smoking was no longer permitted inside the neighborhood watering hole, but the smell of cigarettes was baked into the paneled walls of the narrow room in a stucco building on Irving, three blocks from the house where I'd grown up in the Sunset. Big John's grandson, Joey, now handled the day-to-day operations and lugged the kegs up from the basement. My uncle still showed up six days a week to brew the coffee and make his not-so-secret batter for the fish-and-chips. During the daytime, Dunleavy's had become a gathering spot for the community's seniors. It was a quintessential San Francisco experience to watch Big John serve tea and tell bawdy jokes to a dozen septuagenarian Asian-American men and women sitting in booths decorated with faded photos of Willie Mays and Juan Marichal.

My uncle's expression turned serious as he poured me a cup of scalding Folger's. If you wanted Starbucks, you had to go down the street. "What brings you here at this hour, lad?"

"Family business."

"A little coy for my taste, Mikey. Everybody okay at home? My darlin' great-niece still happy at USC? My little great-nephew still striking out everybody in Marin County?"

"They're fine, Big John."

"Glad to hear it. And how about our soon-to-be Public Defender? You still spending a couple nights a week at Rosie's house?"

"It makes things easier with Tommy—especially during the campaign."

Rosie's house was two blocks from my apartment in the leafy enclave of Larkspur, about ten miles north of the Golden Gate Bridge. After Rosie finished treatments for breast cancer a decade earlier, we became a permanent—albeit unmarried—couple. When Grace was in high school, I started spending two nights a week at Rosie's house. The demilitarized zone between our respective residences became essential for our sanity.

Big John gave me a sly grin. "Why don't you two give up this ridiculous charade and get married again?"

"We weren't good at being married."

"You're older and wiser now, Mikey."

"Definitely older. Not sure about wiser."

"My sources tell me that Rosie is going to win the election."

"They're usually right."

"They're *always* right, lad." He gestured with the meaty hand that hauled in touchdowns when he was an all-city tight end at St. Ignatius six decades earlier. "Come November, she'll be your boss. Gonna be okay with that?"

"Of course." I took a sip of bitter coffee and smiled. "I've been working for Rosie for twenty years."

The gregarious bartender let out a throaty chuckle. Then the back door swung open and a rare bolt of sunlight flashed across the autographed photo of Willie McCovey above the pool table. My younger brother strode in purposefully, gave our uncle a hug, and sat down on the stool next to mine. Pete was a stockier version of the standard Daley family model. His full head of hair and thick mustache used to be a half-shade darker than mine, but now both were silver. The bags under his eyes were more pronounced than usual. Without a word, Big John poured him a cup of black coffee.

"Cheating wife?" I asked Pete.

"Cheating husband. Pays the bills, Mick." His voice was raspier than usual as we exchanged abbreviated pleasantries. He reported that his wife and six-year-old daughter were fine. He took off his bomber jacket, set his iPhone on the bar, and scratched the stubble on his chin. "You said it was an emergency."

"You heard about the Thomas Nguyen case?"

"Yeah. Vietnamese kid at a liquor store in the Tenderloin. The shopkeeper popped his accomplice. Felony murder. Slam dunk for the D.A."

"The trial starts Monday. Nguyen fired Sandy Tran last night. Our office is going to pick up the case."

"Lucky you. I hope you aren't looking for help. My plate's full."

"Nguyen's mother came to see me this morning. She wants me to handle the trial."

"I thought you weren't trying cases."

"I'm not."

My younger brother scowled. "I'm busy, Mick. What's this about?"

"I need to show you something." I put Tommy's photo and dog tag on the bar. Pete and Big John almost bumped heads as they leaned forward to look at them.

My uncle put on the reading glasses hanging from a Giants lanyard around his neck. The color drained from his face as he studied the faded Polaroid. "My God. He looked just like your father. Tommy had aged twenty years."

"You sure it's Tommy?"

"I was in the waiting room when he was born. When was this taken?"

"Two years after his plane went down. Nguyen's mother said that he ejected and landed in a village in North Vietnam."

My uncle swallowed. "Is he . . . still . . . alive?"

"No. Nguyen's mother said he died in '78."

"Where was the U.S. Army?"

"They couldn't find him. Melinda claimed her mother and grandmother nursed him back to health. He died of jungle fever."

Pete was tugging furiously at his mustache. "Why didn't he contact us?"

"He couldn't. It was a remote village."

"Can Nguyen's mother prove any of this?"

"That's where you come in."

My mom always said that Pete had gone to the police academy just to show our dad how tough he was. Pop knew how to bend the rules without getting caught. He retired on his fifty-fifth birthday and died of lung cancer two years later. Pete bent the rules, too, but he *always* got caught. Things came to a head when he and his partner at Mission Station used a little too much muscle breaking up a gang fight on Capp Street. The nephew of a member of the Board of Supervisors ended up with a concussion. The city caved and threw Pete and his partner under a bus when they settled the inevitable lawsuit. Pete was still bitter about it.

I fingered the dog tag. "She gave me the location of Tommy's grave."

"How'd she know? You said she was just two when Tommy died."

"Her uncle showed her the spot."

"Where's he?"

"Dead."

"Figures. You really think you're going to find something?"

"I don't know. Got any contacts in Vietnam?"

"The Peter Daley Investigative Agency has operatives everywhere, Mick." He pointed at the Polaroid. "Where did Nguyen's mother get this picture?"

"From her uncle." I filled in the details. "She says she's Tommy's daughter. If she's telling the truth, it makes us her uncles."

"And it makes Thomas Nguyen our great-nephew and Tommy's grandson." Pete shot a skeptical glance at Big John, who responded in kind.

My uncle removed the towel from his shoulder and pretended to wipe a non-existent spill. The phony Irish lilt disappeared. "She telling you the truth, Mikey?"

"I'm not sure. She knew stuff about Tommy." I told them about the birthmarks and the tattoo.

Big John clutched his reading glasses. "Where has this woman been for the past forty years? Your mom and dad were never the same after Tommy died. At the very least, we might have given Tommy a proper burial."

"Maybe we'll have a chance to do it now."

Pete wasn't convinced. "This picture could have been made with Photoshop. The dog tag could be fake."

"That's why I called you first."

"I can verify whether the photo was taken with a Polaroid. I know a guy who can do a chemical analysis to tell us roughly when the film was manufactured."

"That's a start."

"What's your gut, Mick? You think she's legit?"

"I took her through her story three times. She didn't change a single detail."

"She could be a really good con artist."

His instincts were as finely tuned as Rosie's. "How soon can you check out her story?"

"Gimme a couple of hours to talk to my sources at ICE. It may take a day or two to get somebody on the ground in Vietnam."

I handed him a sealed evidence bag. "This is a lock of Melinda's hair. I need your guy at UCSF to compare it against Tommy's baby teeth to see if she's his daughter." I gave him a card with a swab of Thomas Nguyen's saliva. "And I need him to tell us if Thomas is Melinda's son."

"I'll have it by the end of the day. Where you going now, Mick?"

"To meet my new client."

6
"I WAS JUST SITTING IN THE CAR"

Thomas Nguyen's hollow eyes stared at me across a metal table in an airless interview room inside the Stalinesque San Francisco County Jail #2, which had been shoe-horned between the old Hall of Justice and the 101 Freeway in the nineties. The wags at SFPD dubbed the monstrosity at Seventh and Bryant the "Glamour Slammer." While he didn't appear agitated or violent, there was no way that I could have stopped him if he had leapt across the table to come after me.

The sullen young man spoke to me in a monotone. "You really my great-uncle?"

"Don't know. You really my great-nephew?"

"That's what my mom tells me."

"She telling the truth?"

"Don't know."

"Neither do I." I couldn't tell if the attitude came from teenage angst, genuine indifference, or the fact that he had spent nine months in jail. He wouldn't be a sympathetic witness if we had to put him on the stand. "Keep your voice down. They're listening."

"I got nothing to hide."

"Yes, you do."

His soft features were similar to his mother's, but his broad shoulders and blue eyes hinted at the possibility of Daley genes.

"Can you get me out of here?" he asked.

That was always the first question. "No."

His eyes darted over my shoulder. "You my lawyer?"

"Not yet."

"Then why are you here?"

I wanted to see if he looked like Tommy. "Your mother requested a Public Defender."

"You gonna handle my case?"

"If you qualify, our office will represent you. We'll decide on staffing later."

He finally looked me in the eye. "What if we can prove that you're my great-uncle?"

"I'll consult with my superiors. In the meantime, if you want me to consider the possibility, you need to tell me the truth about everything. It's my only absolute rule: you lie, you die. Understood?"

"Yeah." He leaned forward. "Where do you want to start?"

"Why did you fire Sandy Tran?"

"She wanted me to take a plea for second degree murder."

"Might have been the best deal you were going to get."

"I was just sitting in the car."

"That's enough to get you convicted of felony murder."

"I'm not going to trial with a lawyer who thinks I'm guilty."

Tommy might have said the same thing. "What were you doing in Tho's car?"

"We were going to a party in Daly City."

"How well did you know him?"

"Pretty well. He was a couple of years ahead of me at Galileo."

"Why did he drop out of school?"

"He didn't quit. They threw him out for selling weed. He needed the money. His dad left when he was a baby. His mom is addicted to crystal meth. She lives in a shelter."

"Where did he live?"

"With his mother when she had a room. Sometimes on the street. He stayed with us a couple of times."

"Was he ever arrested?"

"Once or twice. He never did any time."

"You got the name of his supplier?"

"We never talked about that stuff."

"Work with me, Thomas. The D.A. will be more accommodating if you give her something."

"I got nothing."

This wasn't helpful. Then again, it was never ideal to try to garner favor from the prosecutors by having your client snitch. The D.A. might not believe him. More important, it could get your client killed. "You lived with your mom?"

"Yeah."

"How far was the liquor store from your apartment?"

"Couple blocks."

"How often did you go to the liquor store?"

"Every once in a while."

"What about Tho?"

"Don't know."

Short answers were unsatisfying. "Did either of you know the owner?"

"I'd seen him a couple of times. I don't know about Duc."

"What happened at the store?"

"Don't know. We stopped to buy beer. Duc went inside. I stayed in the car."

"Did you give him money?"

"No. He was going to pay."

Sure he was. I asked what happened next.

"A police unit rolled up and a cop went inside. A few minutes later, two more cop cars showed up. One of the cops stuck me in the back of a squad car. They said Duc was dead."

"Did you hear any shots?"

"No. I had my earbuds in."

"Anybody leave the store while you were waiting outside?"

"Don't know. I wasn't paying attention."

We'd look for witnesses. "Who shot Tho?"

"The store owner."

"How do you know?"

"He admitted it."

"Any chance it could have been somebody else?"

A shrug. "I guess."

"The news said Tho pulled a gun."

"Don't know."

"You could see it in the security video." This was a bluff. I hadn't seen it.

His tone turned more emphatic. "I don't know, man."

"They found a gun on the floor. Tho's prints were on it."

"I don't know how it got there."

"You didn't know that he was packing?"

"No."

"Come on, Thomas."

The telltale hesitation. "I knew he had a gun, but I didn't think he had it with him that night. Like I said, we were going to a party. You don't bring a gun to a party."

"Was he planning to sell weed?"

"Maybe. Don't know."

"Did you know he was going to rob the store?"

"No."

"And you never asked."

"Right. We just wanted to get some beer for the party."

Enough. "I've spent twenty years representing guys like you and Tho. I've heard every line from people who are a lot better at lying than you are. I don't care if you're my brother's grandson. If you aren't telling the truth, this is the last time you're going to see me. Understood?"

His Adam's Apple bobbed. "Yeah."

"Last chance. Did you know that Tho had a gun?"

"No."

It's your story and you're sticking to it. "How'd the gun get onto the floor?"

"Beats me."

"Any chance it was planted by the owner of the store or the cops?"

"Don't know. Maybe."

"If Tho didn't have a gun, why did the owner shoot him?"

"Ask him."

"I will." I stood and turned toward the door.

"Where you goin'?" he asked.

"To talk to the lawyer you fired last night. I want to know if you lied to her, too."

7

"THE PATRON SAINT OF LOST CAUSES"

Sandy Tran sat behind a second-hand desk piled with files. The streetwise defense attorney was barely five feet tall. Her salt-and-pepper hair was pulled back into a pony tail, exposing hoop-style earrings. "Tag, you're it," she deadpanned.

"We haven't even been appointed as Nguyen's lawyer."

"You will." The former Deputy P.D. glanced at a white board listing six dozen active cases. She had just erased *People vs. Nguyen.* "Otherwise, you wouldn't be here."

True enough.

Trial exhibits, storage boxes, and sandwich wrappers were strewn about her stifling office above a dry cleaner down the street from Hastings Law School in the Tenderloin. It reminded me of the original offices of Fernandez and Daley in a remodeled martial arts studio above a Chinese restaurant around the corner from the Transbay bus terminal.

"You okay with the change in the lineup?" I asked.

"Sure. It isn't the first time I've been fired on the eve of trial. Now I can catch up on my other cases. I'd feel worse if I was still getting paid. Thankfully, the Vietnamese community raised some cash. It didn't cover all of my legal fees, but it paid most of my expenses."

I was familiar with the financial realities of running a low-rent criminal defense practice where clients frequently had to choose between paying their lawyer or their bail bondsman. Most opted for the latter. It gave me an even greater appreciation for the steady paychecks and health insurance at the P.D.'s Office. "Mind if I ask you something off the record?"

"Fine with me."

"Did you get yourself fired on purpose?"

"Not this time." She gave me a knowing grin as she played with the collar of a denim work shirt. Her going-to-court suit was in a garment bag hanging from a nail pounded into her door. "I learned that trick from Rosie."

So did I. "You weren't stalling?"

"Nope. Thomas fired me fair and square. He didn't like my recommendation to accept a deal for second degree. If I were in his shoes, I might have done the same thing."

"You think he's going to be convicted?"

"Doesn't look good. Every law professor with half a brain will tell you that the felony murder rule is a joke, but that makes no difference out here in the real world. Watch the security video. The facts aren't in dispute. Tho walked into the store and reached inside his pocket. The owner thought he was pulling a gun and shot him in self-defense. Malice aforethought is imputed to Thomas even though he was in the car. End of story. Thanks for coming. Drive home safely."

"Can you see Tho pull the gun?"

"You can see him reach inside his pocket."

"You didn't answer my question. You sure he had a gun?"

"You can't see it in the video. The cops found a gun on the floor next to his body. His prints were on it. That was good enough for them."

"Did they find anybody else's prints on the gun?"

"The shopkeeper. He told them that he found it under Tho's body and disarmed it."

"Maybe he planted it."

"Now you'll have the privilege of trying to sell it to the jury."

I may have no choice. "Was Tho the registered owner of the gun?"

"There are no weapons registered in his name. And the serial number and the identifying information were removed."

"Very professional for a small-time drug dealer. Was anybody else in the store?"

"The owner's son and daughter, a security guard, a customer, and a deliveryman. The son worked at the store. He was standing next to his father when Tho came inside. The daughter went to a movie with a friend who dropped her off at the store. She was waiting for her father to drive her home. She was doing her homework at her father's desk behind the deli counter."

"And the guard?"

"He was behind the counter over by the window. The son and guard corroborated the owner's story. The daughter said that she didn't see Tho come inside. The others were in the back. They didn't see anything, either."

"Did the guard have a gun?"

"It's the Tenderloin, Mike."

"Why didn't he use it?"

"He said he was looking out the window when Tho came in. By the time he realized what was happening, Tho was dead."

"Was the guard licensed and bonded?"

"No, just armed and dangerous. He's the owner's nephew. He's no longer working at the store. Evidently, he wasn't very effective."

So it seems. "Anybody else come or go? Passersby? Homeless people?"

"The only other witness would have been Tho. Unfortunately, he's still dead."

"Did you hire a PI?"

"Yes. His name is in the file. Feel free to talk to him. He didn't find any other witnesses."

Or nobody wanted to get involved.

She pointed at a half dozen boxes with the *Iron Mountain Storage* logo. "I'll send the files to your office. Which chump is going to inherit this mess?"

"Don't know yet."

"You gonna do it yourself?"

"Rosie and I haven't discussed it." Technically, that was a lie, but short of a whopper. Besides, it was none of her business.

She responded with a throaty chuckle. "Mike Daley—still the patron saint of lost causes. I heard you were already over at the Glamour Slammer to see Thomas."

"I was." There were no secrets at the Hall. "Unless Judge McDaniel approves a delay, his trial starts Monday."

"You could have sent a deputy. You wanted to talk to him yourself."

"It's a murder trial on a short timeline."

"It will help Rosie's campaign if you get an acquittal."

"Not necessarily. Besides, this has nothing to do with politics." That much was true.

"Either way, Thomas is your headache now."

It was an opening. "Is he a headache?"

"Compared with most of my clients, no. He isn't a bad kid. No convictions, but he's been picked up for shoplifting a couple of times. I'm sure he's smoked some weed. In this neighborhood, it's impossible to avoid the wrong people."

"Was Tho the wrong people?"

"Absolutely. He got tossed out of Galileo for selling marijuana behind the football stadium. He was arrested a couple of times for possession, but the charges never stuck, and they couldn't nail him for selling."

"Anything more serious?"

"He was hauled in for an armed robbery at a 7-Eleven in the Excelsior, but the charges were dropped. Seems the primary witness disappeared."

"You think Tho had anything to do with it?"

"Don't know."

"Did he ever do time?"

"A couple of days in juvie on a possession charge when he was fifteen."

"You got the name of his supplier?

"If I did, I would have cut a better deal for Thomas."

"Family?"

"Tho's father is long gone. His mother is addicted to crystal meth. When she's clean, she lives in a shelter. You can talk to her if you'd like, but you won't get much."

"Thomas seems pretty smart. His mother said he got into State."

"He's filled with hormones, attitude, and unrealistic expectations. If you were eighteen, would you cop to second degree murder?"

"If it was the best deal I could get."

"You understand the system. He doesn't."

True. "Did he ever lie to you?"

"He claimed he didn't know that Tho had a gun. I still don't buy it. Guys in this neighborhood talk about three things: girls, cars, and guns."

"You sure Tho was packing?"

"Pretty sure."

"Any idea where he got the piece?"

"He probably stole it or picked it up on the street."

"What do you know about the shopkeeper?"

"His name is Ortega Cruz. He's owned the store for almost thirty years. Divorced. Lives in the Mission. A nineteen-year-old son who works at the store. A seventeen-year-old daughter who goes to Mercy High. No arrests. No domestic violence. No alcohol or drugs."

"He had an Uzi behind his counter."

"Actually, it was an AR-15 bought legally in Nevada.

Passed the background check."

"It's illegal here unless it's modified to comply with California law."

"It wasn't modified. The cops confiscated it."

"Maybe he's trigger happy. Had he ever used it?"

"He shot a robber a couple of years ago. The guy survived, but he died a year later at Pelican Bay."

"Did Cruz ever threaten anybody else?"

"Nothing reported to the cops."

"You think it was a good idea to have a semi-automatic weapon in a store?"

"No, but I don't write the gun laws." She opened her top drawer. "You want to see my nine-millimeter? It's a sweet little piece."

"That won't be necessary." She wasn't the only attorney I knew who was packing. "You aren't leaving me with any good options, Sandy."

"There *are* no good options, Mike. That's why I recommended a deal."

"I trust you requested a delay?"

"Of course, but Judge McDaniel has extended us twice. It won't take long to get up to speed. Unless you find some new witnesses, the trial will take just a couple of days."

We spoke for a few more minutes. As I was heading toward the door, my iPhone vibrated. Rosie's number appeared on the display. Her tone was businesslike. "Judge McDaniel signed the order appointing us as Nguyen's counsel."

No surprise. "Did she grant the extension?"

"She's still thinking about it. Her clerk said that the judge wants to meet with us at one o'clock. The D.A. is sending somebody over."

I glanced at my watch. 11:50 a.m. "There's still a little time. I'll stop at the D.A.'s Office on my way to Judge McDaniel's chambers and see what I can find out."

8
"IT WAS A PROVOCATIVE ACT"

The District Attorney of the City and County of San Francisco flashed the radiant politician's smile that her three ex-husbands and the voters of my hometown found irresistible. Nicole Ward stood behind a custom cherrywood desk in her immaculate corner office on the third floor of the Hall of Justice. In lieu of bookcases filled with legal tomes, her walls were lined with photos of herself with the Bay Area's A-list power brokers. She had just turned fifty-five, but her creamy skin, Botoxed forehead, and perfect makeup made her appear a decade younger.

She repositioned the sleeve of her eighteen-hundred-dollar St. John Knit blazer and extended a willowy hand. "I miss seeing you in court," she purred.

She hadn't appeared in front of a judge in years.

"Great to see you, too, Nicole," I lied. I shook her hand and took a seat in a leather armchair opposite her desk. I admired the framed portraits of her impeccably coiffed twin daughters. Jenna was a Tri-Delt at Stanford. Missy was a DG at Cornell. "How many more tuition years?"

"At least three. Jenna wants to go to law school. Missy is talking about a Ph.D. in psychology. It's tough to make ends meet on a public servant's salary."

"Yes, it is." It's easier when your second ex-husband's venture capital firm was one of the early investors in Facebook.

Her phony smile broadened. "How does Grace like USC?"

"Loves it."

"Glad to hear it."

Sure you are. Over the years, we'd been on opposite sides

of several big-time cases, and we were adept at the Kabuki dance of exchanging fake pleasantries. Now firmly entrenched in the top slot at the D.A.'s Office, Ward was a fixture on local TV and, on occasion, CNN. She had perfected the art of talking and grinning simultaneously while saying nothing of substance.

She pointed at the paunchy Deputy D.A. sitting next to me. "You know Andy?"

"Of course."

Andy Erickson was in his late thirties, but his rumpled appearance and thinning hairline indicated that the stress of being Ward's personal lapdog was taking its toll. I remembered his first day in court a decade earlier when he was assigned to prosecute one of my regulars for assault after he'd gotten into a brawl with a homeless guy over a stolen roast chicken. I got the charges dropped on the condition that I found a job for my client, a former small-time heavyweight prizefighter named Terrence "The Terminator" Love. To Rosie's dismay, I hired Terrence as our receptionist and occasional bodyguard at Fernandez and Daley. The Terminator never missed a day and now worked for us in a similar capacity at the P.D.'s Office. Meanwhile, Erickson grew up to be a competent prosecutor. On occasion, I took him out for a beer. He reciprocated by sharing his dad's seats behind the Giants' dugout. San Francisco is still a small town where everybody in the justice system knows everyone else.

Ward didn't realize that she was still grinning as she tried to feign sincerity. "Everybody says that Rosie is going to win the election. I'm pulling for her. It's always better to have somebody competent running the P.D.'s Office."

"I trust that she can count on your vote?"

"Absolutely." Her forehead looked like it was going to crack as she arched a painted eyebrow. "Give her my best."

"I will." Rosie and Ward detested each other. "People whose opinions I respect tell me that you're going to run for mayor."

"Maybe someday." Her plastic smile widened. "What brings my favorite Public Defender to my office on this fine afternoon?"

As if you don't know. "Thomas Nguyen."

"I heard you paid him a visit."

"I did. You must have more pressing matters than monitoring who comes and goes at the Glamour Slammer."

"The Hall of Justice is my home. I like to keep tabs on my guests."

Especially when they're involved in a case that could get you some T.V. time.

Ward pointed at Erickson and invoked a sugary tone. "Andy is doing an excellent job. We made a generous offer on Tuesday. Frankly, I was disappointed that Sandy Tran couldn't persuade her client to accept a deal for second degree murder."

Nice try. "You heard that we've been appointed."

"We have. Have you assigned a Deputy P.D.?"

"Not yet. Sandy is sending over the files. We have a meeting with Judge McDaniel at one o'clock to discuss an extension. I understand that you're invited, too."

"We'll be there."

"It would make life easier if we can tell the judge that you have no objection."

"Can't help you."

"Sure you can."

"No, I can't. We've been extended twice. Judge McDaniel is getting impatient—and I don't blame her."

Your concern is noted. "I'm asking you as a matter of professional courtesy. It will be difficult to get up to speed by Monday."

"It's an open-and-shut case. The facts aren't in dispute."

"There's no such thing as an open-and-shut case. The facts are *always* in dispute."

"Not here." Ward pointed at Erickson. "Give Mike the highlights, Andy."

He deserved better than to be treated like a trained seal.

Erickson spoke as if he was reading from a script. "Nguyen and Tho stopped at Alcatraz Liquors on Eddy Street. Tho went inside. Nguyen stayed in the car. Tho reached inside his pocket and started to pull a gun. The owner of the store—one Ortega Cruz—shot him in self-defense. It was caught on the security video."

"He needed a half dozen bullets to defend himself?"

"The Bushmaster fires a lot of rounds in a hurry."

No kidding. "Tho didn't pull a gun."

"It was in his pocket."

"No, it wasn't."

"Yes, it was. His prints were on it."

"It could have been planted."

"It wasn't."

"The shopkeeper's prints were on the gun, too."

"He found it under Tho's body and disarmed it. We offered Nguyen a deal for second degree murder with a sentence of fifteen years. He's only eighteen. He'll be out when he's thirty-three. Sandy probably told him to take the deal."

True. "He didn't go inside the store."

"It's still felony murder."

"Tho didn't pull the trigger."

"Doesn't matter."

"Yes, it does. *People v. Washington.* The felony murder rule applies only if the shooter is the defendant or an accomplice, not if he's the intended victim."

Erickson glanced at Ward, who switched to a more subdued smile. "Glad you're still keeping up with the law—even if you aren't trying cases anymore."

That's gratuitous. "Washington was decided in 1965."

"I know. *People v. Lima* was decided in 2004. *People v.*

Concha was decided in 2009. Both cases came to the same conclusion: if a defendant or his accomplice engages in a 'provocative act' and his intended victim kills one of them in a reasonable response, the defendant is guilty of murder even though he didn't pull the trigger."

In fairness to Ward, it was a reasonably accurate summary of the law. "Nguyen was outside in the car. How was that 'provocative'?"

Her grin finally disappeared. "Tho's behavior was a provocative act that's imputed to Nguyen."

"Since when is walking into a store a 'provocative act'?"

"It is if you pull a gun."

"You don't know for sure that he did."

"The owner of the store found it under his body. Tho's prints were on it."

"So were the shopkeeper's."

"He disarmed it."

"Maybe he's a trigger-happy nutjob who keeps an Uzi behind his counter."

"Actually, it was an AR-15 purchased legally in Nevada."

"Last time I looked, it was illegal in California."

"The police confiscated it."

"They should have arrested him."

"He acted in self-defense. They gave him a warning."

"Are they planning to give it back?"

"No. It's an illegal weapon."

"And you decided not to press charges."

"He wasn't arrested."

It was a convenient excuse. "Does he own any other guns?"

"Several. All licensed and registered."

One of which is undoubtedly under the counter at his store. "You think it's a good idea to have a semi-automatic rifle in a liquor store in a crowded neighborhood?"

"That isn't the issue, Mike. You know that if it were up to

me, those weapons would be banned. The shopkeeper bought it legally. He used it in self-defense. End of story."

"Come on, Nicole."

"*You* come on, Mike. Sandy Tran argued this issue. Judge McDaniel ruled in our favor. The law is well-established. An act is provocative if its natural consequence is dangerous to human life. Tho walked into a liquor store in the Tenderloin at night with a gun. It created an inherent danger to human life— the shopkeeper's and his own."

"You're ignoring the fact that 'provocative act murder' is always second degree."

"Only if malice was implied. In this case, Tho's actions constituted express malice which is imputed to Nguyen."

"The gun could have been planted by the shopkeeper to support a bogus self-defense claim."

"You can see if that flies with a jury."

"You really think justice will be served by putting this kid away for life?"

Ward invoked the sanctimonious tone that won elections and drove defense lawyers crazy. "I have no choice, Mike. It's my job to enforce the law as it's written."

My ex-wife wasn't the only person running for office. "At the very least, you shouldn't object to an extension."

"That's up to Judge McDaniel."

9
"I'VE ALREADY EXTENDED
THIS TRIAL TWICE"

Judge Elizabeth McDaniel glared at me over the top of her reading glasses. "Haven't seen you in a while, Mr. Daley."

"I'm not spending much time in court."

"Our loss."

Rosie always said it was a bad sign when a judge started with flattery. "You're very kind, Your Honor."

"Have a seat, Mr. Daley." Betsy McDaniel was an elegant woman in her early sixties who attended pre-dawn Pilates classes with Rosie. If you listened attentively to the good-natured Superior Court veteran, you could still hear a trace of an accent from her native Alabama. "It isn't every day that I get a visit from the head of the Felony Division."

"Co-head, Your Honor."

"Only until Rosie wins the election."

"Judges aren't supposed to make endorsements."

"Just expressing an opinion."

She sat down on her black leather chair behind a mahogany desk in her paneled chambers on the fourth floor of the Hall, where she enjoyed an unobstructed view of the slow lane of the freeway. Her bookcases were jammed with legal treatises, French literature, and Donna Leon mysteries. The former prosecutor had spent two decades at the D.A.'s Office before her appointment to the bench, and she relished every minute that she spent in her tightly run courtroom. It was a poorly kept secret that she planned to go on senior status at the end of the year to spend more time with her three grandchildren whose framed photos were lined up on her credenza.

She nodded at Andy Erickson, who was sitting next to me. "Ms. Ward isn't joining us?"

"Afraid not, Your Honor. She had another appointment."

"Local news or CNN?"

He couldn't mask a sheepish grin. "Both."

"You're a good sport, Andy." Her tone became serious as she turned to me. "Seems we need to talk about Thomas Nguyen."

"We do. We've contacted Sandy Tran to arrange for an orderly transition of the files. That leaves us with timing issues."

Erickson interjected. "Your Honor—,"

"We'll hear from you in a moment." The judge pointed her reading glasses at me. "The facts are simple. You don't need an extension."

"We were appointed an hour ago. We haven't seen the files."

"Sandy will get you up to speed. I've already extended this trial twice."

"We had nothing to do with those motions."

"Understood, but that's irrelevant to me. You have four days and the full resources of the P.D.'s Office."

"This is a murder trial."

"I'm aware of that."

"We haven't even seen the prosecution's witness list."

"You can count them on two hands: the store owner, his son, his daughter, a security guard, a customer, a deliveryman, the first officer at the scene, the Medical Examiner, a couple of crime scene techs, and the homicide inspector. There is no question about cause of death. There are no forensics issues." She looked at Erickson. "Any additions to the witness list?"

"No, Your Honor."

"Good." She turned back to me. "You can interview witnesses over the next couple of days. You'll want to spend time with Sandy and her investigator. Finally, you'll need to talk to your client about whether it makes sense to put him on the stand." She waited a beat. "Or you can sit down with Andy when we're finished and iron out a plea."

"Our client has instructed us not to accept a deal."

"Then we'll see you in court on Monday."

"Thomas Nguyen has no criminal record. He's just a couple of years older than your grandson, Betsy."

"My grandson isn't on trial for murder, Mike."

"If he was, you would want his lawyers to have adequate time to prepare."

"This case isn't going to be decided on forensics or expert testimony. There is no dispute about what happened."

"Yes there is. We have reason to believe that Duc Tho was unarmed."

"They found a gun under his body with his fingerprints."

"It could have been planted. They also found the fingerprints of the shopkeeper on that weapon."

"I've already ruled that the security video is admissible. You can show it to the jury and make your case."

I will. "My client was sitting in the car. He was in the wrong place at the wrong time."

"We've covered this territory. It doesn't change the law."

"This is a contorted interpretation of the felony murder rule."

"I've ruled on that issue. If you want to try again, you can take it up on appeal. I've never been a fan of the felony murder rule, but I have to follow the law."

"There was no malice aforethought."

"There was under the felony murder rule."

"Which doesn't apply in this case. Neither Nguyen nor Tho pulled the trigger."

"This issue was briefed and decided. Tho walked into the store with a gun. That's a provocative act imputed to your client."

"We don't know if he really had a gun."

"We're going in circles. You can make your case to the jury."

"Then give us a few extra days. I'm asking for a delay in the interests of justice."

"When lawyers have nothing better, they always offer a platitude about the 'interests of justice.' I can't postpone every trial just because a client fires his attorney. We'll start jury selection at ten o'clock on Monday morning."

"But Your Honor—,"

"I've ruled, Mr. Daley.

* * *

Rosie answered her cell on the first ring. "Where are you?" she asked.

"Leaving the Hall." I pressed my iPhone against my right ear as I walked through the crowded lobby. "Jury selection starts Monday."

"Terrific. I need you at the office. Pete just got here. We need to talk."

10
"WE NEED TO DO THIS BY THE BOOK"

Rosie's oven-like office smelled of perspiration and coffee as Pete spoke to me in a somber tone. "Melinda's story checked out. She's Tommy's daughter. Her son is Tommy's grandkid. My DNA guy is ninety-nine-point-ninety-seven percent sure." His mouth turned up. "We get to welcome a new niece and great-nephew into the family, Mick. You wanna break the good news to Big John?"

"I'll let you have the honors."

Rosie wasn't amused. "You can plan your family reunion later. We just received the files from Sandy Tran. We need to decide who will sit first chair."

Easy call. "I will."

"No, you won't."

"We discussed this, Rosie."

"We didn't agree, Mike."

No, we didn't. "The circumstances have changed."

"Our procedures haven't."

Here goes. "We're the co-heads of the Felony Division. We decide on staffing. We don't have time to wait until our regular meeting on Monday morning."

"You have a conflict of interest."

"I have a personal interest, but no conflict."

Pete interjected. "Maybe I should wait outside."

"Stay here," Rosie snapped. "He's *your* great-nephew, too." She pointed two fingers at me. "You may not have a technical legal conflict, but you have a personal one."

"With whom?"

"Me. Your job description doesn't include trying cases.

You don't have time."

"I'll make time."

"It's a bad idea to represent a family member."

"I just met him. I'll treat him like any other client."

"Sure you will. Besides, you can't do this yourself."

"I was hoping to persuade you to sit second chair."

"Not a chance, Mike."

"Then give me Rolanda."

"No."

"Please."

"No *way*. I'm not going to put my niece in the middle of your family mess."

Rolanda Fernandez was the daughter of Rosie's older brother, who ran a produce market in the Mission. She had spent her summers during college and law school working for us at Fernandez and Daley. Rolanda graduated at the top of her class from my alma mater, Boalt Law School, at UC-Berkeley. She'd turned down an offer from a corporate firm downtown that would have paid her almost twice as much as she was making at the P.D.'s Office to follow in her aunt's footsteps. She was one of our most promising attorneys.

I tried again. "It would be an excellent experience for her. She's young, smart, and ambitious. And she isn't related to Thomas."

"She's still your niece, and she's definitely related to *me*."

"That doesn't present a legal conflict."

"I don't like it."

"She needs to learn how to deal with the media in a high-profile case. She's ready and she has time. She just pled out that gang shooting at Hunters Point."

Rosie thought about it for a long moment. "It might make sense."

"It *does* make sense." It was a rare instance where the truth lined up with my story. I was also hoping for an even more unusual occurrence—that I might win an argument with Rosie.

"I want to talk to her first," she said.

"Fine." She was going to give Rolanda an easy out.

"You'll also need an investigator."

I pointed at Pete. "I already have one."

"He doesn't work for us."

"He works for me."

"Then it's on your dime."

"Fine." I turned to Pete. "We may need to work out a payment plan."

"We always do."

"Would you mind waiting outside for a minute? Rosie and I need to talk."

"Sure, Mick." He headed into the hall.

Rosie made no attempt to conceal her displeasure. "We need to do this by the book, and I have some non-negotiable conditions. First, you're going to treat Rolanda well and give her plenty of responsibility."

"Of course."

"Second, our resources are limited."

I was on my own. "I know."

"Third, I don't want you and your brother playing cops-and-robbers. If you're going to look for witnesses in the Tenderloin, you're going to be extra careful."

"Agreed." For the most part.

"Fourth, I don't want you to say a word to the press until I issue a statement."

"Okay. What are you planning to say?"

"The truth. We've been appointed to handle Nguyen's case. We've just discovered that he's your great-nephew. We followed our usual procedures. If they want any additional information, they should talk to you."

"You worried about political fallout?"

"There's always fallout, Mike. If you screw up, it could

reflect poorly on me. I've worked hard on this campaign. If you embarrass me, I will never forgive you."

"Our client is entitled to representation. If we get an acquittal, it could help you."

"Not necessarily. If you act like a slime ball or you get Nguyen off on a technicality, it could cut against me."

"You're saying we can't win even if we win?"

"You're the one insisting on handling this case yourself."

"I'm prepared to take that risk."

"*You* have nothing to lose."

That was true. "My great-nephew could go to jail for the rest of his life."

"You didn't even know that he was your great-nephew until five minutes ago."

I left it there. It was better to let Rosie have the last word.

The seven-foot, three-hundred-twenty-pound frame of our secretary, legal assistant, security guard, and muscle man, Terrence "The Terminator" Love, filled Rosie's doorway. His high-pitched voice sounded out of place for a guy who looked like Shaquille O'Neal. "Where do you want me to put the files for the Nguyen case?"

"The conference room," I said. "Please tell Rolanda that I need to see her."

"I will." The light reflected off The Terminator's shaved dome. "Rolanda's first chair?"

"No, I am."

His pockmarked face rearranged itself into a wide smile, exposing a gold front tooth—a souvenir of his first paycheck from Fernandez and Daley. "You're trying cases again?"

"Just this one."

"Must be something special."

"It is." Terrence was perceptive for a guy who had spent much of his youth beating the daylights out of his opponents and drinking copious quantities of malt liquor. "I'll explain later. In the meantime, I need you to cancel my appointments for the next week."

"Just like old times. By the way, Melinda Nguyen is here to see you again."

"Tell her I'll be out in a few minutes."

"Will do." He left Rosie's office and closed the door behind him.

Rosie spoke to me in a thoughtful tone. "You sure you want to do this?"

"Absolutely." I thought about our boss, who was sitting down the hall. Robert Kidd had served with distinction as Public Defender for almost three decades, and he had always been supportive—even when I tested the limits of our procedures and his patience. "We should probably clear this with Robert."

She grinned. "I already did."

11

"WE HAVE A FEW CONDITIONS"

Melinda's voice was tense. "I didn't expect to hear from you so soon."

"We're very resourceful." I grabbed a Diet Dr Pepper from the mini-fridge behind my desk. "Something to drink?"

"No, thanks."

Pete was sitting on my windowsill and nursing a Coke. I looked straight into my newfound niece's eyes. "The good news is we've been approved to represent Thomas. The bad news is the judge rejected our request for a delay, so jury selection starts Monday." I waited a beat. "We got the results of the DNA tests. Want to reconsider anything you've told us?"

Her eyes darted to Pete, then back to me. "No."

"There's a ninety-nine percent chance that you're Tommy's daughter and Thomas is your son. That's good enough for us."

"Mr. Daley, I don't know what to say."

"For starters, you can stop calling me 'Mr. Daley.'"

"Do you want me to call you 'Uncle Mike'?"

"Just 'Mike' is fine." I pointed at my brother. "Call him 'Pete.' And thank him for getting this information so quickly."

"Thank you, Pete." She took a moment to get her bearings. "Does this mean you're willing to handle Thomas's case?"

"Yes. My colleague, Rolanda Fernandez, will be assisting me. She's an excellent attorney. She's also Rosie's niece."

"I'm very grateful."

I hope you'll feel the same way when the case is over. "We have a few conditions. First, you and Thomas are going to treat Rolanda respectfully."

"Of course."

"Second, if I find out that you or Thomas has lied to us about anything, all bets are off."

"Understood."

"Third, you're going to write down everything you know about yourself, your uncle, and every member of your family who came to the U.S. We're going to check with ICE. If anything is untrue, you're going to have some major legal issues."

"Okay."

"Fourth, you're going to tell us everything you know about your son, Duc Tho, their friends, the guy who owns the liquor store, and anybody else who may have been in the vicinity that night. We've been told that Tho was tossed out of Galileo for selling marijuana. Somebody was supplying him. We need to know if anybody was working for him. We may want to offer that information to the D.A."

"Sandy Tran asked me the same thing. I don't know much about Duc Tho."

"Then you have four days to use your connections in the Vietnamese community to find something. It may be our only bargaining chip. You also gave us the name of the village where my brother is buried." I handed her a pad of paper. "I want you to draw us a more detailed map."

"I-I can't give you a street address. It was in the jungle."

"We have connections with the Vietnamese government." *No, we don't.* "Write down the exact location or you get a Deputy Public Defender."

"I don't know if anything is still there."

"Give us as much as you can."

She drew a rudimentary map. "We lived along a creek two miles north of Cib Tran Quang. There was a dirt road and about ten huts. There was a well at the south end of town and a tree about a hundred feet west of the well. That was our cemetery. I don't know if there are still any markers. My father and mother are buried under that tree."

* * *

"Heard from your contacts in Vietnam?" I asked.

Pete took a sip of warm Coke. "Working on it."

We were sitting in my office. Melinda had just left. "Any idea how long it might take to get a read on this?" I asked.

"Longer than it took to get the DNA results."

"I'm going down to the Tenderloin. I want to talk to the owner of the store."

"I'll come with you."

"Meet me there in an hour. I want to spend a few minutes with Rolanda. Then I want to talk to the homicide inspector in charge of the investigation."

* * *

My iPhone vibrated as I was walking out of my office. I didn't recognize the number on the display. As soon as I heard the smoker's hack, I regretted my decision to answer.

"Mr. Daley? Jerry Edwards, *San Francisco Chronicle*."

"Good to hear from you," I lied. Edwards had been the *Chronicle*'s in-house pit bull for three decades. Depending on the time of day and how much bourbon he'd consumed, the award-winning investigative reporter operated on a narrow spectrum between angry and hostile. "What can I do for you?"

"I heard you paid a visit to Thomas Nguyen."

"I did."

"I understand his case has been kicked over to the P.D.'s Office."

"It has."

"Judge McDaniel didn't grant your request for a delay."

"She didn't." It was a matter of public record that the trial was set for Monday.

"According to your ex-wife, you're going to handle the trial yourself. I didn't realize you were trying cases again."

"This one landed on our doorstep at eight o'clock this

morning. We need somebody with experience to get up to speed right away."

"Your ex-wife issued a statement saying that Thomas Nguyen is your nephew."

"Great-nephew."

"You shouldn't be spending the taxpayers' hard-earned money defending your relatives. It's a conflict of interest."

"He went through our intake procedures and qualified for our services. We have a legal obligation to provide counsel."

"He's your nephew."

"Great-nephew. I met him for the first time this morning."

"You didn't know his mother?"

"I met her this morning, too."

"That's a very interesting coincidence, Mr. Daley."

"My older brother died in Vietnam a long time ago."

"I know. I was at Cal when he was the quarterback. Nguyen's mother just happened to wander into your office a couple of days before her son is going on trial?"

"Yes. His case will be handled like any other client's."

"I'll be watching. If he receives special treatment, I will make sure that you and Ms. Fernandez are held accountable."

12

"IT HAPPENED VERY FAST"

"Any surprises on the prosecution's witness list?" I asked.

Rosie's niece pulled at her straight black hair—a gesture she'd picked up from her aunt. "Not really, Mike."

Rolanda Fernandez was eleven when I first met her at her father's produce market in the Mission. Now on the wrong side of thirty and a veteran of five years at the P.D.'s Office, her hair had flecks of gray and crow's feet were making inroads at the corners of her eyes. I was immensely proud of her—even though she made me feel old.

At two-fifteen on Thursday afternoon, we were sitting in the windowless office that she shared with two Deputy P.D.s who were in court. The clutter reminded me of my days as a rookie P.D. The walls were filled with photos of defendants, victims, and crime scenes. Files covered the mismatched desks. Rolanda's going-to-court suit was draped over her chair. The only personal item on her desk was a framed photo of her boyfriend.

I pointed at the picture. "How's Zach?"

"Pretty good. He'll be home for a couple of days next week."

She and Zach had met in law school. They shared an overpriced studio apartment in the Mission around the corner from the house where Rosie had grown up, but it was a stretch to say that they lived together. Zach worked for one of the big firms downtown. He had spent three years living out of a suitcase in Las Vegas working on a class action. I liked him, but I thought he was more committed to his job than his girlfriend.

"Any light at the end of the tunnel?" I asked.

"There are kids who haven't started law school yet who will be working on this case when I'm retired. It was mentioned in *abovethelaw* last week."

Abovethelaw.com is the go-to website for the skinny on who's who and what's what at the mega-firms. Its editors are among the most influential players in the legal profession. The managing partners of the power firms are terrified of them.

"Any chance of a settlement?"

"Unlikely. It's a lethal combination of too many clients with deep pockets and big egos and too many lawyers who bill by the hour."

I had little to offer. "They pay him well."

"They do."

"Still glad you became a Public Defender?"

"I wouldn't trade places with him."

"Neither would I." I thought about the five interminable years I'd spent at a soulless mega-firm at the top of the Bank of America Building after Rosie and I split up. I took the job because I needed the money. It was an experience that I wouldn't wish upon anybody except the soulless partners who fired me because I didn't bring in enough high-paying clients. "Thanks for jumping in on short notice."

"I had time."

This was technically true, but she could have filled her plate with other cases. "Rosie didn't try to talk you out of it?"

"Let's just say that she gave me every opportunity to decline your generous offer."

I'll bet. "I'm glad we'll finally have a chance to try a case together. It will be good experience for you. It might even be fun."

"I'll wait until it's over before I thank you for the privilege."

It was like talking to Rosie 2.0. "Anything you want to ask

before we start?"

"Is Thomas Nguyen really your great-nephew?"

"Yes."

"Does that make him my cousin?"

"Sort of. Ask Grandma Sylvia. She has the final call on family matters."

"Where do you want to start?"

I pointed at the prosecution's witnesses listed on her whiteboard. "Let's go through the lineup."

She took off her glasses. "The first officer at the scene will probably lead off. The Chief Medical Examiner will confirm that Tho died from six shots to the chest. The forensics expert will confirm that the bullets were fired from the shopkeeper's gun—an AR-15. The shopkeeper and his son will say that Tho was about to pull a gun. That supports self-defense, and you can bet their stories will match up. The security guard will corroborate their testimony."

"What about the daughter?"

"She's on their witness list, but she said that she didn't see Tho come in the store."

I did a quick mental calculus on the SFPD and other law enforcement personnel who would testify, all of whom I knew. The first officer at the scene was a solid career cop, but he'd been suspended a couple of times for beating up detainees—something we might be able to use. The evidence techs were competent and experienced. It would be difficult to shake them.

I looked at the last name on her board. "Ken Lee is the homicide inspector?"

"Yeah. You know him?"

"He's good. As far as I know, he's clean." I studied the witness list. "Any holes?"

"There are *always* holes, Mike. We just need to find them."

Good answer. I asked about the shopkeeper.

She looked at her laptop. "Ortega Cruz. Sixty. Has owned the store for twenty-six years. His parents came from Mexico. He was born here. Lives in the Mission. Divorced. A nineteen-year-old son works at the store. A seventeen-year-old daughter goes to Mercy High."

"Does your dad know him?"

"No."

Rolanda's father knew everybody who was anybody in the Mission. "Criminal record?"

"A couple of traffic tickets. No arrests."

"What do you know about the AR-15?"

"Purchased legally in Nevada. He has a full arsenal. About a dozen weapons are registered in his name."

"Does he know how to use them?"

"He was in the army and he belongs to a gun club in South City. His credit cards indicate that he's bought a lot of ammunition."

"Sandy Tran told me that he shot somebody a couple of years ago."

"It happened during an attempted armed robbery. The perp survived, but he died later at Pelican Bay. No charges were filed against Cruz. Self-defense."

"This may be a recurring theme. If we can show that Cruz has an itchy finger, it might mitigate the self-defense claim."

"He runs a liquor store in the Tenderloin. I'm surprised that he hasn't shot more people."

That's fair. "Any evidence that he has a temper?"

"Nothing in the police report."

"What about the divorce?"

"Long and acrimonious."

"Domestic abuse?"

"Nothing on record."

"This isn't helping."

"You take your facts as they come, Mike."

Yes, you do. "We should talk to his ex-wife and kids. The son works at the store?"

"Yeah. Graduated from high school. Dropped out of City College. He was at the store when Tho walked in. He corroborated his father's story."

No surprise. "Criminal record?"

"Three hits for shoplifting and two for buying weed. Did community service."

I asked about the daughter.

"Honors student at Mercy High. Never been in trouble. Doesn't work at the store." She confirmed that the daughter went to a movie with a friend who had dropped her off at the store. "Her father was going to drive her home."

"Where was she when the shooting started?"

"At her father's desk in an alcove behind the deli counter. She ducked under the desk when her father started shooting."

"It must have been awful."

"No doubt."

"Who else was there?"

"The security guard was standing next to the shopkeeper when Tho walked in. Seems his only qualification was the fact that he was the owner's nephew. Currently unemployed."

"Criminal record?"

"Two arrests for grand theft auto and one for armed robbery. The armed robbery was pleaded down and he got probation."

Not a terribly solid citizen. "Others?"

"A deliveryman and a customer were in the back. They said they didn't see Tho come inside. They ran out the back door when the shooting started."

"So the only witnesses are the shopkeeper, his son, and his nephew?"

"Correct."

It wasn't much. "Did Tho have a cell phone?"

"A throwaway purchased for cash the day before he was killed."

"No smartphone?"

"A lot of people can't afford an iPhone, Mike. Or maybe he was sophisticated enough to use an untraceable throwaway."

"E-mail? Facebook? Twitter? Instagram? Social media?"

"Nothing. He had a laptop, but he didn't use it much."

"Crime scene photos?"

Rolanda took out a stack of five-by-sevens. "These are pretty grim, Mike."

They always are.

She laid them out on her desk. "It's a narrow store," she said. "The register is on the right as you walk in. Tho was standing about five feet from the counter when he was shot."

The grisly color photos showed Tho's body on the linoleum floor. His gray hoodie was drenched in blood. His eyes were closed. "Sandy Tran said Tho was packing."

"Ortega Cruz said that he found a Kel-Tec P-3AT underneath him." It was a light, cheap, semi-automatic pistol at the high end of the Saturday Night Special food chain. "Yellow marker number six."

I compared the photos before and after Tho's body had been removed. The pistol was within the outline of Tho's body. "Serial number?"

"The identifying information was removed."

"Very professional for a twenty-one-year-old drug dealer. Did they find the gun in his pocket?"

"No. According to the shopkeeper, it was underneath him. They found Tho's prints on the gun."

"Anybody else's prints?"

"The shopkeeper's. He said he got his prints on the gun when he disarmed it."

Interesting. "You believe him?"

"I don't believe anybody."

"We can argue that he planted the gun."

"I know."

"You sure that Tho walked in with a gun?"

"The shopkeeper and his son said he did."

"What do *you* think?"

She answered honestly. "I don't know."

"The felony murder charge will turn on whether Tho committed a provocative act. If we can show that he was unarmed, we can argue that there was none."

"It's still self-defense if the shopkeeper thought he had a gun, even if he was mistaken."

"Maybe he didn't like Tho or acted unilaterally."

"It will be hard to prove."

"We don't have to prove it. We just need to argue it. Video?"

"Yes." Rolanda's fingers flew across the keyboard of her laptop as she pulled up the security video. "Two cameras. One in front and one in back. The one in back was broken." I looked over her shoulder as she cued the video. "It happened very fast."

Rolanda's office was silent except for the buzzing of the clock. The grainy black-and-white footage was shot from a fixed camera mounted on the ceiling above the cash register.

I saw a rack of potato chips near the front of the store. Then I got my first glimpse of Duc Tho during the final seconds of his life. He had a slight build and the wisp of a beard. A hoodie was pulled down over his forehead. The white numerals in the upper left corner indicated that he walked into Alcatraz Liquors at ten-forty-seven and thirty-three seconds. He glanced at the chips and turned toward the counter. It was difficult to see his features. His hands were inside his pockets.

Tho glanced to the left of the register. He smiled or smirked—it was hard to tell. His mouth opened briefly, which suggested that he might have said something—there was no audio. He was still turning as his eyes opened wide for an instant before a hail of bullets blew open the center of his chest. He fell backward into the chips, leaned to his right, and toppled out of camera view. He was probably dead before he hit the floor. Rolanda stopped the video at ten-forty-seven and thirty-eight seconds. Tho had been inside the store for less than five seconds.

Rolanda pushed "Play" again. The shopkeeper rushed into the frame to check on Tho. Then he dropped out of camera view. A moment later, he stood up and pulled out his cell phone. The video ended.

"The shopkeeper could have planted the gun," I said.

Rolanda nodded. "It's possible."

"Run it again."

We watched it again. And again. We studied it in slow motion and in real time. Rolanda enhanced the footage. Tho's right hand never left his pocket.

After the fifth viewing, I sat down next to my niece. "Judge McDaniel is going to let the prosecution introduce this video into evidence. You think he said something to the shopkeeper?"

"Hard to tell. We'll need a lipreader."

"What else did you see?"

"A kid getting shot."

"What *didn't* you see?"

"A gun."

"Exactly. That's one possible line of defense: no gun—no robbery—no provocative act."

Rolanda put on her glasses. "Where do we start?"

"You keep going through the files and the video. I'm going to talk to Inspector Lee."

13
"PROFESSIONAL COURTESY"

The world-weary homicide inspector took a swallow of coffee and tossed his paper cup into an overflowing trash can. "Heard you went to see Thomas Nguyen."

"I did."

"Saw a tweet from Jerry Edwards. Nguyen is your nephew."

"Great-nephew."

"Interesting."

Five years earlier, Inspector Ken Lee had earned a Medal of Valor for his undercover work in busting a Chinatown drug ring run by a small-time thug named Raymond "Shrimp Boy" Chow, who moved up the criminal food chain to cleaner and more lucrative work bribing local officials. Eventually, Chow ended up in jail on a murder charge after he ordered the hit on one of his business associates. Lee was rewarded with a promotion to homicide, where he was paired with the legendary Roosevelt Johnson, who had started his career walking the beat in the Tenderloin with my father. A couple of years later, Roosevelt retired for the third and final time, and Lee had worked alone ever since. Now in his mid-forties, he still had boyish good looks, but his hair was mostly gray, and he had a degenerating hip.

He gave me a half-hearted handshake. "Figured you'd show up sooner or later."

"Guess it's sooner."

He was sitting at a dented metal desk in the bullpen housing SFPD's homicide inspectors on the fourth floor of the Hall. The fluorescent lights buzzed and an overworked window fan recirculated sauna-like air.

I sat down and ignored the disdainful glares of Lee's colleagues who were grinding out reports. This was going to be a finesse game where I had no leverage, so I wanted to engage him. I pointed at the photo of his daughter. "Is Elizabeth in college?"

"Not yet. She's a junior at Lowell."

"How's life with a teenager?"

"Easier than when I worked undercover. She lives with my ex-wife."

I responded with an understanding nod. "Grace is a freshman at USC."

"I heard. How does a fellow Cal guy feel about that?"

I grinned. "Bad parenting, but it seems like a good fit for her."

He didn't return my smile. "How do you pay for a private school on a P.D.'s salary?"

"USC gave her a scholarship."

"Think I can get the same deal for Elizabeth?"

"Maybe. Tell her to apply early."

He laced his fingers behind his head. "How much longer you gonna do this?"

"I can start collecting my pension in seven years, six months, four days, one hour, and twenty minutes. Realistically, I'm not going anywhere until Grace and Tommy finish college."

"My younger daughter is only ten. I still have at least a dozen years."

"It'll be here before you know it." Given San Francisco's precarious finances, I hope there will be a few bucks left in the till when my number comes up. One of the reasons Rosie decided to run for P.D. was the possibility of a bigger retirement package. Welcome to the world of public pension roulette.

Lee touched the lapel of his Men's Wearhouse suit jacket. "Heard you're representing Thomas Nguyen. When did you start trying cases again?"

"Now. Betsy McDaniel won't give us an extension. Jury selection starts Monday."

"You really just found out that this kid is your nephew?"

"Great-nephew. I met him for the first time this morning. His mother, too."

"How long has she lived here?"

"Thirty years. She never contacted us."

"Interesting family dynamics. This kid is your older brother's grandson?"

"Yup."

"I thought he died in Vietnam."

"He did. We were told it was in a plane crash. Turns out he died a few years later."

"You're absolutely sure this kid is your great-nephew?"

"The DNA tests checked out."

"How did you get results so fast?"

"Pete has a guy at UCSF."

"Figures. He doing okay?"

"Fine. Keeps busy."

"Good." He clasped his fingers in front of his face. "And now I suppose you want my help."

"Professional courtesy."

"I don't recall any from you on the Davis case. You knew his alibi witness was lying."

The other homicide inspectors were now watching us. "She lied to me, too."

"You should have known."

"I know." Three years ago, I helped a client of less-than-stellar character beat an armed robbery charge when his sister-in-law provided a less-than-truthful alibi. Two weeks later, my client shot a police officer during a traffic stop. The cop ended up in a wheelchair. "I'm sorry."

"So am I. Either way, I don't have to talk to you."

I recited a defense lawyer's catechism. "You have a legal obligation to provide information that might exonerate my client."

"There is none."

The games begin. "Nguyen was just sitting in the car."

"I didn't invent the felony murder rule."

I had to grovel. "Please, Ken."

An eye-roll. "I'll give you five minutes of professional courtesy."

It was better than nothing. "What happened at the store?"

"This is where I'm supposed to tell you to read my report."

"Can you give me the highlights?"

Another eye-roll. "Tho went inside and started to pull a gun. The owner shot him in self-defense. End of story."

"I watched the security video. You can't see a gun."

"Doesn't matter. Ortega Cruz thought Tho was going to shoot him. Cruz found the gun under the body. Tho's prints were on the handle. A jury will put the pieces together."

"They found Cruz's prints on the gun, too."

"He disarmed it."

"He could have planted it."

"Sure. Sell it to the jury."

Gee, thanks. "Why didn't Tho fire the gun?"

"He never had a chance."

"Had he ever been inside the store?"

"A couple of times."

"Criminal record?"

"Arrested for shoplifting and possession. Did a few weeks in juvie, but never spent any time with the big boys."

"We heard he got thrown out of Galileo for dealing weed."

"We didn't have enough evidence to charge him."

"Do you know the name of Tho's supplier?"

"If I did, I would have arrested him."

"You must have found something on his cell phone or computer."

"He had a throwaway phone."

I was using up my remaining four minutes quickly. "We heard that the owner of the store had an acrimonious divorce. Domestic violence?"

"I'm a homicide inspector, not a marriage counselor."

"Does Ortega Cruz have a criminal record?"

"A few traffic tickets."

"Arrests?"

"He was hauled in on a battery complaint a couple of years ago after he threw a homeless guy out of his store. The charges were dropped."

"Has he ever shot anybody else?" I wanted to see if Lee would provide any details.

"He shot an armed robber a couple of years ago. The guy died at Pelican Bay. No charges were filed against Cruz. Self-defense."

This was consistent with the information in the file. "I heard he used a Bushmaster."

"An AR-15 purchased legally in Nevada. We confiscated the weapon and we aren't giving it back. Nobody outside of the U.S. Army should have an assault rifle."

"I presume he has another weapon at the store?"

"A handgun. Purchased legally. Licensed and registered."

"Did he know how to use the Bushmaster?"

"Spent time at a range in South City. Also served in Vietnam, but didn't see combat. Honorable discharge."

"Did he know Tho?"

"He said he'd seen him in the store a couple of times. Never gave him any trouble."

"Has Cruz ever threatened anybody?"

"About a year ago, a guy pulled a knife. Cruz grabbed his

rifle and held him until a unit arrived."

"We'd like to talk to him."

"He's dead."

Hell. "How many times has the store been robbed since Cruz shot Tho?"

"None. Word is out—Cruz has a weapon and isn't afraid to use it."

It was an effective—albeit heavy-handed—message of deterrence. I asked about Cruz's kids.

"Tony dropped out of City College. Isabel is a junior at Mercy. Tony has a couple of hits for buying weed and shoplifting, but he's never done time. Isabel's clean. No gangs, drugs, or other trouble."

We'd check. "I heard that Tony and Isabel were at the store that night."

"Tony works there. Isabel was waiting for her father to drive her home. Tony will corroborate his father's story. Isabel didn't see anything."

"Any chance Tony shot Tho?"

"Not according to his father."

"Maybe Ortega was trying to protect his son or daughter."

"Not likely, Mike."

"Mind if we talk to them?"

"I can't stop you. They're under no obligation to talk to you."

And their father is protective and owns multiple weapons. "Did either of them know Tho?"

"Nope." He glanced at his watch. "Your five minutes ended five minutes ago."

"Any chance Ortega Cruz was into other stuff? Drugs? Alcohol?"

"He's a deacon at St. Peter's."

When I was a rookie priest at St. Anne's, I learned that deacons weren't always saints. "Violence? Fights? Problems with his neighbors?"

"Nothing reported to us."

It was a more equivocal answer than I had expected. "How does he feel about the Vietnamese community?"

"He's made a living selling them booze."

"It doesn't mean he likes them. Who else was in the store that night besides the son and the daughter?" I wanted to see if Lee's answer matched up with the information in the file.

"A deliveryman and a customer who didn't see Tho come inside. They left through the back door. A security guard was behind the counter near the window. His name is Hector Cruz. Twenty-four. He's Ortega's nephew." He confirmed that Hector had two arrests for grand theft auto and one for armed robbery.

"Was he armed?"

"A piece registered to his uncle."

Great. "Loaded?"

"They're more effective that way."

"Did he know how to use it?"

"His uncle took him to the range a few times."

"Did you consider the possibility that he shot Tho?"

"His uncle admitted that he pulled the trigger."

"You can't see who fired the shots in the security video. Maybe Ortega is protecting his son or his nephew."

"Either way, the shooter acted in self-defense."

"Nguyen told me that Tho didn't have a gun."

"He's mistaken."

"We'll put him on the stand."

"Be my guest. Andy Erickson will take him apart on cross." He stood up, signaling that our conversation was coming to an end. "You got nothing, Mike. The kid should have listened to Sandy Tran and taken the plea."

"I heard that Ignacio Navarro was the first officer at the scene."

"He was."

"Is he still on suspension?"

"He just came back to work." He glanced at his watch. "Time's up."

14

"I'M UNDER ORDERS"

Sergeant Ignacio Navarro's leathery face transformed into a circumspect smile. The one-time all-city defensive tackle at Mission High stroked his silver mustache and spoke to me in a guttural voice. "How's Pete?"

"Fine."

Three decades earlier, Navarro had shown my brother the ropes at Mission Station. He struggled to shoe-horn his two-hundred-and-sixty-pound frame into an overburdened chair at his new post at the public information desk in the bowels of Tenderloin Station, a windowless bomb shelter at the corner of Eddy and Jones, two blocks west of Alcatraz Liquors.

"When did you get back to work?" I asked.

"Last week." His voice filled with contempt. "I haul in a serial rapist. He takes a pop at me when I'm putting him into my unit, so I defend myself. Next thing I know, he hires a lawyer, the city rolls, and I end up here in the dungeon. Your dad never had to put up with this crap. How do they expect us to serve and protect when the bureaucrats at City Hall won't watch our backs?"

"You have a right to defend yourself."

"Damn right."

I glanced at his half-eaten turkey sandwich next to the *Chronicle* sports section on his otherwise empty desk. Navarro was suspended after he'd cracked the skull of a man who had done time for rape, pimping, and dealing ecstasy. The prisoner wasn't going to win a Presidential Medal of Freedom, but this sort of police behavior was frowned upon—especially since the guy's hands were cuffed behind him. Navarro probably would have gotten away with it if a bystander hadn't recorded the incident on his iPhone and showed it to a reporter at Channel 5. My dad never had to worry about seeing himself on YouTube.

He took a draw from a can of Sprite. "Heard you got the Nguyen case."

"I did."

"Heard he's your nephew."

"Great-nephew. Tommy was his grandfather."

"No kidding." He set down his drink. "I didn't know he had a kid."

"Neither did I. We thought Tommy died in a plane crash. Turns out he died a couple of years later."

"Your dad never said much about him."

"It was hard."

"Why didn't Nguyen's mother contact you sooner?"

"Long story."

"I got time."

I didn't, but I wanted to keep him talking. "She was afraid of being deported. Ken Lee said you were the first officer at the scene."

"I was, but I'm not talking."

"Please, Ignacio."

"I'm under orders. My lieutenant says I'm not supposed to talk about anything but the weather."

"You're the public information officer."

"You aren't the public."

"What do you do all day?"

"I follow orders."

Despite his rough edges, Navarro was a straight shooter. "You're on the witness list."

"You'll find out everything I know at trial."

"You have a legal obligation to provide any exculpatory evidence."

"There isn't any."

"If you give me a little help now, I might be able to convince my client to take a deal."

"Andy Erickson told me to keep my mouth shut. He's a smart guy."

"Yes, he is." I didn't like begging, but I had no choice. "We go back a long way, Ignacio. Please tell me what you saw."

"Off the record?"

No such thing. "Of course."

He finished his sandwich. "Tho was dead. The shopkeeper found a gun under his body. He disarmed it and left it on the floor. The shopkeeper admitted that he'd shot him. Said it was self-defense. His son corroborated his story. So did the security guard. His daughter didn't see anything. Your great-nephew was out in the car dicking around, so we brought him in for questioning. Next thing I know, our esteemed District Attorney decided to charge him with felony murder."

"You think it was a good idea?"

"I have no opinion."

"Who called it in?"

"Ortega Cruz."

"You know him pretty well?"

"Yeah. Been in business for a long time."

"How long did it take you to get there?"

"About two minutes. I went by myself."

"Who else was there?"

"Cruz's son and daughter, a security guard, a customer, and a deliveryman. Their names are in the report."

"Why didn't the guard stop Tho before he came inside?"

"Because he's a screw-up. Name's Hector Cruz. He's Ortega's nephew. Big dumb kid with a phony uniform, a fake badge, and a real gun. He's lucky he didn't shoot himself."

"Where was everybody when Tho came in?"

"Read the statements. Ortega was behind the register. His son was standing next to him at the deli counter. The daughter was doing her homework at a desk behind the deli counter. The guard was over by the window. The customer and the deliveryman were in the rear. They bolted out the back door when the shooting started."

"You got names?"

"The deliveryman is Odell Jones. Works for Budweiser. The customer is Eugene Pham. Works at a restaurant on Larkin. Their contact info is in the report."

"Any chance somebody else was there?"

"Not according to the witnesses."

Not exactly a complete denial. "Did anybody outside see anything?"

"This is the Tenderloin, Mike. Nobody saw nothing."

"Did the owner know Tho?"

"He said he'd come in the store a couple of times. Never gave him any trouble."

His story was consistent with the information from Inspector Lee. "You ever shop there?"

"Occasionally. Most of the time, I went over to pick up shoplifters or investigate an armed robbery."

"How often did that happen?"

"Shoplifting happens almost every day. You can count on an armed robbery at least once a month. Ortega has us on speed dial."

"He kept a gun behind the counter."

"You gotta protect yourself."

"I understand this wasn't the first time he'd used it."

"He shot somebody a couple of years ago in self-defense. No charges were filed."

"Has he ever pulled a gun on anybody else?"

"About a year ago, he pulled his piece on a guy who flashed a knife. He kept the gun on him until we got there and made the arrest."

"Was it the same Bushmaster that he used to shoot Tho?"

"No. It was a Glock. We would have confiscated a Bushmaster."

"Is Ortega a good guy?"

"He isn't a bad guy. He doesn't take crap from anyone."

"Any funny business in the store? Selling booze or cigarettes to minors? Drugs? Numbers? Hookers?"

"He used to take bets. Nowadays, people run book on their iPhones."

"Any run-ins with his neighbors?"

"A couple of years ago, he beat up a homeless guy who was pissing in his doorway. A few months ago, he caught a kid spraying graffiti on his door. He put a gun to the kid's head and told him he'd blow it off if he ever caught him again. Nobody pressed charges."

"Sounds like Cruz has a temper."

"So would you if people were pissing on your door."

"I wouldn't put a gun to their head."

"You might if it happened twenty times."

Maybe. I asked him about the son.

"Tony isn't a brain surgeon, but he's a decent kid. He partied a little too much in high school and got picked up a couple of times for buying weed, but he's kept his nose clean for a couple of years."

"What about the daughter?"

"Good kid. Honors student at Mercy. Never been in trouble."

"How much did she see that night?"

"More than she should have. Her father yelled at her to duck under the desk when Tho came in. She didn't see him get shot, but she heard everything."

"She must have seen the body."

"She did. Must have been horrific."

"Is she going to testify?"

"Not my call, but I doubt it. She didn't see Tho come in the store and her parents are dead-set against it."

"Can't blame them. And the security guard?"

"Hector is a lug who lives with his mother. He didn't make it through City College, so he went to work at the store. He has two hits for grand theft auto. He's still on probation for an armed robbery charge that he pleaded down. Ortega fired him after Tho got shot."

I was getting nowhere. "Did you know Tho?"

"Only by name. Garden-variety street punk."

"I heard he did some work for one of your neighborhood drug dealers."

"He was a low-level errand boy who sold weed."

"You got the name of his supplier?"

"No."

"Would you tell me if you did?"

"After I arrested him." He made a dramatic gesture of picking up the paper. "I gotta get back to work."

*   *   *

Pete's number appeared on my iPhone. "Where are you, Mick?" he asked.

"Leaving Tenderloin Station. Where are you?"

"Across the street from Alcatraz Liquors. You said you'd be here an hour ago."

"I was talking to Ignacio Navarro. You got anything?"

"My mole at ICE pulled our niece's immigration file. Her story checked out. I have a source at the State Department checking on the village in Vietnam. We'll know more in a day or two."

"Any info about Tho's drug connection?"

"I made a couple of calls, but I haven't heard back yet. How soon can you get here?"

"Ten minutes."

"Hustle, Mick. Cruz's son is working by himself. This may be our only chance to talk to him alone."

15
"I TOLD YOU NOT TO
TALK TO ANYBODY"

The fidgety young man with the slicked-back hair, wispy mustache, and indifferent expression stood behind the deli case next to the cash register. He glanced over my shoulder, touched the stud in his left ear, pulled the sleeve of his Jay-Z T-shirt, and spoke to me in a monotone. "Yeah?"

My dad always said that you should start with sugar. "Two turkey sandwiches on French rolls, please. Lettuce, tomato, mayo, mustard. Two bags of Doritos and a couple of coleslaws."

"Uh, okay."

You have a knack for customer service. "Got a couple of chocolate chip cookies?"

"I might."

Teenagers. "Thanks."

Pete and I were the only other people in the store. Alcatraz Liquors was shoe-horned between a nail salon and a tattoo parlor on the ground floor of a century-old five-story residential hotel on Eddy Street. The cash register, deli case, and ATM took up one side of the narrow room. There was a battered desk with a TV tucked in a nook behind the deli counter. The opposite wall was lined floor-to-ceiling with cheap liquor and boxed wine. The refrigerator in the back was loaded with domestic beer and malt liquor. A hand-lettered note between the beef jerky and the lottery display reminded customers that cold, hard cash was the only coin accepted in this realm.

At five-ten on Thursday afternoon, the front door was

propped open in a futile attempt to lure a breeze inside a business without air conditioning. The stench of exhaust fumes and urine overwhelmed the aroma of salami, potato salad, and sourdough. A homeless guy was sitting on a milk crate in front of the store, a mixed-breed puppy sleeping peacefully at his feet. Many of the passers-by wore housekeeping or food service uniforms. Few spoke English.

I watched the young man slice my roll. "How's business?"

He didn't look up. "Crappy. People can't afford booze if they aren't working."

True. The Tenderloin was still a bastion of reality in San Francisco's expanding tech Neverland. I tried to appear nonchalant as I looked at the security camera above the register. I was standing near the spot where Tho had been gunned down. Pete was pretending to examine the wine selection. In reality, he was memorizing the layout.

I tossed a bag of jerky onto the counter. "How long have you worked here?"

"About a year. My dad owns this place."

"Probably works his ass off."

"So do I."

Sure. "You gonna take over after he retires?"

"We'll see. This isn't Wal-Mart."

"You still in school?"

"Nah. I took a few classes at City College. I didn't like it."

Pete set a gallon box of Burgundy on the counter. "How bad is this stuff?"

The kid grinned. "Pretty bad."

"Perfect." Pete smiled. "It's a gift for somebody I don't like—my idiot brother-in-law."

I always enjoyed watching him work. He didn't have a brother-in-law.

"What's your name?" he asked the kid, knowing the answer.

"Tony."

"I'm Pete. Could you do me a favor? Would you mind if I use your bathroom? I know this isn't Starbucks, but I gotta take a leak really bad." As Tony was thinking about it, Pete added, "I'll buy another jug of this fine wine and there will be a nice tip for you."

Sensing a windfall, Tony handed Pete a key attached to a coat hanger. "Down the hall, turn left, go through the storage room, and follow the smell."

"Got it." Pete headed down the aisle. Tony went back to work on our sandwiches.

"My brother," I said. "Any siblings?"

"My sister is a junior at Mercy. She's going to college."

"Good for her. You live here in the neighborhood?"

"We live with my mom in Daly City. My dad's in the Mission."

"When I was a kid, we lived on Garfield Square. You know the produce market at 24th and Alabama?"

"Yeah."

"The owner used to be my brother-in-law. I get along with him better than I do with my ex-wife." I glanced outside. "My dad was a cop here in the Tenderloin. You think it's sketchy now, you should have seen it in the sixties. I played baseball at S.I."

"I ran track at Jefferson."

We exchanged small talk until Pete returned and gave Tony the key. "Thanks, man."

"No problem." Tony put our sandwiches, Doritos, coleslaws, two plastic forks, and some napkins into a paper bag. I handed him two twenties and told him to keep the change. He gave us an inquisitive look. "What are you doing down here?"

Pete answered him. "We heard you made excellent sandwiches."

"What are you really doing?"

"Trying to fix a problem." Pete placed three twenties on the counter. "I'm going to level with you, Tony. We're looking for information about Thomas Nguyen."

The kid looked at the bills. "I don't think I should accept these."

Pete added two more twenties to the pile. "It's a gratuity for helping me pick the wine. My brother works for the P.D.'s Office. He was just appointed to represent Nguyen."

"I got nothing to say."

I put another twenty on the counter. "If you can help me persuade my client to take a plea bargain, you won't have to waste your time in court next week."

He stashed the money inside his pocket. "He's lucky he didn't get shot."

"I heard. Did you know Duc Tho?"

"I'd seen him a couple of times."

"Do you know any of his friends?"

A hesitation. "'fraid not."

"We heard he made ends meet by dealing weed."

"I don't know anything about it."

And you wouldn't tell us if you did. "Anybody we might talk to off the record to get a little skinny on Tho's business?"

"You're talking to the wrong guy."

I wasn't convinced. "What happened that night?"

"Tho came in and tried to rob us. My dad shot him in self-defense. We called the cops. Your client was outside in the car. The cops arrested him."

"Where were you when Tho came inside?"

He pointed at the floor. "Right here."

"And your dad?"

"Behind the register."

"Anybody else?"

He used his thumb to point behind him. "My sister was

sitting at my dad's desk. She didn't see anything." He gestured toward the window. "My cousin, Hector, was over there. He was our security guard. He didn't see Tho come in, either."

"How could he have missed him?"

"He was talking on the phone."

"You saw Tho come inside?"

"Yeah."

"And you saw him pull a gun?"

There was an almost imperceptible hesitation. "I saw him reach inside his pocket."

"Did you see the gun before he got shot?"

"No, but my dad found it under his body."

"You're sure he had a gun?"

"Yeah."

"Did he say anything?"

"'Gimme the money.' That's when my father took him out."

"You still keep a gun behind the counter?"

"A Glock. Licensed and registered to my father. You wanna see it?"

"I'll take your word for it. Ever used it?"

"At the range."

"You a pretty good shot?"

"Not bad."

"Who else was here?"

"A delivery guy and a customer. They were by the refrigerator. They went out the back door."

"We'd like to talk to the security guard."

"He doesn't work here anymore."

"What's he doing now?"

"He's between jobs."

"You know where we can find him?"

"South City."

The back door opened and a man whom I surmised was

Tony's father filled the hallway. Ortega Cruz was an older, larger, and angrier version of his son. Behind him was a teenage girl wearing a Mercy High School uniform. Tony's sister was pretty. Her delicate features were hidden by black bangs matching her eyes.

Ortega's tone was gruff. "Tony taking care of you?"

"He's been very helpful."

Tony interjected. "He's Nguyen's lawyer."

His father frowned. "I told you not to talk to anybody."

"I didn't say anything."

The elder Cruz turned to me. "Get out of my store."

"I'm trying to persuade Thomas to take a plea. The police said you acted in self-defense."

"I did."

"Then please give us five minutes of your time."

He thought about it for a moment. His voice softened as he spoke to his daughter. "Tony will take you home, Isabel. I'll see you tomorrow."

16
"IT WAS HIM OR ME"

Ortega Cruz spoke to me in a gravelly voice. "The D.A.'s Office told me that I don't have to talk to you."

"You don't." I was in no position to bargain. "I'm asking for a favor."

Cruz jabbed a finger at me. "It was him or me. I'm sorry the kid died, but you do what you gotta do." He punched a button on the register and frowned as he noted the day's receipts. His work shirt was drenched in sweat as he sat on a stool behind the counter. His tone turned surprisingly melancholy. "You got kids?"

"Yeah." I hadn't expected the question. "A daughter in college and a ten-year-old son." I pointed at Pete. "His daughter just turned six."

"Put yourself in my shoes. A punk comes into your store and demands money. You're standing between your son and your nephew. Your daughter is a few feet away. You have a second to react. What would you have done?"

"Just what you did." *Well, maybe not.*

"Exactly."

"My client didn't even come inside the store. You think it's right to put away a kid for murder for sitting outside in the car?"

"That's up to you lawyers. I told the cops the truth: I shot the kid in self-defense. They decided to arrest your client. The D.A. decided to charge him."

"What if he was your kid?"

"I would have told him not to hang out with a lowlife like Duc Tho."

"How do you know that he was a lowlife?"

"He tried to rob me."

"That's fair." I pointed at Tony's graduation photo behind the counter. "Your son is a good kid."

"Yeah." His tone was halfhearted. "He's working."

"For me. If I didn't give him this job, he would be on the street with punks like Tho. He wants to play videogames and hang out with his girlfriend."

"He'll figure it out. Despite our best efforts to screw up our kids, they somehow manage to turn out okay."

"I hope so." His eyes lit up as he glanced at a photo of his daughter. "Isabel is going to college."

I wanted to keep him talking. "I trust that you and your wife are on the same page?"

"Yes. And it's my ex-wife."

"Sorry."

"It is what it is. We split up ten years ago. Maria got tired of the long hours and the late nights. The kids live with her in Daly City. The schools are better."

There was undoubtedly more to the story. "I'm divorced, too. We try to keep things civil around the kids." *And at the office. And in bed.* "Does Isabel come here often?"

"Every once in a while."

"I heard she was here the night that Tho was shot."

"She was. She was sitting at my desk doing her homework."

"How much did she see?"

"Enough. She didn't see Tho come inside the store. I told her to get under the desk when I realized that I was going to have to protect us. She heard everything."

"Did she see the body?"

"Yeah."

I shook my head. "Is she okay?"

"It's getting better."

"She's on the prosecution's witness list."

"I know. They said that she wouldn't have to testify."

"If I can convince my client to take a plea bargain, she won't need to go to court."

Cruz was now engaged. "What else do you need to know?"

I glanced at the homeless guy sitting on his doorstep. "You have much trouble?"

"The usual: shoplifters, gangbangers, drug dealers. Haven't had an armed robbery in a few months. You know what bugs me the most? I get here at five a.m. and my doorway already smells like piss. I wash it down. By noon, it smells again. How would you feel?"

"Not great."

"Welcome to the American Dream. My alarm that goes off twice a week. I know the cops at Tenderloin Station. I bring them sandwiches. I make them a platter at Christmas. It doesn't matter."

"You pay protection money to the gangs?"

"Everybody does. Makes no difference. I hired my nephew as a guard, but he didn't pay attention, so I let him go."

"What do you do for security now?"

He reached under the counter and showed me a Glock. "It's cheaper and more effective. And it doesn't come in late and steal my beer."

"You know how to use it?"

"I go to the range every Sunday after church. Tony and Isabel come with me."

The family that shoots together . . . I nodded at Pete. His turn.

He pointed at the deli counter. "Is that where Tony was standing when Tho came in?"

"Yeah."

"And your nephew?"

"Over by the window. He was talking on his cell phone. He didn't even see Tho."

"How long was Tho inside the store?"

"Not long. A few seconds."

"Did he say anything?"

"'Gimme the money.'" Cruz shrugged. "You think I wanted to shoot him when my kids were here? I did what I had to do."

"I would have done the same thing." Pete's tone remained even. "He pulled the gun as he was walking up to the counter?"

"Yeah."

"What was it?"

"A Kel-Tec P-3AT."

He knew guns. Pete kept pushing. "You saw it?"

"He was pulling it out of his pocket."

"He pointed it at you?"

"He was about to."

"So you took him out first."

"I had to."

"I understand. I used to be a cop. Now I teach self-defense at Richmond Rod & Gun. You should come by. I'll show you some stuff."

"Maybe I will."

"Where do you shoot?"

"Jackson Arms in Daly City."

"Tell Andy that Pete Daley says hi." Pete gave him a conspiratorial wink. "You get a clean kill on Tho?"

"Middle of the chest."

"Nice. How many bullets?"

"Six."

"Any misses?"

"None. He was dead before he hit the floor."

"What'd you use?"

"Bushmaster AR-15. I bought it in Nevada a couple of

years ago."

Pete feigned approval. "Nice action. They gonna give it back?"

"I don't know."

"More reason for us to wrap up this case quickly." Pete glanced at the nine-millimeter on the counter. "Very reliable. Where'd you get it?"

"Jackson Arms."

"You got more?"

"A couple. Everything I got is legal—go ahead and check me out."

"We don't need to."

Yes, we do. Pete glanced at me, and I re-entered the discussion. "You a good shot?"

"Sharpshooter. Tony's even better."

"Did you know Tho?"

"He came in the store a couple of times."

"Ever give you or Tony any trouble? Shoplifting? Hassling you or your customers?"

He shook his head a little too emphatically. "No."

"Was he carrying when he came in the other times?"

"He didn't show it."

"Do you know anything about his family?"

"Just what I've read in the papers."

"You know any of his friends?"

"No."

"We heard he was dealing dope. You know his supplier?"

"No."

"Why did he pick your store?"

"Because he was an idiot. Lots of kids like him in this neighborhood."

"Like what?"

"Young. Stupid. Unemployed. Doing drugs. Looking for trouble."

"Vietnamese gangs give you trouble?"

"*All* the gangs give me trouble."

"You ever talk to the cops about it?"

"Yeah. They'd need to put a cop on every corner before it would make any difference."

"How do you deal with it?"

"You buy a gun. And you can't be afraid to use it."

It wasn't a terribly satisfying answer, but I understood it. "The D.A. told us that there was a customer in the store when Tho came in."

"Eugene Pham. Lives around the corner. Works at a sandwich shop on Larkin. Nice kid. Never gives me any trouble."

Cruz divided people into two categories: those who gave him trouble and those who didn't. "We heard there was also a deliveryman."

"Odell Jones. Works for Bud. Been coming in for years.

"We'd like to talk to him."

"He's on the road all day. His territory goes out to the Sunset and down to South City."

"We'd also like to talk to your nephew. Any idea where we might find him?"

"San Bruno."

"Address?"

"Moreland Drive."

Huh? "County Jail?"

"Yeah. I figured you knew."

"Knew what?"

"Hector was picked up for buying crystal meth from an undercover cop last night. I'm getting him a lawyer and putting together money for bail." He gave me a knowing look. "I might let him stay down there for one more night to teach him a lesson."

17

"I DON'T NEED A P.D."

San Francisco County Jail #5 looked like an elongated Costco perched above the 280 Freeway in the rolling hills of San Bruno about fifteen miles south of downtown San Francisco. I was sitting at one of the stationary tables in the common area of a jail pod that was much nicer than its dingier counterpart at the Glamour Slammer. If you're arrested in San Francisco, you'll want to book a room down here.

Hector Cruz's droopy eyes stared at me across the table. "Who are you?"

"Mike Daley. I'm with the Public Defender's Office."

"I don't need a P.D. My uncle got me a lawyer."

"You have a nice uncle. Your lawyer gave me permission to talk to you. I represent Thomas Nguyen. You're on the prosecution's witness list."

"My uncle told me not to talk to anybody."

"If you help me convince my client to accept a plea bargain, my friends at the D.A.'s Office might go easier on you." *That's sort of true.* "Anything you tell me is attorney-client privileged." *That's a bald-faced lie.*

"Can you get my charges dropped?"

"Maybe." *Not a chance.* "Why are you here?"

"They're saying I bought crystal meth from an undercover cop."

"Did you?"

"It was a set up."

It always is. "What's the cop's name?"

"I don't know."

I'll find out. "He sold you the stuff?"

"He tried, but I didn't buy."

They never do. "Then why did he arrest you?"

"He said that I offered to pay him, but I didn't."

Of course not. "Did money change hands?"

"Not exactly."

"There seems to be a misunderstanding. Was he wearing a wire?"

"Yeah."

You're dead. "So it's your word against his?"

"I guess."

"And the tape."

"I suppose."

"It's entrapment. Your attorney will get it excluded." *Easy for me to make promises that your lawyer won't be able to keep.* "Have they set bail?"

"Ten grand. My uncle said he would loan it to me."

"Is he going to lend you money for a lawyer, too?"

"Yeah."

"You have a *really* nice uncle. Is this your third felony?"

"Could be."

It was conceivable that he was going away for a long time—maybe even life—under California's draconian "three-strikes" sentencing laws. "I can help you."

His sleepy eyes perked up. "How?"

"I have an investigator working on the Nguyen case. I'll ask him to find out what he can about yours."

"The cops won't talk to him."

"Yes, they will. He used to be one of them."

He showed the first sign of interest. "What do you want from me?"

"Tell me what happened the night that Duc Tho was killed."

"He walked into the store, showed a gun, and asked for money. My uncle shot him."

"How long was he inside the store?"

"A few seconds."

"Where were you?"

"Behind the counter between my uncle and the window."

"Did you see Tho come inside?"

"No."

"You just said that you were standing next to your uncle."

"I was looking out the window and talking on my cell."

Some security guard. "Then what?"

"I don't know. By the time I turned around, my uncle had shot him."

"Had you ever seen Tho?"

"A few times. He never gave me any trouble."

"Did you see him pull the gun?"

"No."

"But you heard him ask for money?"

A hesitation. "Yeah."

"What exactly did he say?"

"'Gimme the money.'"

His uncle and his cousin said the same thing. "Anything else?"

"No."

I was tempted to ask him how he heard Tho if he was talking on his cell, but I filed it away as something that I might use later. "You saw the gun?"

"My uncle found it underneath the body."

"Did you see it *before* he was shot?"

"No."

"But you're absolutely sure he was packing?"

"Yeah."

And you aren't going to contradict your uncle—especially since he's paying your bail. I was already looking forward to putting Hector on the stand. "What did you do when the shooting started?"

"I ducked behind the counter and called the cops." He confirmed that Sergeant Navarro arrived within minutes.

"Did you or your uncle touch the body?"

"Just my uncle." He quickly added, "And only to make sure that Tho was dead."

It wasn't as if one of them planted the gun. "Were you packing that night?"

"My uncle's nine-millimeter."

"You know how to use it?"

"I'd shot it at the range."

"Why didn't you take out Tho?"

"Like I said, I didn't see him come in. My uncle shot him before I could react."

"We heard that Tho was selling weed at Galileo."

"I don't know."

"Any idea who was supplying him?"

He shrugged.

"If you can give the D.A. the name of Tho's supplier, they'll go easier on you."

"I don't know. And even if I did, I'd end up dead if I gave them a name."

He knew more. "They can protect you, Hector."

"Sure, they can." He folded his arms. That topic of conversation was now concluded.

I tried another angle. "Are you and Tony close?"

"We hang out a little."

"Is he into drugs?"

"Just beer."

"Did he buy anything from Tho?"

"Tony doesn't do that stuff. Neither do I."

Except for the crystal meth that you tried to buy from the undercover cop. "What did Tony's dad think about his drinking?"

"He didn't like it. Pretty ironic for a guy who runs a liquor store."

I flashed an understanding smile. "Did Tony's dad give him a lot of grief?"

"Yeah. Me, too."

"Like what?"

"Like dropping out of college. And not getting a better job."

"He was on you all the time, wasn't he?"

"He never lets anything go."

"What about Tony's sister?"

"Ortega is a lot nicer to her."

Maybe that's because she's a good student who doesn't get arrested. "It must have been rough on her."

"It was."

I sent up a final flare. "Hector, other than that night, did you ever see your uncle pull the gun?"

"All the time."

* * *

My iPhone vibrated as I was driving down Moreland Drive. There is no cell phone reception inside the jail building or the parking lot. I saw Pete's name on the display. "Where are you, Mick?"

"San Bruno. I just talked to Hector Cruz. He's just like his uncle described him."

"How soon can you get back to the Tenderloin?"

"If the traffic is good, about a half hour."

"Good. I found Eugene Pham."

18

"HE DOESN'T TAKE CRAP
FROM ANYONE"

"I didn't see anything," the twitchy young man insisted. A tattoo of a snake was visible on Eugene Pham's shoulder beneath his soiled white smock. "I have to get back to work."

Pete placed five twenties on the Formica table next to his baguette filled with sour pickled daikon and carrot, cilantro and cucumber—known as Bahn Mi, and colloquially pronounced "bang me." It was the specialty at Saigon Sandwich, a hole-in-the-wall beneath a bright blue awning on Larkin between Turk and Eddy. "This is a gratuity for ten minutes of your time. If you're cooperative, there may be more."

My brother was depleting our modest investigation budget quickly.

Pham covered the bills with his hand and glanced at the kid who was mopping the floor behind the counter. "What do you want to know?"

Pete's tone was even. "Did you know Duc Tho?"

"No."

"Where were you when he came inside Alcatraz Liquors?"

"Back of the store."

"Did you see him pull a gun?"

"I didn't see or hear anything. I ran out the back door when the shooting started."

"Did you see Ortega Cruz shoot Tho?"

"No."

"So you can't confirm that he pulled the trigger?"

"He admitted it."

"But you didn't see it."

"Correct."

"Was anybody else in the store?"

"Ortega, his son, his daughter, and his nephew. There was a deliveryman filling the refrigerator by the deli counter. I don't know his name."

This lined up with everything we had heard so far. Pete kept pushing. "Any chance somebody else was there? Maybe behind the counter or in the storage room or the bathroom?"

"I didn't see anybody else."

"Do you shop there often?"

"Once or twice a week."

"How well do you know Ortega?"

"Not well."

"Has he ever given you any trouble?"

"No."

"We heard he shot a guy a few years ago."

"I read about it in the paper."

"Is Ortega a good guy?"

"I think so, but he doesn't take crap from anyone."

* * *

I lowered the passenger-side window of Pete's decommissioned police-issue Crown Vic parked across the street from Saigon Sandwich. His air conditioner had retired two years earlier. "What did you think of Ortega Cruz?" I asked.

"He kept his cool. He'll be a strong witness."

"What about Tony?"

"He'll say whatever his father tells him to say."

"I need you to have somebody watch Ortega. And talk to his friends, neighbors, and business associates."

"In the works, Mick."

"And find out everything you can about Tony and his sister."

"And his mother," Pete added. "And most important, Tho."

"Yeah." I took a breath of the warm evening air. "You think Pham knows more than he told us?"

"*Everybody* knows more than they've told us, Mick."

"Any chance you can track down the Bud deliveryman?"

"Already did."

"How?"

"Big John."

19

"I GOT THE HELL OUT"

The evening crowd was watching the Giants' game on the big screen at Dunleavy's at seven-thirty on Thursday night. Big John placed an iced tea on the table in front of the stocky deliveryman sporting a polo shirt with a Budweiser logo. My uncle tossed the ever-present dishtowel over his shoulder. "This one's on the house, Odell. You want something to eat?"

"No, thanks, John."

"I'd be grateful if you'd help my two favorite nephews."

"Happy to do what I can, but I didn't see anything."

"Then this won't take long." Big John strolled over to the bar, where he pretended to wash some mugs. In reality, he was listening to us.

"You from around here?" I asked Odell Jones.

"The Bayview. I live in Daly City."

"How long have you been working for Bud?"

"Forever."

"I'm surprised we haven't met."

"I'm never here for long." He took a sip of iced tea. "I understand you're representing Thomas Nguyen."

"We are. Would you mind telling us what you saw that night?"

"Yeah." He glanced at Big John, then he turned back to me. "Nothing."

"Why are you on the prosecution's witness list?"

"Beats me. I was filling the refrigerator in the back behind the deli counter when Tho came in. I got the hell out when the shooting started."

"Why were you there so late?"

"My truck broke down earlier in the day. I was catching up."

"Was anybody with you?"

"No."

"Did you park on the street?"

"No, in the alley." He confirmed that he came in through the back door.

"Who else was in the store?"

"Ortega, his son, his daughter, and his nephew. There was a customer in the back. Vietnamese kid, I think. I don't know his name. Never saw him before. He followed me out the back door."

"Any chance he might have killed Tho?"

"Doubtful."

"Where were Ortega and his kids when the shooting started?"

"Ortega was at the register. Tony was behind the deli counter. Isabel was sitting at Ortega's desk. Hector was over by the window."

"Did you see Tho come inside the store?"

"No."

"Ortega told us that he asked for money."

"Might have. I didn't hear anything."

Pete took a sip of coffee. "How long were you in the store?"

"Five minutes."

"Did anybody else come or go while you were there?"

"I don't think so."

"Any chance somebody else was there?"

"Doubtful."

"There's a storage room and a bathroom in the back. Could somebody have been there?"

"It's possible. What difference does it make?"

"Just curious."

Pete was *never* just curious. He pretended to take a drink from his empty mug. "Had you ever met Tho?"

"No."

"We heard he was dealing marijuana in the neighborhood."

"I heard the same thing. Don't know anything about it."

"Any chance you know who was supplying him?"

"'fraid not."

"How well do you know Ortega?"

"Pretty well. Been delivering to his store for years. He's a decent guy."

"He ever given you any trouble?"

"A couple of times he called my boss to complain when I was late."

"Did he ever threaten you?"

"Not really." He reconsidered. "Well, sort of."

"What do you mean?"

Jones paused. "About six months ago, I came in late. Ortega's place had been robbed the night before, and he was in a bad mood. He showed me his Glock. He said that if I was late again, he'd use it on me." He added, "He wasn't serious."

Jones was getting antsy, and I didn't have time to be subtle. "Does he have a problem dealing with you because you're African-American?"

"I don't think so." He touched the Budweiser logo on his shirt. "I think he has bigger problems with the Vietnamese."

"Why?"

"I don't know. I never ask him about it."

"We heard he served in Vietnam."

"He did."

"You think it has something to do with his time in the army?"

"Not sure. It was a long time ago. It might also have something to do with the Vietnamese gangs in the Tenderloin. They give everybody trouble."

* * *

Big John squeezed his ample torso into the chair across the table from Pete and me. "Get anything useful from Odell?"

"Not much," I said.

"He's a stand-up guy, Mikey."

"I know."

Pete scowled. "You've known him for a long time, haven't you, Big John?"

"Yeah."

"Does he always carry a .22?"

My uncle chuckled. "Just like your daddy. You don't miss a thing, do you?"

"I'm going to take that as a compliment."

"It was intended that way."

"So, does he always pack?"

"He works in some rough neighborhoods and he's been robbed a few times." Big John's impish eyes narrowed. "He didn't shoot Tho, Petey. And if his employer finds out that he's packing, he'll get fired. I don't want that to happen because he helped you."

"Yes, Big John."

My uncle turned to me. "Where are you off to now?"

"The office." I looked at Pete. "You coming with me?"

"No. I'm going to check on a few things."

"Going to play cops-and-robbers?"

"Possibly."

20
"LITTLE THINGS ADD UP
TO ACQUITTALS"

"Did you get anything more on Tho's cell phone?" I asked.

Rolanda was staring at her computer. The aroma of leftover pizza wafted through her office at eight-thirty on Thursday night. "Jibes with what you heard from Inspector Lee. They found a throwaway in his pocket. Bought for cash the day before he died. There was a call to his mother and a call to Thomas."

"This isn't helping."

"It is what it is. Did you and Pete get anything we can use?"

"Not much." I summarized our interviews with Inspector Lee, Sergeant Navarro, the Cruz family, Eugene Pham, and Odell Jones. "Their stories lined up on the big points."

"What about the little points?"

"Ortega and Tony insisted that Tho reached for a gun inside his pocket. Both admitted that they didn't actually see it before Ortega started shooting."

"That's consistent with the video. They'll claim that they thought he was pulling a gun. What about the security guard?"

"He was looking out the window when Tho walked in. He didn't see anything, but he heard Tho demand money."

"That lines up with his uncle and his cousin."

"Except he was talking on his cell phone."

"How did he hear Tho?"

"I guess he heard him out of the other ear."

"Right. Anything else?"

"Ortega's nephew said that his uncle has a temper. The

deliveryman said that Ortega had flashed a gun a few times and he had issues with the Vietnamese community."

"It may prove that Ortega is a hothead who likes to show off a weapon. If he reasonably thought that Tho was pulling a gun, it's probably enough to support self-defense. The fact that they found the gun on the floor with Tho's prints suggests that their concerns were legitimate.

"Ortega's prints were on the gun, too."

"He admitted that he picked it up and disarmed it."

"If we can show that the gun was planted or that he acted unilaterally, we might mitigate his self-defense claim."

"And how do you plan to do that?"

"I'm not sure." I took a bite of pizza. "Let's go back to the evidence. Is there anything proving that Ortega shot Tho?"

"He admitted it."

"He could be lying to protect his son or his nephew or even his daughter. If we can suggest with some credibility that somebody else shot Tho, it calls into question Ortega's self-defense claim and changes the narrative. It also shows that he's a liar. Did the cops check his hands for gunpowder residue?"

"Yes."

"Did they check anybody else for gunpowder residue?"

"No."

"Then we'll ask them why not."

"They found gunpowder residue on Ortega's shirt."

"We'll argue that he could have been standing next to the shooter."

"Get real, Mike."

"There were at least three people within a couple of feet of each other behind the counter—Ortega, Tony, and Hector. If any one of them fired the shots, it's possible that gunpowder residue would have landed on Ortega's shirt."

"The ballistics report indicated that Tho was hit in the chest from shots fired from behind the register."

"Then we'll need to find an expert to argue that he was still turning when he was shot."

"Why?"

"If he was moving, it broadens the theoretical radius from which the shots were fired by a few feet. We can argue that Tony or maybe even the security guard shot him. Is there anything on the video proving that they were standing where they said they were?"

"No. You can't see any of them in the video when the shots are fired."

"Good."

She responded with a puzzled look. "Why is that good?"

"If we can make a decent argument that Ortega, Tony, or Hector is lying about anything, it will impair their credibility on the self-defense claim and cast doubt on everything they told the cops. Juries don't like to convict people based on perjured testimony."

"It will be hard to prove perjury."

"We don't need to prove it. We just need to suggest it. And we will have no trouble bringing the security guard's credibility into question because he was arrested last night for buying crystal meth from an undercover cop."

"How'd you find out?"

"Ortega told me. Turns out he's lending Hector money for bail and a lawyer."

My niece smiled. "Would you lend me money if I'm ever arrested?"

"Absolutely."

"That's why you're my favorite uncle."

"I'm your only uncle."

Rolanda wiped her glasses. "Do you think Ortega is saying that he shot Tho in self-defense to protect his son or his nephew?"

"I doubt it, but we may want to make the argument. If we

can catch him in a lie—any lie—it will work to our advantage."

"Rosie says you're good at the little things."

I hoped that she was referring only to my qualities as a lawyer. "Little things add up to acquittals."

"What about truth and justice?"

"That stuff is nice, too, but our job is to find holes in the prosecution's case and cast doubt on the credibility of their witnesses. Then we let the jury decide."

"Have you always been this cynical?"

"Ask your aunt. I'm just a humble pawn playing in an imperfect legal system. Did you find any dirt on Pham?"

"A couple of shoplifting charges and a speeding ticket. No convictions."

It wasn't much. I asked about Odell Jones.

"He did time for armed robbery thirty years ago. Nothing since."

"He was carrying a gun when Pete and I met with him."

"He's the licensed owner of several handguns. It doesn't mean that he shot Tho."

"Anything on Ortega's ex-wife or daughter?"

"Working on it."

I didn't need to explain the urgency. "Did you talk to Candace?"

"Yes. I e-mailed her a copy of the security video."

"Good." Candace Greene was Rosie's classmate at San Francisco State. She had a Ph.D. in Special Education with an emphasis on teaching children with hearing disabilities. She was a superb lipreader and an accomplished expert witness. "Is she available to testify?"

"Yes. I've already put her on our witness list. Standard rates."

"Perfect."

Pete's name appeared on the display of my iPhone. "Are you still at the office?" he asked.

"Yeah."

"How soon can you get to Gino and Carlo's?"

"Fifteen minutes."

"Good. I chased down the P.I. that Sandy Tran hired to work on this case. Did Rolanda mention who it is?"

"No."

I could hear the chuckle in his voice. "Nick the Dick."

21
"INDEED I AM"

The Rossi Family has operated Gino and Carlo's on Green Street since 1942. The dive bar is housed in a ramshackle two-story building constructed shortly after the 1906 earthquake. Flanked on one side by Caffe Sport and Sotto Mare and on the other by Golden Boy Pizza and Tattoo Boogaloo, Gino and Carlo's has always been popular among cops, firefighters, and blue collar workers because it's one of the few watering holes in North Beach that opens at six a.m. In addition to hosting countless celebrations and memorials, it was also the informal office of the legendary one-eyed muckraking journalist, Warren Hinckle, who held court at a table in the back with capable assistance from his ever-present basset hound, Bentley.

Pete and I were sitting at a table next to the bar in a room that smelled of beer and pretzels. Sitting across from us was a diminutive P.I. who was busy repositioning the fresh red rose on the lapel of his five-thousand-dollar Wilkes Bashford suit. He sounded like Humphrey Bogart. "If you're in your seventies," he was explaining, "you're a septuagenarian. If you're in your eighties, you're an octogenarian. Do you know what you are if you're in your nineties?"

I had to play along. "No idea."

Nick "The Dick" Hanson re-aligned his toupee and took a gulp of chianti. "A nonagenarian."

"Does that mean you're a nonagenarian, Nick?"

He smiled triumphantly. "Indeed I am."

Over the years, for better and worse, my hometown has produced more than its share of characters. It started during the Gold Rush when a failed businessman named Joshua Abraham

Norton started calling himself "Emperor Norton," and proclaimed that he was the emperor of the United States. When he died penniless in 1880, more than 30,000 people lined Market Street for his funeral procession. In the 1890s, the gauntlet passed to Mayor Adolph Sutro, who used his fortune from the Comstock Lode silver mine to build monuments to himself, including the Sutro Baths, an indoor swimming complex next to the Cliff House that was more elaborate than the fantasy pools in Hawaii. The Baths closed when I was a kid, but you can still see the ruins. Over the decades, other luminaries included beat poets Jack Kerouac and Allen Ginsberg, a stripper named Carol Doda who headlined the city's first topless club a few blocks from where we were sitting, and a high-end madam named Sally Stanford who became a restaurateur and later the Mayor of Sausalito. The list would not be complete without mentioning flamboyant lawyers like Melvin Belli, Jake Ehrlich, Vincent Hallinan, Tony Serra, and Nate Cohn.

Nick "the Dick" was one of San Francisco's few remaining characters. The son of a bootlegger was born in North Beach during Prohibition. He drove an ambulance during the bombing of Pearl Harbor and served in the Pacific. He came back home and opened a detective agency next to the Italian Athletic Club across the street from Washington Square Park. Nick was a charter member of the legendary Calamari Club, a group of politicians, lawyers, labor leaders, restaurateurs, newspaper columnists, and other movers and shakers who have been meeting for lunch in the backroom at Scoma's at the Wharf since the fifties. He played liar's dice at the Washington Square Bar and Grill with *Chronicle* columnist, Herb Caen, who dropped his name at least twice a week. After Caen died, he became a regular at Mayor Willie Brown's power lunches at Le Central. In his spare time, he had written a dozen semi-readable mystery novels based loosely on his favorite character: himself.

At four-foot-ten and barely a hundred pounds, he looked like a cross between Edgar G. Robinson and Danny DeVito.

He took a bite of the clam and garlic pizza that Pete had brought in from Golden Boy next door. Gino and Carlo's serves food only on special occasions. He spoke to Pete. "You keeping busy? There's always a place for you at the agency."

"Thanks, Nick. Got more work than I can handle." Pete had worked for Nick for a short time, but preferred being his own boss. "Everybody okay at home? Kids, grandkids, and great-grandkids?"

"Everybody's fine. At last count, the Hanson Investigative Agency employs nineteen members of my extended family. Not bad for an old guy, eh?"

"Not bad at all. You still working cases?"

"A few."

"I thought you retired."

"I got bored."

He couldn't sit still. "I'm helping my big brother with the Nguyen case."

"I heard." Nick arched an eyebrow in my direction. "Is this kid really your great-nephew?"

"Yeah."

"Jerry Edwards is going out of his mind."

"He'll calm down."

"We'll see. From everything I hear, your case is a loser."

"We were hoping you might have found something that would tilt it our way."

"N-L, Mike. Not likely." Nick pushed a slice of pizza toward me. "Try this. The secret to becoming a nonagenarian is garlic."

I couldn't possibly turn him down. "How did you pick up the Nguyen case?"

"Sandy Tran called my son, Rick. He's running the agency now."

Rick may have the title of managing agent, but Nick would always be running the show.

Nick ordered another glass of wine. "Rick handed the case over to my grandson, Nicholas the third. He passed it over to my great-grandson, Dick, who got busy on another case, so I graciously volunteered to step in."

Pete kicked my foot. It took every ounce of self-control to keep me from asking Nick whether they called his great-grandson "Dick the Dick." I gulped some water and turned to the matters at hand. "How much time did you spend on the case?"

"Couple days. I did it as a favor to Sandy. Nguyen couldn't afford us."

"The store owner, his son, and the security guard all told us that Ortega Cruz acted in self-defense. A deliveryman and a customer in the back of the store said they didn't see or hear anything."

"They told me the same thing."

"Did you look at the video?"

"Indeed I did."

"Did you see a gun?"

"Indeed I did not." The charismatic P.I. flashed the smile in the author photo on the dust jacket of his books. "Legally, it probably doesn't matter. The D.A. just needs to show that Ortega Cruz thought his life was in danger. Put yourself in his shoes. A sketchy-looking kid walks into your store with a hand in his pocket and asks for money. You would have been scared, too."

"Maybe we can show that he's a hothead with an itchy trigger finger. He shot a robber a couple of years ago."

"I heard." Nick took another gulp of chianti. "I'm still not hearing anything that's going to get you around a reasonable argument that Cruz acted in self-defense."

"Did you find any other witnesses?"

"A couple of people mentioned that there was a homeless guy who used to hang out in front of Cruz's store. He might have been there that night."

"Got a name?"

"No, but he calls himself the 'Lion of the Loin.'"

"Any idea where we might find him?"

"Not sure. He might have left town." He pointed at Pete. "Fortunately, your new investigator is very resourceful."

"Yes, he is."

He finished his chianti. "I hope your defense isn't going to come down to the testimony of a homeless guy."

* * *

Rosie's name appeared on my iPhone as I was driving west on Geary. "How did it go tonight?" I asked her.

"Shook a bunch of hands, raised some money, and nibbled at some rubber chicken."

"Still glad you decided to go into politics?"

"Looking forward to the day *after* the election."

Me, too. "Is Tommy okay?"

"Fine. Are you heading home soon? Maybe you should come over to the house for a few minutes."

"I'll be there in about an hour. I need to make a stop first."

22
"WHY ARE YOU DOING THIS?"

"Why are you doing this, Mike?"

"Doing what, Roosevelt?"

"Representing Thomas Nguyen.

"It's my job."

My father's first partner and the most decorated homicide inspector in SFPD history was nursing a cup of green tea. At eighty-two, Roosevelt Johnson's melodious baritone was still commanding, but its forcefulness had been tempered by years and a battle with throat cancer. "You could have kicked it over to a Deputy P.D."

"There are extenuating circumstances."

Roosevelt was sitting in a well-used armchair in the living room of a fifteen-hundred square-foot bungalow three blocks from Dunleavy's. He and his wife had bought the place almost a half-century earlier when he was working with my dad. They were the first African-American family in the neighborhood. "Is he really Tommy's grandson?"

"Yes. Pete's DNA guy at UCSF ran the tests."

He gave me the knowing look that I had seen countless times at our dinner table on Sunday nights. "I wish your mom and dad were still here."

"So do I." I glanced at the kitchen and lowered my voice. "How's Janet?"

"So-so. The chemo seems to be working, but she gets tired."

His wife was battling lung cancer. "She's in good spirits."

"She's a fighter. And she puts up a good front." He took a sip of tea. "Why did you want to see me at this hour?"

"I was hoping you would help me with the Nguyen case."

"I'm retired."

Technically, this was true. "I hear you're working on cold cases."

"A couple. With DNA and new technology, sometimes they're worth another look."

"Heard anything about the Nguyen case?"

"I just told you that I'm retired."

For fifty years, Roosevelt always had a suit and tie laid out in the spare bedroom. "You know more about what's going on at the Hall of Justice than our D.A."

"Maybe a little."

I waited.

He cleared his throat. "I read the papers just like everybody else. As far as I can tell, Tho walked into the store with a gun. The shopkeeper killed him in self-defense." He set down his cup. "I've never thought much of the felony murder rule, but you don't have time to get the law changed before the trial starts on Monday."

"Heard any gossip?"

"A little. Your client's odds are lousy. Ortega Cruz said that he killed Tho in self-defense. He found Tho's piece under the body. Cruz's son and nephew will corroborate his story."

"For a retired guy, you seem to know a lot."

"You now know everything that I do."

"Would your opinion change if I told you that I watched the security video and you can't see a gun in Tho's hand?"

"Not necessarily. Cruz will say that he *thought* Tho had a gun. Given the neighborhood, it wasn't an unreasonable assumption. It still supports self-defense."

"What if Tho was shot within a couple of seconds after he walked inside the store, and it wasn't clear if he said anything?"

"You can argue that he acted unilaterally, but it's going to be an uphill battle."

"Any idea where Tho got the gun?"

"The paper said it might have been stolen. Evidently, all of the identifying information was removed."

"Do you know anything about the store owner or the victim?"

"Afraid not. This isn't my case."

"Ignacio Navarro told me that Tho was a small-time drug dealer."

"Seems we didn't have enough evidence to arrest him. We don't know the name of his supplier, either."

"Who told you that?"

"I had lunch with Ignacio a couple of weeks ago during his little sabbatical."

"Do you think the charges against him were legit?"

"No comment."

"Did he tell you anything else about my case?"

"No."

Roosevelt always played it straight with me. "You worked with Ken Lee."

"We were partners when he moved over to homicide."

"Is he a good guy?"

"He isn't a bad guy. He's a good detective, Mike, and he doesn't like to lose. It would be a mistake to go after him. And it would be an even bigger one to underestimate him."

Got it. "You think it's a good idea to prosecute a kid with no criminal record for murder in a case like this?"

"Not my call. You're going to have to try this case based upon the law as it's written. You have the rest of your life to try to change it."

"What's your gut, Roosevelt?"

"Your best bet is to discredit Cruz's testimony or somehow show that he didn't act in self-defense. If he had no reason to be afraid of Tho, there was no provocative act. I have no idea how you're going to prove it."

His instincts were always solid. "That won't be easy."

"You're a good lawyer."

"Any other options?"

"Convince your client to accept a plea bargain. It may be the best deal he's going to get."

"You'll let us know if you happen to hear anything else?"

"Of course. Give my best to Pete."

23
"JUST LIKE OLD TIMES"

"Is Tommy okay?" I asked.

"Fine," Rosie said. At one-thirty on Friday morning, we were sitting at the butcher block table in her kitchen that doubled as her home office. She flashed a tired smile as she took a bite of a reheated burrito. "He's asleep."

Good. "Heard anything from Grace?"

"No."

Figures. "Is your mom here?"

"Yeah." Rosie looked down the hall leading to what used to be Grace's room, and was now Tommy's. Sylvia Fernandez bunked with him during her frequent overnight visits.

"How's her hip?"

"Not great."

At eighty-four, my ex-mother-in-law liked saying that getting old wasn't for sissies. "Are you making any headway on the concept of getting her to move out of the house?"

"No."

Rosie was becoming increasingly concerned that her mother's arthritic hip would cause her to take a fall in the Mission District bungalow that she and her husband had bought almost sixty years earlier for a whopping twenty-four thousand dollars. In San Francisco's insane real estate market, she could probably clear almost two million if she ever decided to sell. Rosie's gentle suggestions that Sylvia move into a condo at an upscale independent living facility had not been well received.

"What time did you get home?" I asked.

"Midnight."

Earlier than usual. "Still enjoying the democratic process?"

"Living the dream, Mike."

The sweet aroma of Sylvia's burritos filled Rosie's two-bedroom house across the street from the Little League Field in Larkspur. The cottage had been built for a teacher almost a hundred years earlier. Rosie had rented it after she and I split up when Grace was two. Raising a kid in San Francisco requires elaborate planning for schools or a trust fund. We had neither the patience for the former nor the wherewithal for the latter, so opted for Marin, where the schools are better. Around the same time, I moved into an apartment two blocks away behind the Larkspur fire station. A couple of years ago, one of our few well-heeled clients bought the house for us as a token of his appreciation after we got his death penalty conviction overturned. It was the closest we'll ever come to winning the lottery.

I took Rosie's hand. "Is your mom okay?"

"She's limping more than usual and she refuses to use her cane."

"Did you talk to her again about giving up her car?"

"Let's not go there now."

"Nothing's easy, Rosie."

"No, it isn't." She waited a beat. "She agreed to stay for the weekend."

"That'll help." We couldn't do our jobs without her. "I trust you explained the situation with Thomas?"

"I did. She thinks you're crazy."

"Just like old times." I opted to change the subject. "How did it go tonight?"

"We raised about five thousand."

"Not bad." When Rosie entered the race, she was excited about the issues and the enthusiasm of the crowds. After six months of endless fundraising, she measured success by the number of dollars collected. "How was the turnout?"

"Modest."

"Any trouble?"

"A couple of people started with the usual stuff that I'm just a carpetbagger from Marin."

Notwithstanding the fact that Rosie was born and raised in the Mission, for political purposes, she was, in fact, a carpetbagger from Marin. It was perfectly legal. Unlike some municipalities, you don't have to live in San Francisco to work for the city government. It was a running joke that half of the SFPD cops lived in Novato. On the other hand, optics are important in politics.

"Did anybody from the press show up?"

"Jerry Edwards."

"Did he ask you about Thomas's case?"

"You think he came just for the popcorn? He accused me of giving special treatment to your great-nephew. He gave me the usual line about keeping an eye on us. Sometimes I think he's watched *The Godfather* too many times."

"Did it make the news?"

"Briefly. I told him that we followed our standard procedures. That didn't satisfy him."

"Nothing does."

"I told him that he should talk to you."

I smiled. "Thanks."

"We haven't heard the last of it, Mike."

No doubt. "Did anybody else mention Thomas's case?"

"No. Everybody was too busy eating the free food and getting hammered."

"You're getting cynical, Rosita."

"I was cynical long before I decided to run for office."

That was accurate.

She finished her burrito. "Are you and your client treating my niece nicely?"

"Of course. Rolanda is an excellent lawyer."

"She said the same thing about you. Any good news on Thomas's case?"

"Not much." I summarized what I knew so far. "Rolanda and I went through the witness lists, police reports, and security video. Tho's hand was inside his pocket when he walked into the store, but you can't see a gun."

"Are you saying that he didn't have a gun?"

"I'm saying that you can't see it in the video. We can argue that he didn't threaten Cruz and there was no provocative act."

"That's the best that you can do?"

"For now."

"How do you explain the gun with his fingerprints under his body?"

"I can't—yet."

"The jury will put the pieces together. Ortega Cruz will testify that he saw the gun—or thought he did—and acted in self-defense. His son will corroborate his story. So will his daughter. And his nephew. That's your provocative act."

She was the unrelenting voice of realism. "Ortega's fingerprints also were on the gun. We'll argue that he made up the whole story about the robbery and planted the gun to make a case that he acted in self-defense."

"He'll say that he got his prints on the gun when he disarmed it. He'll claim that he was protecting himself, his son, his daughter, and his nephew. That's textbook self-defense."

I was too tired to argue. "Then we're screwed."

The crow's feet at the corners of her eyes became more pronounced as she smiled. "You're just the bluebird of happiness tonight, aren't you?"

"It's just the way I'm drawn."

"That's why I will always love you, Mike." She leaned across the table and pecked me on the cheek. "Still glad you decided to handle this case?"

"Absolutely." Rosie's mother emerged from the hall.

"You're up late, Sylvia."

"Actually, I'm up early."

True enough. She was always watching CNN by four a.m. She was wearing a USC sweatshirt over her nightgown—a gift from her granddaughter. She was barely five feet tall, but she carried herself with understated grace. Always impeccably coiffed, she pulled her silver hair back and took a seat next to Rosie.

"Coffee?" I asked.

"No, thanks."

"Rosie tells me that your hip is bothering you again."

"It's fine."

It was her standard answer. "Maybe you should have the doctor look at it."

Her expression and tone turned sharp. "I'll be okay."

It was the signal to change the subject. "Burritos were good."

"Thanks."

"Did Tommy have a good day?"

"He's doing fine, Michael."

I sensed irritation. "Something on your mind, Sylvia?"

"Is Thomas Nguyen really your great-nephew?"

"Yes."

"Pete's sure?"

It always annoyed me that she valued my brother's opinions more than mine. "He's sure."

"Is he guilty?"

"No." Like her daughter, Sylvia always cut to the chase. "He was sitting in the car when Tho was shot."

"The *Chronicle* said that's still felony murder."

"In my humble opinion, it isn't."

"In the judge's humble opinion, it is."

"Thomas is still entitled to a defense."

"He's entitled to a Public Defender. It doesn't have to be

you."

"We need somebody to deal with this right away."

"You're doing this yourself because he's your great-nephew. If this was anybody else, you would have handed it off to a deputy."

That was true.

She wasn't finished. "You're taking time away from your regular duties and your family."

In other words, I was ignoring Rosie and Tommy in the middle of an election campaign. "The trial will last only a few days."

"Then you'll find something else to distract you."

Rosie finally interjected. "That's not fair, Mama."

"Maybe not, Rosita." Sylvia turned back to me. "When Angel got in trouble, you told me that it's a bad idea to represent relatives."

"We defended her anyway. She's our niece. And you told me that family matters."

"You don't even know Thomas Nguyen."

"He's my great-nephew." Sensing that I was about to lose yet another argument, I was grateful for the diversion when Tommy wandered into the kitchen. "Hey, Tom. You're up late."

"Hey, Dad." He was wearing Giants pajamas. "I heard you guys talking."

"Sorry. We didn't mean to wake you." He was a light sleeper who inherited my propensity for worrying. "You feeling okay?"

"I'm fine." He rubbed his eyes. "Why are you here so late?"

"Lawyer stuff."

"The Thomas Nguyen case?"

He watched the news. "Yeah."

"Is he guilty?"

"No." Please don't ask your grandmother for her opinion.

"Is he really your great-nephew?"

It was difficult to keep anything from him. "Yes."

"Does that mean he's my cousin?"

"Sort of."

"Are you going to have to work all weekend?"

"I'll be at your game on Saturday." I darted a helpless glance at Rosie, then I turned back to Tommy. "Why don't you go back to bed? I'll come in and say goodnight."

"Are you going back to work?"

"Not tonight."

"Good."

* * *

A few minutes later, Rosie and I were sitting on the sofa in her living room. "You want to stay tonight?" she asked.

Yes. "I don't think so, Rosita. I promised Rolanda that I would look at our jury questionnaires and I need to check in with Pete."

"Do what you have to do, Mike."

"Is your mother going to be okay with this?"

"Absolutely." She leaned over and kissed me. "At the end of the day, she always comes around."

* * *

The sound of my iPhone woke me up from an uneasy sleep. The red numerals on the clock on my nightstand indicated that it was five-thirty on Friday morning. Pete's name appeared on the display.

"Where are you?" I asked him.

"The Tenderloin."

My eyes struggled to acclimate to the darkness in my one-bedroom apartment that was better suited for a college student than a lawyer. "Did you find Tho's supplier?"

"No, I found his mother."

24
"HE DIDN'T LIKE GUNS"

"We're sorry for your loss, Ms. Tho."

"Thank you, Mr. Daley." Duc Tho's mother clasped her hands as she looked at me through bloodshot eyes. "It's Anita."

"Mike."

At six-fifteen on Friday morning, I was sitting on a wobbly card chair and Pete was standing next to the open window in a dingy room paid for by the city. Anita lived in a single-room-occupancy hotel, or SRO, at Larkin and Ellis, in one of the most dangerous corners of the Tenderloin. A century ago, the mid-rise apartments and hotels within walking distance of Civic Center Plaza were home to middle class families. Over the years, the neighborhood wedged between the theater district and City Hall evolved into a cesspool of drugs, prostitution, and homelessness. It was also where San Francisco housed some of its neediest residents. Among them was Anita Tho.

The room was just big enough to fit a twin bed, a chest of drawers, a desk, and a chair. It smelled of cigarette smoke and bus fumes. The kitchen was a mini-fridge and a hotplate. The sink didn't work. The bathroom was down the hall. The corridor was lined with mattresses and reeked of urine.

"How long have you lived here?" I asked.

"Two weeks."

"How long can you stay?"

"As long as I'm clean."

"One day at a time."

"Yeah."

Anita was a petite woman with sad brown eyes and pouty

lips. She was wearing a cotton blouse and a pair of torn Levi's. Her only jewelry was a gold stud in her left ear. A pack of cigarettes was on her dresser next to a half dozen bottles of prescription medications.

"You from around here?" Pete asked.

"I've always lived in this neighborhood. My parents came over from Vietnam after the war." She said that her mother died when she was twelve. Her father died when Duc was a baby.

"Any other family?"

"A couple of cousins. They stopped talking to me after . . ."

Pete finished the sentence for her. "You started doing drugs."

"Yeah."

"How long has it been?"

"About ten years."

"How did Duc's father react?"

"I wouldn't know. He left when I was pregnant."

"Were you married?"

"I was too young to be married. I was way too young to be a mother, and Duc's dad was way too drunk to be a father."

"How did you support yourself?"

"I worked at a laundry for a while. I tried flipping burgers at the Burger King by the BART Station, but that didn't work out."

"Tough to make ends meet—especially when you have a kid."

"Yeah. I started drinking a little. Then a little more. Then I started smoking weed. Then I tried crack. Then meth."

It was a desperate existence. "Tell us about Duc," I said.

There was a faraway look in her eyes. "He was a good kid who got in with the wrong crowd."

"When did it happen?"

"Middle school. It was my fault. I wasn't much of a role

model. It isn't easy living in a neighborhood where everybody—including your mother—is doing crack."

True.

She kept talking. "He started smoking weed in eighth grade. By then, I was spending most of my time trying to steal enough money to support my habit. When he was a sophomore in high school, he had moved up to harder stuff."

"Crack?"

"Yeah."

"Meth?"

"Probably."

"Heroin?"

"I don't think so. He started selling dope to make a little money. Then he needed to sell more to pay for his habit. That's when they tossed him out of high school." She lowered her eyes. "I should have done something, but I couldn't."

I thought about Grace and Tommy. "Where were you living?"

"When I was clean, we lived in the SROs. When I was dirty, we'd live on the street. Duc would stay with friends sometimes. I'm not proud of it."

"It happens, Anita. Was he ever arrested?"

"A couple of times. He never did time."

"Do you know where Duc was getting the drugs?"

"People in the neighborhood."

"Any chance you might know their names?"

"No."

"Was he still using drugs when he was killed?"

"Yes. Mostly meth. He was drinking, too."

"It must have been very difficult for you."

"It was."

Pete spoke up again. "Did you ever shop at Alcatraz Liquors?"

"Once or twice. I won't go back there now."

"Understood. Do you know the owner?"

"No."

"He's going to testify that Duc tried to rob him. Do you think he's telling the truth?"

She clenched her right fist. "No."

"Why would you say that?"

"Duc wasn't a fighter. He was a little guy with a big heart."

"The owner of the store said that Duc pulled a gun."

"I heard."

"Did you ever see him with a gun?"

"No."

"Is it possible that he had a gun that he didn't show you?"

"No."

"How can you be so sure?"

"He didn't like guns. He was afraid of them."

"How do you explain the fact that they found a gun under his body with his fingerprints?"

"I can't."

Pete looked my way. "Was Duc right handed or left handed?" I asked.

"Left. Why does it matter?"

"The fingerprints were from his right hand."

"That's odd."

"We thought so, too. Would you be willing to testify if we need you?"

"Sure." She pushed out a sigh. "Duc was a good boy, Mr. Daley. He never hurt anyone."

"I'm sure he was. Is there anything we can do to make your life a little easier?"

She responded with a melancholy smile. "It might be nice if you bought me some breakfast."

25
"HE'S FUNDAMENTALLY A GOOD MAN"

"What can I get you?" the waitress asked.

"Scrambled eggs, bacon, wheat toast, and another cup of coffee," I said.

"Coming up."

Maria Cruz trudged toward the kitchen in JoAnn's Café, a diner squeezed between a Filipino bakery and a barber college on El Camino Real in South San Francisco. At nine-twenty on Friday morning, the breakfast crowd had dwindled, and the lunch patrons wouldn't show up for a couple of hours. I was the only customer at the counter. I had already bought breakfast for Anita Tho, so I wasn't hungry, but I had to order something. Trial preparation isn't good for a diet.

Maria returned and refilled my coffee. She was mid-fifties and her gray hair was pulled back into a bun. "Your eggs will be out in a minute."

"Thanks." I smiled. "How long have you worked here?"

"About ten years."

"I appreciate your hospitality."

"Pays the bills." She seemed grateful for a kind word from a less-than-demanding customer. "You look familiar."

"I get that a lot."

"No, I've seen you. Are you an actor?"

"'fraid not."

"Politician?"

"Worse. I'm an attorney."

"You seem like a decent guy for a lawyer."

"I get that a lot, too. I work for the San Francisco Public Defender's Office."

A look of recognition crossed her face. "I saw your picture on T.V. last night."

"My fifteen seconds of fame." I leveled with her. "I'm representing Thomas Nguyen."

She put down the coffee pot. "You know that was at my ex-husband's store."

"I do." I held out a hand. "Mike Daley. You must be Maria Cruz."

Her voice went flat. "I am."

"I'm sorry for troubling you here at work. I spoke to your ex-husband and your son yesterday. I was hoping that I could ask you a few questions."

She glanced at the manager, who responded with an inquisitive look. She held up a hand to reassure him. Then she turned back to me. "I want you to leave my kids alone."

"I will. If you answer a few questions, I promise that I won't bother Tony or Isabel."

Her tone became sharper. "This has been very hard on both of them—especially Isabel."

"It must have been horrible for her. Did she see your husband shoot Duc Tho?"

"No, but she saw the body."

"I'm so sorry."

"So am I."

"Has she talked to a counselor?"

"She talked to our priest. It's helped a little."

"And Tony?"

"He won't talk to anybody. It was hard for a few months. Then he seemed to be doing better. Now he's getting nervous about the trial."

"He won't have to do much."

"He's sensitive."

I hadn't seen that part of his personality. "I have a nineteen-year-old daughter. I can't imagine what Isabel and Tony have been through."

"We're doing the best that we can."

"If you help me, I might be able to convince my client to accept a plea bargain. If he does, Tony and Isabel won't have to testify next week."

Her lips formed a tight ball. "What do you want to know?"

"Tony and your ex-husband told me that Tho threatened them with a gun and demanded money."

"He did."

"I understand that Ortega shot a robber a few years ago."

"He did."

"How did he feel about it?"

"Badly."

"How did *you* feel about it?"

"Terrible." She swallowed. "I wanted Ortega to sell the store. The hours are terrible and the neighborhood is dangerous. He deals with shoplifters and homeless every day. On bad days, somebody will pull a gun or a knife. We could never take a vacation. He came home angry every night. It was no way to live."

"Is that why you got divorced?"

"In part. We never saw him."

"I heard he has a temper."

"A little."

"Were you afraid of him?"

"No."

"Were the kids?"

"Sometimes."

"Hector told me that Ortega yells a lot."

"Sometimes." She held up a hand. "He's fundamentally a good man. He's very protective of the children and me. Those are good things."

"Yes, they are."

She glanced at her watch. "I need to take care of my other

customers."

"Thanks for your help, Maria. I know this must be very hard for you and your children."

"It is."

"If there is anything that I can do to help you, please let me know. And I don't think it will be necessary, but we might need to ask you to testify at the trial."

Her eyes turned to ice. "I will be available, but I want to make two things clear. First, I want you to leave my children alone. Second, I will not testify against my ex-husband."

* * *

"How did it go with Cruz's ex-wife?" Pete asked.

"Not great." I pressed my iPhone against my ear as I inched northbound on the 101 near the airport. "She's very protective of her kids. She said her ex-husband is a decent guy with a temper."

"Is she prepared to testify about the temper?"

"No."

"That doesn't help."

No, it doesn't. "You find anything we can use?"

"Maybe. How soon can you get back to the Tenderloin.?

"Give me a half hour."

"Meet me in front of Glide Memorial. I found the 'Lion of the Loin.'"

26
"THE LION OF THE LOIN"

"What took you so long, Mick?"

"Traffic."

Pete smirked. He loved telling people that our mother used to drive faster than I did. He pointed at a rail-thin man of indeterminate middle age sitting on a milk crate next to the shopping cart holding his belongings in front of Glide Memorial Church in the heart of the Tenderloin. "This is Brian Holton."

I inhaled the fumes from the cars barreling past us at one-thirty on Friday afternoon as I shook his calloused hand. "Maybe we could talk inside where it's quieter."

Pete answered for him. "Brian wants to keep an eye on his stuff."

Got it. It was hot outside, but Holton was wearing a soiled Burberry overcoat that cost its original owner over a thousand dollars. His eyes were red and his puffy face was covered by gray stubble. Homeless people age faster than the rest of us. "You from around here?"

"Palo Alto. Gunn High School. San Jose State. I worked security in the tech industry after I got back from my third tour in Afghanistan."

Rosie always said that there was a fine line between those who lived with roofs over their heads and those who didn't. "Army?"

"Marines."

"Where do you live?"

"Here and there." His melancholy smile revealed a missing front tooth. "I had a nice set-up under the Bay Bridge, but the cops made us move. My stuff got stolen in the Mission. I've been here in the Tenderloin for a couple of years."

"Ever tried the shelters?"

"Too many rules."

It was a common sentiment. I pointed at the imposing Methodist church that became a pillar of outreach and health services in the neighborhood when the legendary Reverend Cecil Williams arrived in the sixties. "They have a lot to offer here."

"I come in for meals sometimes."

"How long have you been on the street?"

"Almost ten years." His tone was businesslike. "I got into some bad drugs. My wife left me and things went downhill."

"How about the VA?"

"They tried."

"I'm not a social worker, but I know some people who might be able to give you a hand."

"I've been through the system a couple of times. There's an industry in this town of people trying to help guys like me. Sometimes I think they're more interested in keeping their grant money than doing anything for us."

I didn't push him. "I'm representing Thomas Nguyen."

"I heard." He pulled a can of malt liquor from his pocket, opened it, and took a long draw. "Vietnamese kid going on trial Monday."

"He also happens to be my great-nephew. I understand you know everybody in the neighborhood."

"They call me the 'Lion of the Loin.'"

I feigned admiration. "Who gave you that name?"

"I did."

Thought so. "I understand that you were in front of Alcatraz Liquors the night Duc Tho was killed."

"I might have been."

"Would you mind telling us what you saw?"

He held out a palm. "You lawyers get paid for your time. So do I."

I slipped him two twenties. "You understand that the size of your gratuity depends upon the quality of your information."

"As it should be."

"And you will be much more valuable to us if you're prepared to testify."

"I charge a premium for that service. You'll also need to provide a suitable wardrobe and cover my incidental expenses."

"We'll take care of it." The P.D.'s Office had a closet filled with donated clothing. "Were you at Alcatraz Liquors on the night Tho was shot?"

"Yes."

"What were you doing there?"

"Hanging out. Ortega used to slip me a few dollars to keep the troublemakers away."

"How did you manage that?"

"I told people that Ortega had a gun and he wasn't afraid to use it."

I handed him another twenty. "Where exactly were you when Tho went inside?"

"Outside the front door."

"Anybody with you?"

"No."

"Did Tho say anything to you when he went inside?"

"No."

"Was he carrying?"

"Probably. In this neighborhood, you assume that everybody is packing until proven otherwise. It's a matter of self-preservation."

"Did you see a gun?"

"No, but he wouldn't have shown it."

"Did Tho say anything to Ortega?"

"He might have. I didn't hear anything."

"Did you see Ortega shoot him?"

"No. And as soon as I heard shots, I got the hell out of there."

"Any chance somebody other than Ortega shot Tho?"

"Doubtful. He admitted it."

"Any chance Ortega or Tony planted the gun on Tho?"

He smiled. "Anything's possible."

I asked him if he had talked to the police.

"Briefly. I told them the same thing that I just told you."

"Did you ever see Ortega pull his gun on anybody?"

"Many times."

"Did you ever see him shoot somebody other than Tho?"

"No, but I've seen him show the gun. Hell, he pulled it on me a bunch of times. That's one of the reasons that I don't hang out in front of his store anymore."

"You think he would have shot you?"

"Probably not, but you never know."

"He used to have a security guard."

"I know. I heard that Hector is in San Bruno again. What did he do this time?"

"He was picked up for buying crystal meth from an undercover cop."

"He should have known better. How long is he going to be down there?"

"Until his uncle pays his bail. I understand that Hector and Ortega didn't get along."

"Hector has a knack for finding trouble. This isn't the first time that Ortega has bailed him out."

"Does Hector know the dealers in the neighborhood?"

Holton smiled. "If he did, he wouldn't have tried to buy from an undercover cop."

"Do *you* know the dealers?"

"A few."

"What about undercover cops?"

"They're harder to pick out."

I changed direction. "How does Tony get along with his father?"

"The same way I got along with my father when I was nineteen."

I was starting to like the Lion. "You got kids, Brian?"

"My son just turned seventeen. He and his mother moved to L.A. I haven't seen them in years."

"Sorry."

"Me too."

"Does Tony know how to use a gun?"

"Yeah. His father taught him how to shoot, but Tony doesn't like going to the range."

"He doesn't like guns?"

"He doesn't like hanging out with his father."

Got it. "What about his sister?"

"I used to see her at the store every once in a while. Isabel is smarter than Tony, and her father treats her better." He frowned. "I can't believe she was there that night. What a nightmare. I don't know if she saw Ortega shoot Tho, but she must have seen the body."

I thought of Grace. "Did you know Duc Tho?"

"I'd seen him in the neighborhood."

"Do you know any of his friends?"

"Nope."

"We heard he was selling weed to the kids at Galileo."

"Wouldn't surprise me."

"You know the name of his supplier?"

A hesitation. "No."

"Could you find out?"

"Maybe. That's going to require a payment at super-premium rates."

"We can work that out." I probed for a few more minutes,

then I handed him a business card wrapped in five twenties. "This is a down payment. Can we give you a lift somewhere?"

"No, thanks."

"You got a cell phone?"

"No."

Pete handed him a throwaway cell. "You do now. We'll be in touch."

* * *

Pete's tone was philosophical. "I was hoping that he knew more, Mick."

"I didn't expect much."

We were sitting in his car at two o'clock on Friday afternoon. It had been an ungodly long couple of days, and we were just getting started.

Pete frowned. "I'll keep an eye on him. And I want to do some checking here in the neighborhood."

"You want company?"

"It might be better if I did this by myself."

* * *

Rolanda's text came in as I was driving back to the office. "Meet me at Stonestown Mall as soon as you can," it read.

"Why?" I texted back.

"I found Ortega Cruz's daughter."

27

"DO YOU THINK THEY KNOW?"

"Where is Isabel?" I asked.

In her faded jeans and Warriors T-shirt, Rolanda could have passed for a college student. She pointed at the Apple Store between the Olive Garden and the Nordstrom's at the south end of the Stonestown Galleria. "Inside."

"How long has she been here?"

"Almost an hour."

It was impossible to get out of an Apple Store in less time. "How did you find her?"

"I played a hunch. This is where we used to hang out after school."

Rolanda's alma mater, Mercy High, was across Nineteenth Avenue. When I was a kid, Stonestown was a fifties-vintage, open-air mall. When we got good grades and we were a little flush, my mom and dad used to take us for burgers at the Red Chimney after church. Several ownership changes and remodels later, the now-indoor facility looked like every other mall in the U.S. Stonestown was in the Lakeside District near Mercy, St. Ignatius, Lowell, and Lincoln High Schools, as well as City College and San Francisco State. Not surprisingly, at three o'clock on Friday afternoon, its two-story concourse was filled with young people.

"You managed to find her in the middle of a crowded mall?" I said.

Rolanda responded with a mischievous smile. "I checked her Facebook page. Her parents should tell her to update her privacy settings."

Very resourceful. "Is she alone?"

"She's with a girlfriend. How do you want to play this?"

"For now, we just watch." A couple with matching Lowell High hoodies strolled past us arm-in-arm. "She saw me yesterday at her father's store. If either of us is going to talk to her, it should be you."

"Agreed."

We tried to blend in as we took up positions at either end of the Apple Store. Well-dressed kids texted their friends as they wandered past us. I found a spot near the entrance to Nordstrom's. Rolanda camped out in front of Victoria's Secret. Twenty years ago, we would have looked conspicuous. Nowadays, the ubiquitous smartphones gave us cover.

Five minutes went by. Then ten. I wondered whether my time could have been better spent reviewing files or looking for witnesses. I held my iPhone to my ear and pretended to talk to somebody. I was hoping to hear from Pete, but he had maintained radio silence since our visit with the Lion.

Fifteen minutes later my phone vibrated. Rolanda's name appeared on the display. "Isabel is leaving the store," she said.

"I see her. Follow her, but don't get too close."

"Got it."

The Isabel Cruz who walked out of the Apple Store with her friend looked nothing like the quiet teenager I'd seen briefly at her father's store the night before. She was wearing a skin-tight white blouse cinched up to reveal her naval, along with a pair of short shorts. Her long black hair was pulled back into a French twist. Her face was caked with makeup. A designer backpack was slung over her shoulder. She and her friend could have passed for sisters. They stared intently at their iPhones as they started walking toward the central atrium.

I punched in Rolanda's number on my speed dial. "You see her?"

"Yeah."

"I'm guessing those aren't official Mercy High uniforms."

"They aren't."

"Did you dress that way?"

"All the time. We used to change after school. It made it easier to get the boys from St. Ignatius to buy us stuff."

A long time ago, I had been one of those boys. "Did your father know about this?"

"Of course. Did your father know that you and your brothers used to come over here after school to hit on the girls from Mercy?"

I loved my niece. "Absolutely."

"I gotta roll, Mike."

"I'll be right behind you."

Isabel and her friend ambled past the Michael Kors store and the Armani outlet. They managed to avoid other shoppers even though their eyes were focused on their iPhones. They stopped briefly at Sunglass Hut, but they didn't buy anything. They paused again at the French Bakery, then decided to go up the escalator. Rolanda followed them. I counted to ten, then went upstairs, too.

When I reached the second floor, I was overwhelmed by the unique aroma of the American mall food court. Isabel and her friend considered the possibilities among the usual options: Starbucks, Panda Express, Korean Barbeque, Hot Dogs on a Stick, the San Francisco Soup Company, frozen yogurt, and Mrs. Fields. They opted for slices from Village Pizza, and sat down at one of the modular tables under the skylight. Rolanda found a seat a short distance away and pretended to look at her iPhone. I sat down a little farther away and hid my face behind my phone. I was concerned that Isabel might recognize me, but I realized that she was more interested in texting.

My iPhone vibrated again. A text from Rolanda read, "Now what?"

I texted her back. "We wait."

"How long?"

"Not sure. Can you hear anything?"

"Not much. Can you?"

"Nothing."

"Can you get closer?"

"Probably not." I glanced over at her and held up a hand. She responded with an impatient frown.

I thought of Pete as we continued to watch Isabel and her friend eat pizza, drink soda, and send texts. My brother always said that the most important attributes for a P.I. were patience, perseverance, and a low-maintenance digestive system.

At four o'clock, Isabel got up and bought some frozen yogurt. Her pal bought a cookie. They returned to their seats and resumed texting.

At four-thirty, Isabel and her friend took a break from their phones and looked around.

I sent Rolanda a text reading, "They're looking for somebody."

We waited a few more minutes. Then Isabel's face broke into a wide smile. Her friend stood up and smiled, too, as two athletic young men approached them. The taller one was African-American and wore a City College sweatshirt. The shorter was Asian-American and sported a San Francisco State hoodie. City College took a seat next to the friend. Hoodie grinned and sat down on Isabel's lap. She laughed as Hoodie pulled her close and kissed her long and hard. After they separated, she smiled as he wiped the lipstick from his mouth.

I glanced at my iPhone, where I found a text from Rolanda. "Didn't see that coming," it read.

I looked up again. Isabel, her friend, and the two boys were gathering their belongings. I shot a text to Rolanda. "Take a photo."

The text came back immediately. "Already did. Do you want to follow them?"

"Yes. Maybe we can get a license number."

"You don't want to talk to her?"

"Not while the others are around."

I looked over at my niece, who nodded.

We followed them outside, where they got into a rusted Nissan Sentra parked near the McDonald's. The boy who had kissed Isabel got behind the wheel, and Isabel sat in the passenger seat. The others got into the back. I typed in the license number on the notepad of my iPhone.

"You got a name on the boyfriend?" I asked Rolanda.

"Henry Minh."

"How did you find him so quickly?"

"There are about a thousand pictures of him on her Facebook page. He's a junior at State. He lives at 27th and Kirkham."

"Lowell?"

"Lincoln."

"Good student?"

"Not bad."

"Good citizen?"

"As far as I can tell. No criminal record. You want me to follow them?"

"No. I'll get Pete to have somebody watch her."

"Did Isabel's mother or father mention a boyfriend?"

"No."

My niece gave me a sideways look. "Do you think they know?"

I watched the Nissan drive up to Nineteenth Avenue. "Probably."

My iPhone vibrated. Pete's name appeared on the display. "Where are you, Mick?" he asked.

"Stonestown. I need you to have somebody keep an eye on Cruz's daughter and her boyfriend."

"Will do. In the meantime, meet me at the Tennessee Grill in twenty minutes."

It was a cop hangout a few blocks north of Stonestown. "You got something?"

"Yeah. Somebody who knows somebody who knows the undercover cop who busted Ortega Cruz's nephew."

"How did you find him?"

"Roosevelt."

28
"WE'RE LOOKING FOR BIGGER FISH"

The veteran cop took a bite of chicken-fried steak and washed it down with a Coke. "Heard you got the Nguyen case."

"We did."

"Heard your client is going down."

"Not without a fight."

"Wouldn't expect anything less from you, Mike."

Lieutenant Phil Dito had been a classmate of Pete's at the academy. He had grown up around the corner from Big John's saloon. Three of his seven brothers were SFPD. The rest were firemen. He was a solid cop and a stand-up guy. Built like a mini-fridge, he had been an undersized, but tenacious offensive lineman at St. Ignatius when Tommy was the quarterback.

Phil, Pete, and I were sitting at a Formica table in the back of the Tennessee Grill, a diner on Twenty-third, down the hill from Taraval Station. A counter ran the length of the narrow room, and booths lined the opposite side. Faux wood paneling ran halfway up the walls. Except for an occasional fresh coat of olive green paint, it looked the same as it did when it opened in 1952. The menu hadn't changed, either. The Tennessee wasn't the sort of place that would garner Michelin stars, but you never left hungry. It was popular with the cops who worked up the hill. It also served as Phil's auxiliary office.

Pete took a swallow of his Lou's Special, a concoction of scrambled eggs, corned beef, mushrooms, spinach, and garlic that came with a generous side of crispy hash browns and toast. "We're off the record," he said. "Phil's doing us a favor."

"Understood." I took a sip of black coffee. "Do you know

something about our case?"

Dito frowned. "Just what I've read in the papers."

Not helpful. "It's always good to see you, but why are we here?"

The leather-faced cop gulped down the remnants of his dinner. He grabbed a handful of paper napkins from the metal dispenser and wiped the grease from his face. "I heard you went to see Hector Cruz."

"I did. He's the nephew of the guy who said he shot Duc Tho."

"I know."

"Hector was there that night. He was working security at the store."

"I know that, too."

I was going to have to do this at Phil's pace. "Do you think Hector shot Duc Tho?"

"I doubt it."

I was getting impatient. "What aren't you telling us?"

Pete finally interjected. "Phil knows the undercover cop who arrested Hector."

Finally. "Would you mind giving us his name?" I said.

Dito shook his head. "Then he wouldn't be undercover anymore."

True. "Would you be willing to ask him a few questions on our behalf?"

"I already did."

"What did you find out?"

"Hector is an idiot."

Thank you for bringing it to our attention. "The kind who might have shot Duc Tho?"

"Unlikely. He's never done anything violent. He used to steal cars. Now he's a small-time drug mule who runs errands for another slightly-less-small-time guy."

"Do you have the name of Hector's supplier?"

"Working on it."

"Any chance it was Duc Tho?"

"Not as far as we can tell."

"Do you know the name of Tho's supplier?"

"I don't know that, either."

"You guys went to a lot of trouble to set up an undercover sting to arrest a low-level guy."

"We pick the low-hanging fruit first. At the risk of mixing metaphors, we're looking for bigger fish. If we can get Hector to give us the name of somebody higher in the food chain, we'll go after them next. Eventually, we'll work our way to the big guys."

"He's charged with a felony."

"He committed a felony."

"You think the D.A.'s Office really wants to put him away for a long time?"

"Honestly, I doubt it. At the end of the day, they'll probably just lean on him until they're satisfied that he's given them everything he knows. Eventually, they'll cut a deal with his lawyer."

"That's all that you've got?"

"Afraid so. I'll let you know if I hear anything else."

I reached for the check. "We appreciate your time, Phil. Give my best to Diane."

"I will."

* * *

Pete was hunched over a cup of coffee. "Sorry, Mick. I thought that Phil had more."

"No worries. I knew it was a longshot."

We were still sitting in the back of the Tennessee Grill at five o'clock on Friday afternoon. Dito had left. I was dead tired and dreading the Friday afternoon traffic for my drive downtown. I had ruled out heading home to Marin. I had to prepare for trial and the traffic on the Golden Gate Bridge on a

Friday afternoon would have been unbearable.

Pete gripped his mug tightly. "You got anything we can use, Mick?"

"Not much."

"We still have all weekend."

"I know. Do you have somebody watching Isabel Cruz?"

"Yeah."

"She has a boyfriend."

"I know. I have somebody watching him, too."

* * *

I was driving on the Golden Gate Bridge at eleven-thirty on Friday night when Pete's name appeared on my iPhone. "I hope this means you found something," I said.

"I have somebody watching Isabel and her boyfriend. They spend a lot of time together."

"That's the way it usually works."

"I went through their Facebook pages, Instagram feeds, and social media."

"Legally?"

"Absolutely. Seems Isabel's dad isn't crazy about the fact that she's going out with a Vietnamese guy."

"How does this impact our case?"

"It probably doesn't."

"Not the answer I wanted to hear."

"Can you meet me at noon tomorrow in the alley behind Saigon Sandwiches?"

"Sure. Why?"

"The Lion of the Loin wants to see us."

"I'll be there."

"Bring some cash. And you might want to bring Terrence the Terminator. The Lion said this could get a little dicey."

29
"I THINK I'M ENTITLED TO A BONUS"

The Lion of the Loin smiled. "Nice to see you again, gentlemen."

At noon on Saturday, the alley behind Saigon Sandwiches was strewn with expended needles and smelled of urine.

"Good to see you, Brian," I said. "I understand you have some information for us."

"I might. Who's your friend?"

"This is Terrence." The Terminator was standing next to me, arms folded. He looked even more intimidating than usual as the afternoon sun reflected off his bald dome. "He's my executive assistant."

Brian the Lion was sitting on a red milk crate. His shopping cart was parked within arm's length. The Tenderloin was less imposing in the daylight, but still dangerous. The parade of homeless people, alcoholics, drug dealers, and petty criminals were out on their daily search for money, food, and other necessities or, as the case may have been, vices.

Pete pulled up another crate and sat down next to Holton. "You have something for us?"

"You recall that I expect to be compensated for my services."

"I do." Pete slipped him two twenties.

"I'll need a little more."

"We'll need a little information first."

"I can't give you the information until you give me another hundred."

"That won't work for us."

"It'll have to. And I'll need another hundred for my

business associate."

"And who would that be?"

A razor-thin young man with a scar across his cheek and an American flag tattoo on his bicep emerged from behind a Dumpster. "This is Eduardo."

I extended a hand. "Nice to meet you, Eduardo." It probably wasn't his real name. "Do you have some information for us?"

Holton answered for him. "He does, but he'll need a hundred first."

"That's a lot."

"That's the price."

I pulled out my wallet and slipped five twenties into Eduardo's hand.

His blank expression didn't change as he turned around and started walking away.

"Where are you going?" I asked.

Holton answered for him. "Eduardo's part in this transaction is now concluded."

"You still haven't provided any information."

Holton pointed at Terrence. "We'll need a little help from your friend."

The Terminator held up a massive hand. "What do you want me to do?"

"Buy us lunch."

"I don't understand."

I was running out of patience. "I'm not paying you another nickel until you tell us what's going on."

Holton was enjoying himself. "You're going to give your assistant two hundred dollars. He's going inside to order a 'Tenderloin Special' from Eugene Pham. He's going to give Eugene the money and tell him to keep the change."

"I don't like it."

"Nothing is going to happen. Terrence will be out in a

minute. I'll stay here with you until he comes back."

I turned to Terrence. "You don't have to do this."

"I'll take care of it."

I handed him ten twenties and he headed inside. Pete and I waited with the Lion. Five minutes later, Terrence emerged with a brown paper bag, which he handed to me.

"Four Bahn Mi," he said. "One for each of us."

I opened the bag and handed sandwiches to Pete and Terrence. Then I gave Holton a sandwich. "So, what's the information?"

Holton answered for him. "Check the bottom of the bag."

I found a baggie containing a dozen pills. "Ecstasy?"

Holton nodded. "Yes. The Tenderloin Special. I trust you understand why I sent your assistant inside instead of me."

"I do." I had just committed a felony. Except for the fact that Pete, Terrence, and I had just engaged in criminal activity, the result was useful. "You could have just told us that Pham was supplying drugs to Duc Tho."

"I could have, but I wanted you to see it for yourself."

"I take it you got this information from Eduardo?"

"Yes."

"Is he available to testify?"

"No. As far as ICE is concerned, Eduardo does not exist."

"Then we'll need you to testify that Pham was Tho's supplier."

"I can't help you there, Mike."

Pete, Terrence, and I weren't about to admit to the police or the D.A. that we were buying drugs from Pham.

The Lion stood up and put his crate into his shopping cart. "I would think that this information might be useful to the D.A. You'll have to figure out the best way to present it. If you package it properly, it might create some leverage to negotiate a plea bargain for your client."

"It might."

He held out a hand. "In that case, I think I'm entitled to a bonus."

30
"WE HAVE SOMETHING TO OFFER"

The District Attorney of the City and County of San Francisco glanced at her Cartier watch. "I have to be over at Channel 7 in an hour."

"This won't take long," I said.

Nicole Ward pointed at Erickson. "Andy will be here if we run out of time."

At 5:30 on Sunday evening, Rolanda, Erickson, Ward, and I were meeting in Ward's office. Erickson was dressed in jeans and a Giants' cap. Ward was wearing an Aidan Mattox ensemble. We had contacted her almost twenty-four hours earlier. She said that she couldn't meet with us until today because she had "prior commitments." My guess was that she was preparing her wardrobe for her TV appearance or she wanted to watch the Niners game.

"We have something to offer," I said.

Ward responded with the politician's smile. "We're listening."

"We're off the record."

"For now. You know the dance. You proffer information. We check it out. If it's useful, we might be inclined to discuss terms."

Yup, that's about it. "We know the name of Duc Tho's supplier."

Ward and Erickson exchanged a glance. It was Erickson who responded. "How did you obtain this information?"

"A confidential source came to us." I wasn't going to mention Pete or Terrence. "We think this information will be valuable to you."

Ward smiled broadly. "We already know that Eugene Pham was Tho's supplier. Our Tenderloin Drug Task Force has been watching him."

Crap. I hope they weren't watching him yesterday when Terrence went inside and bought some ecstasy. "Why haven't you arrested him?"

"Tho isn't the only person he supplied. We're hoping to catch a few more fish before we bust him."

"You should have told us about it."

"I didn't want to compromise an ongoing undercover operation."

"You have a legal obligation to provide information that's relevant to our case."

"We are required to provide information that would tend to exonerate your client. The fact that Pham was supplying drugs to Tho has no bearing on your case—except perhaps if you are looking for leverage in negotiating a plea bargain."

True. I turned to Erickson. "You still should have told us about it, Andy."

"Not in this case. In other circumstances, I might have done so as a matter of professional courtesy. When we have undercover operatives at risk, I need to err on the side of caution."

I didn't like it, but I understood.

Ward flashed a smug grin. "I take it this means that you won't be proffering additional evidence at this time?"

"Correct."

"I'm going to do something that I wouldn't ordinarily do. I'm going to reinstate our offer to plead this case down to second degree. It remains open until ten o'clock tonight. Interested?"

"No."

"You have a legal obligation to take our offer to your client."

"I will."

"If I don't hear from you, we'll see you in court tomorrow morning."

31

"YOU NEED TO MAINTAIN
YOUR COMPOSURE"

Thomas's response to Ward's offer was a succinct "No."

"You sure?" I asked.

His eyes narrowed. "I'm not pleading guilty."

The Glamour Slammer was quiet at seven o'clock on Sunday evening. Thomas and I were seated at a metal table in a consultation room. An over-muscled deputy was standing outside the locked door. I was grateful that I didn't have to conduct this discussion through a Plexiglas divider.

Thomas chewed on his finger. "Do you think they might make me a better offer?"

"Unlikely."

"I'm not going to plead guilty."

"Nobody is saying that you killed anyone."

"They're trying to convict me of murder just the same."

"It's a legal technicality."

"It's legal crap. If I plead guilty, I'm admitting that I'm a murderer. I'm not going to do it. If twelve people convict me for sitting in the car, then it will be on their conscience."

"You might end up in jail for a long time."

"I'll be there for a long time if I plead guilty. At least if we go to trial, there's a chance, right?"

"Yes."

"How good of a chance?"

I didn't pull my punch. "Not great."

"How not great?"

"I'd say your odds of being convicted are better than fifty-fifty."

"That's reassuring."

"We don't have great cards."

"How are you planning to play them?"

"We want to show that somebody other than Ortega Cruz could have shot Tho. It's difficult because Ortega admitted it and Tony and Hector will corroborate his story."

"How does that help?"

"If somebody else shot Tho, they can be tried independently for murder. It also blows up Cruz's story that he acted in self-defense. More important, there's no provocative act, which means you can't be convicted of felony murder."

"You have no evidence that somebody else did it."

"We'll argue that Tony or Hector shot Tho. They were in a position to do so."

"So was Ortega." His expression turned skeptical. "You're just going to throw stuff up against the wall to see if it sticks, aren't you?"

Yes. "More or less."

He sighed. "We're done, aren't we?"

"You never know with a jury. I've had cases where I figured I had a sure winner and my client was convicted. Other times I thought my client was guilty as hell and the jury let them off. It's a crapshoot."

"What would you do if you were in my shoes?"

I considered my answer for a moment. "I'd go to trial."

"Then that's what we'll do."

"I'll have some clothes ready for you when you get to court tomorrow."

"What difference does it make?"

"A lot. Trials are theater. The jury will be watching you. I want you to sit quietly and pay attention. Don't say anything unless I tell you to do so. You need to be very respectful of the judge, the jury, and the prosecutors."

"I'll try."

"Most important, I need you to maintain your composure. Trials are unpredictable. Unexpected stuff happens. The prosecutors will say things to try to get a reaction from you. You need to stay calm. Understood?"

"Yes."

I waited a beat. "There's something else that I need to discuss with you. We may want you to testify."

His eyes grew larger. "Me?"

"Yeah."

"Why?"

"To tell the jury that Duc was unarmed and didn't intend to rob the store. And to give the jury a sympathetic face."

"I'm not sure that I can do it."

"It will be short and you'll follow my lead. It will show the jury that you're a decent guy who was in the wrong place at the wrong time."

"Won't the prosecutor have a chance to do cross examination?"

"Yes. It could get a little rough, but I don't think they'll lean on you very hard. Nobody is suggesting that you shot Tho."

He nodded. "Anything else?"

"We'll see you in court at ten o'clock tomorrow morning."

32
"YOU GOT NOTHING"

I was walking into my office when my iPhone rang. "Jerry Edwards. *San Francisco Chronicle*," the voice said.

As if I don't remember where you work. "What can I do for you, Jerry?"

"My sources tell me that you haven't been able to work out a plea bargain for your client."

"Who's your source?"

"Nicole Ward."

"She called you?"

"I saw her on TV."

Excellent reporting. "I can confirm that we have not reached a plea bargain."

"So we're still on at ten o'clock tomorrow?"

"Yes."

"Any update on your case?"

He was fishing. "No."

"Any new evidence?"

"No."

"I find it hard to believe that a fine attorney like yourself who is working with an excellent private investigator like your brother has been unable to find any information that might be helpful to your client's case."

Flattery isn't going to work. "Sorry."

"Is there something that you can't tell me?"

A lot. "No."

"You're sandbagging me, aren't you?"

Absolutely. "No."

"Come on, Mike."

Enough. "You've been around the block enough times to know that I have no legal obligation to tell you anything about my case."

"I can help you in the court of public opinion if you give me something I can use."

"You know that lawyers don't share information about evidence and strategy on the eve of trial. That would be malpractice."

"They do if they think it would help their client. You got nothing."

True. "I'll see you in court in the morning, Jerry."

* * *

I sat down at my desk and punched in the number of an old friend. An overly cheerful voice picked up on the first ring.

"Hanson Investigative Agency. Bernadette speaking. How may I help you?"

It was Nick's great-granddaughter. "It's Mike Daley, Bernie. How've you been?"

"Just fine, Mr. Daley."

"Have you finished law school?"

"Almost. I'm in my third year."

"That's great."

Between classes at USF Law School, she made a few bucks working at Nick's agency.

"What can I do for you, Mr. Daley?"

"Is Nick around?"

"Senior, Junior, Third, or Fourth?"

"Senior."

"One moment please."

Despite my foul mood, I smiled. I envisioned Nick the Dick sitting in his office in North Beach with his feet up on his cluttered rolltop desk, clutching an unlit cigar, and fingering the rose in his lapel.

"How ya doin', Mike?" he asked.

"Not bad, Nick."

"I hear you're going to court tomorrow."

"We are. Thanks for directing us to the Lion of the Loin."

"Did Pete find him?"

"Yes."

"Did he provide any useful information?"

"No."

"Sorry, Mike."

"You got anything else that we can use?"

"I'm afraid not. So how you gonna play it?"

"The usual, Nick. Smoke and mirrors."

His tone turned serious. "No kidding, Mike. What are you gonna do?"

"Our ballistics expert will testify that the shot could have been fired by somebody other than Ortega Cruz. Our lipreader will argue that Tho never threatened Cruz."

"That's it?"

"We'll try to blow enough smoke to make the jury think that somebody other than Cruz shot Tho. If that doesn't work, we'll argue that he lost his temper and didn't act in self-defense."

"Seems thin."

"It is."

"You got a Plan B?"

No. "I was thinking of putting you on the stand."

"What exactly do you want me to say?"

"I don't know. We'll have to wing it. If nothing else, it will entertain the jury and it will be fun."

He chuckled. "You think it will work?"

"It can't hurt. You always told me that if you can't prove your case to the jury, you should try to amuse them."

"It works."

"I know. Are you available to testify if we need you?"

"Indeed I am."

* * *

Roosevelt's voice was tinged with melancholy. "How are you holding up, Mike?"

"Not bad."

"You sound tired."

"I am."

"I saw Jerry Edwards on the news. He said you're going to trial in the morning. Anything I can do to help?"

"Got a minute to give me a reality check?"

"Sure. What have you got?"

"Not much."

He listened without interrupting as I described the evidence. After I finished, the phone went silent for a moment. I envisioned him stroking his mustache as he ran through various scenarios in his mind.

Finally, he cleared his throat. "Doesn't sound like you have anything that will get you a slam-dunk acquittal."

"We've come to the same conclusion. How would you play this?"

"I'd try to show that somebody other than Ortega Cruz could have pulled the trigger. It's a variation on the old 'SODDI' defense."

It was an acronym for "Some other dude did it."

Roosevelt was still talking. "If the jury thinks there's a decent argument that somebody else shot Tho, you eliminate Cruz's self-defense claim. More important, you cast doubt on everything he's said. Maybe the jury will think that he's protecting his son or nephew or even his daughter."

"We were thinking the same thing."

"What is the lipreading expert going to say?"

"She's prepared to testify that it's inconclusive whether Tho ever asked for money, or, for that matter, whether he said anything at all."

"If that's the case, it also could mitigate the self-defense claim."

It was still a stretch. "What about the gun that he allegedly found under Tho's body?"

"That's a problem," he acknowledged.

"Cruz's fingerprints were on that gun."

"You can make the argument that he planted it, but he'll say that his prints got on the gun when he disarmed it."

True. "Do you think we should put Thomas on the stand?"

He considered his answer for a moment. "Probably, but only if you think the jury will have empathy. If he appears callous or arrogant, it will cut against you. You'll want to play up the fact that he was outside in the car, which means that, arguably, he's a victim, too."

"Do you think Erickson will go after him on cross?"

"Doubtful. He'll try to get him off the stand as fast as he can."

I cut to the bottom line. "Do you think we should accept a plea for second degree?"

"Based upon my limited knowledge of the evidence and the fact that I've never met your client, I would say that it would minimize the potential damage."

"What's your gut, Roosevelt?"

"Tho was in the store for only a couple of seconds before he was shot. You might want to argue that there wasn't enough time for Ortega Cruz to develop the requisite fear in order to have acted in self-defense."

"Roosevelt?"

"Yes?"

"Thanks."

33
"YOU NEED TO MESS THINGS UP"

"Any additions to the prosecution's witness list?" I asked.

Rolanda shook her head. "No."

"Did you submit our final list?"

"Of course."

"Any objections?"

"Erickson wanted to know why we included Ortega Cruz's wife and daughter."

"To give them something to think about."

"Are you planning to call them?"

"Not unless we find a good reason."

"Thought so."

At eleven o'clock on Sunday night, Rolanda, Pete, Rosie, and I had gathered around the table in the conference room at the P.D.'s Office. Trial binders, file folders, witness lists, poster boards, and exhibits were scattered haphazardly. Two empty pizza boxes were stashed in the corner. The recycling bin was filled with empty soda cans.

"How are we coming along on jury questionnaires?" I asked.

"Almost finished."

"Good." I pointed at Rolanda's laptop. "All set to show the security video?"

"Yes."

"Other exhibits ready to go?"

"Yes."

"I'll want you to handle the cross on some of the prosecution's witnesses. And I'll need you to do the direct exam of some of our witnesses when we present our case."

"I'm ready. I've been preparing with the best attorney I know."

"Thank you."

She pointed at Rosie. "I meant her."

I know.

My ex-wife smiled triumphantly. "Still glad Rolanda is second chair?"

"Absolutely. And we're very grateful for your help, too."

"My pleasure."

I turned back to my niece. "I think it might be better if you handle our closing argument."

"Sure. Why?"

Because I want to give you the experience. "You're more likeable than I am."

She grinned. "Nobody's more likeable than you are, Mike." She quickly added, "Happy to do it."

"Great. There's still the small matter of deciding what you're going to say. We need to think about this tonight. If things go as planned and jury selection goes quickly, we'll get to closing arguments in a few days."

"Rosie and I have outlined some scenarios. I'll be ready."

Always three steps ahead. I turned to Rosie. "Have you given any more thought about whether we should ask for a bench trial?"

"Yes. The answer is no."

We'd been going back and forth on this issue since Friday. "May I ask why?"

"Judge McDaniel."

"Betsy has always given us a fair shake."

"I know, but she's already ruled that the felony murder rule is applicable. She doesn't think much of it, but she comes in with a predisposition to apply the law as it's written. She could have thrown this case out months ago, but she didn't."

"You think we'll have a better chance with a jury?"

"It's always a crapshoot, but if we're lucky, they'll be reluctant to convict your great-nephew of murder when he didn't pull the trigger."

I looked over at Rolanda. "Do you agree?"

"Yes."

I posed the same question to Pete, who nodded. He had a good feel for how non-lawyers would react to various scenarios.

"Then it's settled. We'll ask for a jury."

We talked about jury selection for a few minutes. Then we spent another hour going through the jury questionnaires (abbreviated version), my opening statement (short), the prosecution's witness list (also short), our witness list (even shorter), and our trial exhibits (few). We brainstormed ways to make the cops look sloppy and the prosecution's witnesses look untrustworthy. We spent an hour trying to come up with plausible arguments to suggest that Ortega Cruz somehow didn't act in self-defense.

It was almost midnight when Rosie leaned back in her chair. "What's the narrative?" she asked.

I knew this was coming. It was one of the first things that she had taught me when I was a rookie Public Defender. You need to tell the jury a compelling story with a beginning, a middle, and an end. More important, you need a coherent and easy-to-digest theme that you can explain in a couple of sentences. "Thomas was just sitting in the car," I said. "Good kid, wrong place, wrong time."

"It might not matter under the felony murder rule."

"It's a bad law."

"It isn't the jury's job to rewrite the law."

"There was no provocative act. You can't see the gun in Tho's hand."

"Ortega Cruz will testify that he saw it—or thought that he did."

"Then our theme is to argue that Ortega Cruz is a trigger-happy nutjob who lied about a robbery to cover up a homicide. No robbery-no provocative act-not guilty."

"Not bad."

Pete smiled. "I like it. You need to mess things up."

"What do you mean?"

"Ortega Cruz is going to say that he shot Tho in self-defense. His son, his nephew, and maybe his daughter are going to corroborate his story. You need to discredit them—even if you need to play dirty. If you have to, put the Lion of the Loin on the stand and get him to say that Ortega is a crackpot who liked to show off his AR-15. Show that the son is a weakling who is afraid to stand up to his father. Show that the nephew is an idiot with a criminal record. If one of them cracks, maybe the others will, too. Juries don't like liars—especially when they shoot people."

"Ortega admitted that he shot Tho."

"Make the argument that he was trying to take the rap for his kid."

"You think we should accuse Tony of killing Tho?"

"The system isn't pretty. You're always standing on your soapbox and lecturing everybody about providing a zealous representation for your client and letting the system sort things out."

Guilty. "What if Tony was your kid?"

"I'd meet you out in the parking lot with a tire iron." Pete turned serious. "Do what you have to do, Mick. And watch your backside."

I didn't like his tone. "What is it?"

"Just a hunch that the D.A. knows more than they've told you."

"They always do. Something in particular?"

"One of my sources saw Ken Lee down at the jail in San Bruno earlier this evening."

"He has a lot of active cases."

"He wouldn't have gone down there on a Sunday night if it wasn't urgent."

34

"CAN YOU WIN?"

"How do you like working with Rolanda?" Rosie asked.

"She's terrific."

I felt her warm breath on my cheek as she leaned over and kissed me. "Thanks for looking after her."

The light from her clock radio reflected her eyes as I hugged her. "My pleasure."

We were lying in Rosie's bed at three-thirty on Monday morning. The trial would start in six and a half hours.

Her full lips transformed into a whimsical smile. "Remember how we used to get ready for big trials when we first met?"

"How could I possibly forget?" When we were baby Public Defenders, Rosie and I made love the night before trial. "I learned a lot about preparation from you."

"And you learned a little about the law, too."

"I think it put us into the right frame of mind."

"I don't know about you, Mike, but I wasn't thinking much about the trial when we were doing our pregame warmup."

"To be honest, neither was I." *Beautiful Rosie.* I kissed her again. "Do you think we were serving our clients' needs adequately?"

"Absolutely. We were also serving our own needs more than adequately. Good lawyers need to multi-task, Mike."

"Yes, they do. Do you still think it's a good idea to prepare for trial this way?"

"Are you questioning my methods?"

"No. I'm questioning my stamina."

"Get over it. It's worked well for a long time. Besides, I

haven't come up with anything better." Her tone turned serious. "You ready to roll?"

"Yeah."

"Can you win?"

"I don't know."

Her expression was bemused. "Not wildly confident, are we?"

"No, we're not."

"Maybe we need to have a little more warmup sex."

A fine idea. "Your mother will be up any minute."

"We'll be quiet."

"I promised Rolanda that I would meet her at the office at seven."

She glanced at her watch. "That gives us three and a half hours."

"Let's save a little something for the post-trial victory celebration."

"You'd rather go to the office than make wild, passionate love to me?"

"I'd rather make wild, passionate love to you than anything else in the world."

"What's stopping you?"

"My responsibilities to my client and deference to Father Time."

"Lame, Mike."

"I know."

"I would like to take this opportunity to remind you that you insisted on handling this case yourself even though we have an office full of excellent attorneys."

"Seemed like a good idea at the time."

"And now?"

"Maybe not."

She reached over and touched my cheek. "Are you going to be okay, Mike?"

"Yeah."

"Is there any chance that you'll be able to get Thomas off?"

"There's always a chance."

"Any idea how you might do it?"

"Rolanda or Pete will come up with something. They're very resourceful."

"I'll see you in court, Mike."

"You're coming to cheer us on?"

"Wouldn't miss it."

35
"ALL RISE"

"All rise," the bailiff said.

At ten o'clock sharp on Monday morning, Judge McDaniel emerged from her chambers and walked briskly to the bench. She never used a gavel. "Please be seated."

Three standing fans pushed around the heavy air in her windowless courtroom. Rolanda and I stood at the defense table on either side of Thomas, who had traded his orange jail clothes for a charcoal suit. Andy Erickson was at the prosecution table. Ken Lee was standing next to him. As the in-charge homicide inspector, he was the only witness allowed in court during testimony. Melinda was seated behind us in the front row of the gallery. Rosie was in the back. Otherwise, the defense side was empty.

The prosecution had a bigger turnout. Nicole Ward was sitting behind Erickson and chatting up Jerry Edwards, who was one of only three members of the fourth estate observing the trial. His counterparts from the *Oakland Trib* and the *San Jose Mercury* were in the back row alongside three courthouse regulars. A sketch artist from the *Chronicle* was sitting on the aisle, pencils poised. A criminal law professor from USF and two of his students sat in back of Ward. They were probably going to write yet another law review article about the felony murder rule.

Judge McDaniel turned on her computer and pulled the microphone toward her. "Good morning," she said to nobody in particular. She nodded to the bailiff. "Please call our case."

"The People versus Thomas Nguyen." He recited the case number and noted that the charge was first degree murder.

"Would counsel please state their names for the record?"

"Andrew Erickson for The People."

"Michael Daley and Rolanda Fernandez for the defense."

"Any last-minute issues?"

Erickson was first. "Your Honor, the public would benefit from seeing this trial. We therefore renew our request to have these proceedings televised."

"Denied. Mr. Daley?"

I invoked a deferential tone and made a futile request for the record. "Your Honor, we respectfully ask that you reconsider your ruling regarding the application of the felony murder rule. Under well-established California law, we believe that it does not apply where the deceased was killed by the intended victim of the original crime."

"Noted and denied. Anything else, Mr. Daley?"

"No, Your Honor."

"Let's pick a jury."

* * *

Under Judge McDaniel's diligent and artful choreography, jury selection moved more rapidly than usual and consumed only two full court days—which seemed glacial to our potential jurors, but represented a breakneck pace for the lawyers. At two-fifteen on Wednesday afternoon, four men and eight women filled the vinyl-covered swivel chairs in the jury box. We chose four women as alternates. It wasn't a bad draw for us, but it was hard to predict which way they would lean. We had neither the time nor the resources to hire a jury consultant or conduct mock panels, so Rolanda and I relied on an informal survey of our colleagues, and, to a greater extent, our instincts. The conventional wisdom says that defense attorneys should pick jurors who can be confused or manipulated. In short, we're supposed to look for idiots. Bonus points are awarded to those with gripes against the justice system.

I've never liked painting with such broad strokes. While most people—including me—abhor the concept of jury service, I've found that jurors generally try to do the right thing. We looked for thoughtful people who would have trouble living with themselves if they put away a kid for sitting in his friend's car. Erickson wanted jurors who would follow the law.

Judge McDaniel addressed the jury in her grandmother voice. "Ladies and gentlemen, you are performing an important civic task, and the court appreciates your service."

The young woman with the nose ring who worked at the Verizon Store on Market Street shifted in her seat and chewed her gum more forcefully.

The judge's tone was serious. "For obvious reasons, I must ask you to turn off your cell phones." She recited the usual warning that the jurors are not allowed to talk to anybody or each other about the case. "Do not do any research on your own or as a group. Do not use a dictionary or other reference materials, investigate the facts of law, conduct any experiments, or visit the scene of any event involved in this case. If you happen to pass by the scene, do not stop or investigate." She also told them not to read about it in the papers or online. "Finally, I must remind you not to post anything about this case on Facebook, Twitter, Instagram, Snapchat, WhatsApp, or social media. If you tweet or text about this case, I will hold you in contempt and it will cost you money. Understood?"

The jurors and alternates nodded.

"Good." She looked at the prosecution table. "Mr. Erickson, do you wish to make an opening statement?"

Of course he does.

He stood up and buttoned his gray suit jacket. "I do, Your Honor."

"I would ask our jurors to give you their undivided attention."

Erickson kept his eyes on the jury as he walked to the lectern and placed a single note card next to the microphone. "Ladies and gentlemen, my name is Andy Erickson. I represent the State of California. I appreciate your service, and I am grateful for your attention."

It was a little smarmy, but not over the top.

"I know that your time is valuable. I promise to get you home as soon as possible."

He had crossed the line into patronizing.

Erickson nodded with authority. "The facts of this case are not in dispute."

Every prosecutor tries to sell the idea that the facts aren't in dispute.

"On December fourteenth of last year, a young man named Duc Tho walked into Alcatraz Liquors on a dangerous street in the Tenderloin. Duc demanded money and reached inside his pocket. Not surprisingly, the owner of the store feared for his life. He pulled a weapon that he had acquired legally and shot Duc in self-defense. Sadly, he died at the scene." Erickson nodded again. "It was a great tragedy."

His sentiment was sincere, but his delivery was melodramatic. I was also pretty sure that he would not refer to Ortega Cruz again without including the words "self" and "defense."

Erickson pointed at Thomas. "The defendant is Thomas Nguyen, who is sitting between his attorneys at the defense table."

All eyes turned to Thomas. It was a standard—and effective—maneuver. The first thing you learn as a baby prosecutor is that you always point at the defendant. It's sort of like throwing out the first pitch at a baseball game.

Erickson nodded again. He was good at nodding. "The defendant was a friend of Duc's. The defendant was sitting outside in Duc's car when Duc went into the liquor store.

Under California law, the fact that Duc went inside to commit a felony was sufficient to make the defendant guilty of murder under a legal doctrine called the 'felony murder rule.'"

Notwithstanding Erickson's incessant repetition of the word "defendant," I understood his choice of language. He would try to dehumanize Thomas by not mentioning his name. Conversely, he would refer to Tho by his first name to paint him more sympathetically and to remind the jury that there was, in fact, a victim in this case.

It's considered bad form to interrupt during an opening statement, but I wanted to let the jury know that I was paying attention. More important, I wanted to break up Erickson's flow. I stood and invoked an understated tone. "Objection, Your Honor. Please remind Mr. Erickson that opening statements are limited to discussing facts and not making legal arguments."

Judge McDaniel responded with a perfunctory nod. "Please, Mr. Erickson."

"Yes, Your Honor." As expected, he picked up exactly where he had left off. "Under California law, there are two elements to every crime. In legal jargon, we call them *actus reus* and *mens rea*. But that's the only Latin that you're going to hear from me."

Smart move. Jurors hate it when lawyers talk Latin.

Erickson moved a step closer to the jury. "In plain English, the two elements are a criminal act and a criminal intent. You need both to find a defendant guilty."

He was absolutely right, but that didn't stop me from complaining. "Objection, Your Honor. Mr. Erickson is arguing the law again."

Technically, my objection was legitimate. In reality, it was likely to have no effect on Erickson's presentation or the eventual outcome of the case.

"Sustained." Judge McDaniel showed her first hint of

irritation, which should have been directed at me, but played to the jury as impatience with Erickson. Courtroom dynamics are frequently unfair. "Please stick to the facts, Mr. Erickson."

"Yes, Your Honor." He was still facing the jury. "We know for a fact that the defendant was sitting in the car. We also know for a fact that the shopkeeper shot Duc in self-defense— he admitted it."

Last time. "Objection, Your Honor. Stating that something is a fact doesn't make it factual. It is a fact that the shopkeeper *said* that he shot Mr. Tho. However, his state of mind at the time remains an open issue."

I was starting to try her patience. "Sustained."

I glanced at Rolanda, who closed her eyes. It was a signal for me to shut up. I was starting to sound whiny.

Erickson moved in front of the jury where I couldn't see his face. "You might be wondering how the defendant committed a crime if he was outside in the car. Under California law, if somebody is killed during the commission of a felony, the acts of the individual who causes the death can be attributed to another person who participates in the felony. In this case, the shopkeeper's act of shooting Duc Tho is imputed to the defendant."

Erickson paused to let the concept sink in. As far as I could tell, the jury was with him.

"Let's talk about the second element. You're probably wondering how somebody outside had the requisite criminal intent to be convicted of murder."

There was no sign that the jurors were, in fact, pondering this question.

"Under California law, if someone enters a business with an intent to commit a felony or in circumstances creating an inherent danger to the people inside, that person is deemed to have the requisite criminal intent. In legal terms, we call this a 'provocative act.'"

It wasn't the most eloquent explanation of the legal concept of a "provocative act," but it was easy to follow and close enough.

Erickson put his hand on the rail of the jury box. "In such circumstances, the criminal intent of the perpetrator is imputed to his accomplice. In this case, Duc's criminal intent is attributed to the defendant. Consequently, the combination of a criminal act and criminal intent means that the defendant is guilty of murder."

This elicited a skeptical look from the software developer from Google who was sitting next to the woman from the Verizon store.

Erickson walked back to the lectern. "Ladies and gentlemen, your job is to determine the facts of this case and apply California law as it is written. At the end of the day, I am confident that you will find the defendant guilty of felony murder."

He picked up his note card, unbuttoned his jacket, and returned to his seat.

Judge McDaniel turned to me. "Did you wish to make an opening statement, Mr. Daley?"

"Yes, Your Honor."

I could have chosen to defer my opening until Erickson had finished his case, but I wanted to speak to the jury right away. I glanced at the handwritten note that Rolanda had placed on the table in front of me which read, "Simple."

I walked to the lectern and worked without notes. "Ladies and gentlemen, my client, Thomas Nguyen, has been wrongly accused of a crime that he did not commit. In fact, he did not commit any crime at all. Thomas did nothing except sit in a car outside of the store where Duc Tho was killed. Duc entered a liquor store in the Tenderloin and was shot in cold blood by the shopkeeper, who claims that he acted in self-defense because Duc threatened to rob him. Except there was no robbery. And there was no threat. Mr. Erickson presented you with a contorted interpretation of a discredited doctrine called the felony murder rule. It's a terrible law that doesn't even apply in this case. However, since the prosecution is insisting on pursuing these spurious charges, we have no choice but to dispute them and demonstrate why they are wrong."

I was doing exactly what I had just accused Erickson of doing: arguing the law instead of stating the facts. This was intentional. I was trying to goad him into objecting and appearing defensive. To his credit, he didn't take the bait.

"Mr. Erickson says that the facts are not in dispute. He's wrong. Even if the felony murder rule was a good law—which it isn't—he isn't applying it properly. He's going to try to convince you that Thomas should be responsible for the shopkeeper's act of shooting Duc Tho. That's unfair to Thomas. And it's not the way the law is supposed to work.

"Mr. Erickson is right about one thing—it's your job to determine the facts and apply the law. But I would add something else. You need to use your good judgment and common sense. Thomas didn't have a gun. Neither did his friend. Duc Tho went inside and was shot in cold blood. You shouldn't convict a high school senior of murder for sitting in a car. Maybe Mr. Erickson wants to punish somebody because Duc Tho is dead. Maybe he doesn't know any better or he can't do any better. But I know that you do and you will."

Except for a subtle nod by the Google guy, there was no reaction from the jurors. I walked back to the defense table and sat down.

Judge McDaniel turned to Erickson. "Please call your first witness."

"The People call Sergeant Ignacio Navarro."

It was a logical place to start. Navarro was the first officer at the scene.

36
"THERE WAS BLOOD EVERYWHERE"

The veteran cop tapped the microphone and nodded reassuringly to the jury. "My name is Sergeant Ignacio Navarro. I've worked at Tenderloin Station for twenty-four years."

You wouldn't have suspected that the polished professional in the navy suit was the same guy who had stonewalled me in the basement of Tenderloin Station.

Erickson was standing at the lectern. You never crowd a strong witness. "How many homicides have you seen over the course of your career?"

"About two dozen." Navarro testified in the clipped cop dialect that jurors expect after watching countless episodes of *Law & Order* and *CSI*.

"How many resulted in a conviction?"

"Objection," I said. "Relevance." I was trying to distract them.

"Sustained."

Erickson continued as if he hadn't heard us. "Sergeant, were you working at Tenderloin Station at ten-forty-seven p.m. on December fourteenth of last year?"

"Yes."

"Do you recall what you were doing?"

"Processing a detainee who had been arrested for public intoxication."

"Were you escorting the prisoner to a holding cell?"

He smiled at the jury. "Actually, I was carrying him."

I didn't want him to build empathy. "Your Honor, we will stipulate that Sergeant Navarro was working at Tenderloin

Station on the night of December fourteenth of last year when a nine-one-one call came in regarding a shooting at Alcatraz Liquors."

The judge was pleased. "Thank you, Mr. Daley."

Erickson introduced a printout into evidence and handed it to Navarro. "Do you recognize this?"

"It's the nine-one-one log for the night of December fourteenth of last year."

"Does it show a call at ten-forty-seven and forty seconds?"

"Yes." Navarro pretended to study the report. "A person identifying himself as Ortega Cruz, the owner of Alcatraz Liquors, placed the call. A second call came in at ten-forty-eight and thirty-five seconds from Hector Cruz, the security guard. Both reported shots fired. Ortega said that he had shot and killed a man in self-defense during an attempted armed robbery. Hector confirmed his story. Nine-one-one dispatch called us immediately."

Erickson had put the first points on the board. To convict someone of murder, you need a victim. For good measure, he played the nine-one-one tapes. It was overkill, but it got the jury's attention.

Erickson lobbed another softball. "What did you do when the call came in?"

"I signed out a police unit and drove the two blocks to Alcatraz Liquors."

Erickson introduced a poster-sized diagram of the store and placed it on an easel between the jury and the witness box. In our world of elaborate computer graphics, the simple low-tech depiction was effective.

Erickson pointed at the drawing. "Sergeant, could you please confirm that this accurately represents the layout of the store?"

"It does."

"What time did you arrive?"

"Ten-fifty-one p.m."

"What was happening outside?"

"A crowd had gathered. I instructed everyone to remain orderly. I called for backup and an ambulance. Among other things, a Honda Civic was illegally parked in front of a fire hydrant. We later determined that it belonged to the victim, Duc Tho."

"Was anybody in the car?"

"The defendant, Thomas Nguyen."

"Is he in this courtroom?"

"Yes, he is." Navarro pointed at Thomas. "He is sitting between the attorneys at the defense table."

Erickson had another score. He had placed Thomas at the scene.

Thomas leaned over and whispered, "Can you do anything?"

"Not yet."

"What happened next?" Erickson asked.

"I was met in the doorway by the owner of the store. He identified himself as Ortega Cruz. He confirmed that there was no longer an active shooter inside. I followed standard procedure and searched him. I determined that he was not armed. Then we entered the store."

"What did you find?"

"A body on the floor later identified as Duc Tho. There was blood everywhere. I surveyed the scene and determined that nobody was in immediate danger."

"Did you find any weapons inside the store?"

"Yes. An AR-15 rifle and a Glock nine-millimeter handgun were on the counter. There was a Kel-Tec P-3AT handgun on the floor next to Mr. Tho's body. Mr. Cruz informed me that he was the licensed owner of the AR-15 and the Glock. He confirmed that he had shot Duc Tho in self-defense with the AR-15. The Glock had been in the possession of his nephew,

Hector, the security guard. Mr. Cruz said that he had found the Kel-Tec under Mr. Tho's body."

"Were you able to determine the registered owner of the Kel-Tec?"

"No. All of the identifying information had been removed."

"Were any of the weapons loaded?"

"No. Mr. Cruz informed me that he had disarmed all three firearms and gave me the unused bullets. In accordance with standard procedure, I re-checked the weapons to make sure that they weren't loaded. As a safety precaution, I maintained custody of all weapons until backup arrived a few minutes later. I logged in all three firearms and the unexpended ammunition into evidence."

I didn't expect him to say that he planted the gun.

"Who else was there?"

Navarro confirmed that Tony, Hector, and Isabel were present. "I searched Tony and Hector and determined that they were unarmed."

"Did you search Mr. Cruz's daughter?"

"No. Per standard procedure, I waited for a female officer to arrive. Isabel was very upset and I did not believe that she posed a threat."

"Could you please show us where you found the deceased?"

Navarro pointed at the diagram. "On the floor in front of the cash register."

"Did you attempt to administer first aid?"

"Yes. He was dead."

"Move to strike," I said. "Sergeant Navarro is not qualified to determine whether the victim was deceased."

"Sustained. The jury will disregard Sergeant Navarro's statement."

Erickson held up a hand. "Sergeant Navarro, based upon your decades of experience, did it appear to you that the victim was seriously injured?"

"Yes. I'm not the Medical Examiner, so I couldn't make an official pronouncement. There was no pulse. It was apparent that the victim's major organs had been hit by gunfire." He confirmed that EMTs arrived within minutes and attempted to resuscitate Tho. "They were unsuccessful. The victim was pronounced dead at the scene."

"Could you please describe Ortega Cruz's demeanor?"

"He was upset, but he demonstrated good judgment by identifying himself and cooperating. He confirmed that he had used the AR-15 to shoot Mr. Tho in self-defense after he announced his intention to rob the store."

"Did you place him under arrest?"

"No. After backup arrived, I drove Mr. Cruz to Tenderloin Station, where he provided a full statement. He admitted that he had shot Mr. Tho in self-defense."

Erickson nodded triumphantly. "In self-defense," he repeated.

If you say "self-defense" again, we'll turn it into a drinking game.

Erickson walked over to the cart and introduced the AR-15 into evidence. "Is this the weapon that Ortega Cruz used to shoot Duc Tho?"

"Yes."

Erickson next picked up the Glock and showed it to Navarro, who confirmed that Hector had been in possession of the weapon when Tho had walked into the store. He went through a similar exercise to have Navarro identify the Kel-Tec.

"Mr. Cruz's son was present when you arrived. Could you describe his demeanor?"

"He was upset."

"Did you question him?"

"Yes. He confirmed that Duc Tho had walked inside the

store, reached inside his pocket, and demanded money. He said that his father had shot him in self-defense."

Erickson asked about the security guard.

"Hector Cruz also confirmed that Duc Tho had entered the store and demanded money. His uncle shot Tho in self-defense."

Not surprisingly, their stories matched up.

"Did you question Mr. Cruz's daughter?"

"Briefly. She was extremely upset. She said that she didn't see Duc Tho enter the store or hear him say anything."

"Did she see her father shoot Mr. Tho?"

"No. At her father's instruction, she ducked under the desk when Mr. Tho entered the store and demanded money. She heard shots fired from there."

"Was anybody else was in the store?"

"A customer named Eugene Pham and a Budweiser deliveryman named Odell Jones were in the back of the store. They left through the rear door. We found both men in the alley and questioned them. Neither of them saw Mr. Tho enter the store."

Erickson had what he needed. "No further questions, Your Honor."

"Cross exam, Mr. Daley?"

"Yes, Your Honor."

Rolanda jotted a note on the pad between us which read, "Little things."

37
"YOU TOOK HIS WORD FOR IT?"

"May we approach the witness?" I asked the judge.

"Yes, Mr. Daley."

I buttoned my suit jacket and I moved in front of Navarro. On cross, I was permitted to ask leading questions. "Sergeant, you arrived at Alcatraz Liquors by yourself, right?"

"Yes."

Unlike during direct exam, his answers would be short. "Do you usually work alone?"

"My partner was off."

"You knew that shots had been fired?"

"I did."

"But you still went by yourself?"

"Part of the job. I requested backup."

"You entered through the front door with your weapon drawn?"

"Standard procedure."

"Were you scared?"

He hadn't expected the question. "I was concerned."

"How long was your weapon drawn?"

"Until I secured the premises and made sure that all weapons were disarmed."

Good answer. "You testified that Ortega Cruz met you when you came in."

"Correct. He admitted that he had shot Duc Tho in self-defense."

He would mention it at every opportunity. "But neither you nor any of your fellow officers saw him shoot Duc Tho, right?"

"Correct."

"How do know that he was telling the truth?"

"I had no reason to disbelieve him."

"You took his word for it?"

"Most people don't admit to killing somebody unless they actually do so."

"Unless they're trying to protect somebody."

"Three witnesses corroborated his account."

"His son, daughter, and nephew. Did you consider the possibility that he was trying to protect one of them? Or did you take their word for it, too?"

"Objection," Erickson said. "Argumentative."

"Sustained."

I pointed at the diagram. "You testified that Ortega Cruz directed you to two weapons on the counter and one on the floor."

"Correct."

I picked up the AR-15 from the cart. "This is the weapon that Mr. Cruz said he used to shoot Duc Tho?"

"Yes."

"This weapon is illegal in California, isn't it?"

Erickson was on his feet. "Objection. Relevance."

"Overruled."

I didn't think the judge would give me that one.

"True," Navarro said. "The AR-15 is illegal in California."

"Did you arrest Mr. Cruz for possessing an illegal weapon?"

"No. We confiscated the firearm and gave him a warning."

"Is it Department policy *not* to arrest people who possess illegal assault weapons?"

"Objection. Relevance."

"Sustained. Please move on, Mr. Daley."

I put the AR-15 back on the cart and picked up the Kel-Tec. "You also testified that this weapon was on the floor."

"Correct. Mr. Cruz informed me that he had found it under

Mr. Tho's body."

"You took his word for that, too?"

"I had no reason to disbelieve him."

"Did you consider the possibility that Mr. Cruz or somebody else had placed the gun under Mr. Tho's body?"

"There was no such evidence. We found Mr. Tho's fingerprints on the handle."

"And Mr. Cruz's prints, right?"

"Yes."

"That doesn't rule out the possibility that somebody else could have put it there."

"Objection. Argumentative."

"Sustained."

"You testified that you checked Mr. Tho for a pulse. Did anybody else touch the body?"

"The EMTs."

"But that was after you arrived. What about Mr. Cruz?"

"He also checked for a pulse."

"And he said he found a gun."

"Correct."

"And his son, daughter, and nephew corroborated his story."

"Yes."

"And you took their word for it."

"Objection," Erickson said. "Asked and answered."

"Sustained."

I may have planted some modest seeds of doubt about his credibility in the minds of the jurors. Or maybe not. I pointed at Thomas. "When did you first meet my client?"

"After backup arrived."

"Was he armed?"

"No."

"Had he entered the store?"

"No."

"Shot anyone?"

"No."

"Attempted to drive away or escape?"

"No."

"Resisted arrest, acted belligerent, or otherwise gave you any trouble?"

"No."

Glad to hear it. "In other words, he was just sitting in the car."

"Yes."

Good. "You testified that you've worked at Tenderloin Station for twenty-four years."

"Correct."

"Have you ever been suspended?"

Erickson was up. "Objection. Relevance."

"Your Honor, Mr. Erickson introduced evidence of Sergeant Navarro's experience and qualifications. We should be able to ask about it, too."

"Overruled."

Navarro's tone remained even. "I've been suspended twice in twenty-four years. The first time involved a bogus claim that my partner and I used more force than necessary to subdue a suspect. That claim was dropped."

"That was because the suspect died, right?"

"My partner and I were exonerated."

That's true. "You were also suspended more recently, weren't you?"

"An unsubstantiated claim that my partner and I used excessive force to subdue a serial rapist."

"Did you?"

"No."

Right. "But you were, in fact, suspended."

"I was."

"And the city paid the victim a substantial settlement,

didn't they?"

"Objection," Erickson said. "Relevance. And any such information is confidential."

"Sustained."

I looked over at the Google guy and arched an eyebrow. Then I turned back to Navarro. "You're back at work?"

"Correct."

"What are your responsibilities?"

"I am the Public Information Officer at Tenderloin Station."

"That's because the Department agreed that you shouldn't be allowed on the street, right?"

"Objection. Relevance."

"Overruled."

Navarro exhaled. "I am approaching retirement and I requested duties that aren't as physically demanding."

You're full of crap. The juror from the Verizon scowled. "No further questions, Your Honor."

"Redirect, Mr. Erickson?"

"No, Your Honor."

When I took my place at the defense table, I saw a note from Rolanda. It read, "Not bad. Trying to show Navarro was lying?"

I leaned over and whispered, "Yeah."

"About what?"

"Anything."

Her mouth turned up.

The judge spoke to Erickson. "Please call your next witness."

"The People call Inspector Kenneth Lee."

38

"IT WAS A SIMPLE CASE OF SELF-DEFENSE"

Ken Lee fingered the snow-white pocket square that was the only adornment of his pressed black suit. "I have been a homicide inspector with SFPD for ten years."

"What did you do before you became a detective?" Erickson asked.

Lee shot a confident glance at the jury. "I worked undercover in Chinatown."

Judge McDaniel's courtroom was getting hotter. I sat on my hands for five minutes as Erickson walked Lee through his spotless record, medals of valor, and community service awards. He was, in fact, a stellar cop.

Erickson moved in front of the witness box. "Inspector, were you called in to investigate the homicide of Duc Tho at Alcatraz Liquors on December fourteenth of last year?"

"Objection," I said. "Assumes facts not in evidence. It's up to the jury to determine whether this case involves a homicide."

Erickson shook his head. "I'll rephrase. Were you called in to investigate the death of Duc Tho?"

"I was."

"What time did you arrive?"

"Eleven-seventeen p.m. Approximately thirty minutes after Mr. Tho was shot."

"Could you please describe the scene?"

"Our officers had secured the entries and established a perimeter. They were monitoring a small crowd outside, assisting medical personnel, and canvassing the area for witnesses. Entry to the restricted area was limited to authorized police personnel pursuant to our sign-in procedure."

I didn't expect him to say that they were letting people trample the evidence.

Erickson pointed at the diagram of the store. "Who was inside when you arrived?"

"Sergeant Ignacio Navarro along with two officers and medical personnel." He confirmed that Tho had been pronounced dead at the scene. "Police photographers, videographers, and evidence technicians were starting to process the scene. The owner of the store was also there."

"What about witnesses?"

Lee named Tony, Isabel, and Hector Cruz, Eugene Pham, and Odell Jones. "They were outside in separate squad cars."

"Why?"

"We separate witnesses to question them independently so they can't compare stories." He noted that Isabel was permitted to sit in the squad car with her mother, who had been called to the scene.

"Where was the defendant?"

"In another squad car."

"What did Ortega Cruz tell you?"

"He had shot Duc Tho in self-defense when he came inside the store, demanded money, and threatened him with a gun. Sergeant Navarro reported that Mr. Cruz had found a Kel-Tec pistol under Mr. Tho's body. We later determined that Mr. Tho's fingerprints were on that weapon."

"Did anyone corroborate Mr. Cruz's story?"

"Yes. His son, daughter, and nephew. All were present when Mr. Tho walked in."

In response to Erickson's question about weapons, Lee confirmed that the AR-15 and the Glock were on the counter, and the Kel-Tec was on the floor. "All three had been logged into evidence and bagged and tagged in accordance with standard procedure."

"Did Ortega Cruz explain why he had shot Mr. Tho?"

"It was a simple case of self-defense."

Erickson glanced at me as if to say, "So there!" Then he turned back to Lee. "Other than the witnesses, did you find any evidence corroborating his story?"

"A security video."

Erickson turned to Judge McDaniel. "We would like to introduce the security video from Alcatraz Liquors from the night of December fourteenth of last year."

"Objection," I said. "We have no way to verify the authenticity of this video."

Erickson fired back. "We've provided affidavits of its genuineness."

"This could have been made by a high school kid on an iPhone."

"Mr. Daley is being melodramatic."

Yes, I was. And I was also sandbagging. Rolanda and I wanted them to introduce the video so that we would have a chance to pick it apart. "Your Honor, this video shows horrific violence. It will be offensive and disturbing to our jurors."

Erickson stayed firm. "We've discussed this issue. It's an essential element of our case."

Judge McDaniel didn't hesitate. "I have already ruled on this issue. It's admissible."

"At the very least," I said, "I would ask you to instruct Mr. Erickson to be judicious."

"So ordered."

"And that you warn the jury that its contents are very disturbing."

"Seems you just did, Mr. Daley."

Yes, I did. "For the record, I think it should come from you."

"The jury is cautioned that the video you are about to see

contains graphic violence."

The woman from the Verizon store exchanged a glance with the Google guy.

One of Erickson's subordinates wheeled in a flat-screen TV and positioned it so that it was visible from the witness box, the bench, the jury box, and the gallery. Erickson spoke directly to the jurors. "This is very short, so I would appreciate your attention. First, we'll show it to you in real time. Then we'll play it in slow motion."

The Google guy was intrigued.

Erickson rolled the video in real time and stopped it an instant before Tho was shot. Then he spoke to Lee. "Inspector, could you please tell us where and when this video was taken?"

"Alcatraz Liquors on December fourteenth of last year. Ten-forty-seven and thirty-three seconds." Lee pointed at the screen. "The date and time are stamped in the corner."

"Where was the camera?"

"Directly above the cash register."

"I'd like you to run the video again in slow-motion. I would appreciate it if you would describe what's happening as we go."

"Of course." Erickson handed the remote to Lee, who narrated as he played the video again. "First you see Duc Tho walking into the store. He turns to his right and faces the register." Lee paused the video. "You can see something bulky inside his right front pocket. His mouth is open. According to witnesses, it was at this point that he demanded money."

Lee started the video again, then stopped it. "Here Mr. Tho is starting to pull a gun from his pocket." He stopped the video just before the shots were fired and handed the remote back to Erickson.

"What did you conclude from this video?" Erickson asked.

"We have visual corroboration that Mr. Tho walked into the store and began removing an object from his pocket that we later determined was a Kel-Tec handgun. This represented a lethal threat to Ortega Cruz and the others in the store. It also corroborated Mr. Cruz's account that he shot Mr. Tho in self-defense."

"No further questions, Your Honor."

"Mr. Daley?"

I walked up to the witness box. "How long was that video, Inspector?"

"Just over three seconds."

"And in three seconds, you were able to determine that Mr. Tho came into the store, turned to his right, demanded money, and pulled a gun?"

"Correct."

"Would you mind if I run this video this time?"

"That's fine."

I started the video in super slow-motion. I stopped it when Tho entered the store. "You would agree that this is where Mr. Tho came inside?"

"Yes."

I advanced the video and stopped it again. "Now he's turned to face the register?"

"Correct."

So far, so good. "You said Ortega Cruz told you that Mr. Tho demanded money."

"Correct."

I pointed at the screen. "His mouth is open. Is this when he demanded money?"

"According to Mr. Cruz, yes."

"What did he say?"

"'Gimme the money.'"

I responded with an inquisitive look. "Did he say anything else?"

"Mr. Cruz couldn't recall."

"But he definitely said the word 'money'?"

"Yes."

I started video again and stopped it right before the shots were fired. "Inspector, you would acknowledge that this is the instant before Ortega Cruz allegedly shot Duc Tho?"

"Yes."

"Can you see the shooter?"

"No."

Good. "So you have no visual evidence of the identity of the shooter, do you?"

"Mr. Cruz admitted it."

I turned to the judge. "Would you please instruct the witness to answer the question?"

"Inspector, please."

Lee's tone dripped with sarcasm. "This video does not show the shooter."

"It's therefore possible that it could have been somebody other than Mr. Cruz, right?"

"Objection," Erickson said. "Calls for speculation."

"Sustained."

One more time. "Did you consider the possibility that Mr. Cruz took responsibility for shooting Mr. Tho to protect his son, his daughter, or his nephew?"

"Objection. Speculation."

"Sustained. Please move on, Mr. Daley."

I pointed at Tho's right front pocket. "Would you agree that Mr. Tho's hand is still inside his pocket?"

"Yes."

"And he was shot a fraction of a second thereafter?"

"Yes."

"You can't see a gun."

"Objection. There wasn't a question."

No, there wasn't. I pretended that I was playing *Jeopardy* and turned my statement into a question. "Would you agree that you cannot see a gun in this frame?"

"We found it under his body."

"You didn't answer my question. Would you agree that you cannot see a gun?"

Lee answered with a grudging, "Yes."

"Inspector, you testified a moment ago that Ortega Cruz told you that he had acted in self-defense when Mr. Tho demanded money and threatened him with a gun."

"Correct."

"Yet you just acknowledged that in this video taken the instant before Mr. Tho died, you cannot see a gun."

"It was inside his pocket."

"But there is no evidence of that from this video, is there?"

"Mr. Cruz was certain that Mr. Tho was pulling a weapon and we found a gun with his fingerprints underneath his body."

"That's what Mr. Cruz told you, but you have no way to verify his story, do you?"

"His son, his daughter, and his nephew corroborated his story."

"They could have been lying."

"Objection, Your Honor. Mr. Daley is testifying."

Yes, I am.

"Sustained."

"No further questions."

I walked back to the defense table and took a seat next to Rolanda, who jotted a note reading, "You okay?"

"Fine," I whispered. "I thought it went pretty well."

39
"MULTIPLE GUNSHOT WOUNDS"

Dr. Joy Siu toyed with the collar of her starched white lab coat. "I am the Chief Medical Examiner of the City and County of San Francisco. I've held that title for two years."

Erickson nodded. "What was your position before that?"

"I was the Chair of the M.D./Ph.D. Program in anatomic pathology at UCSF."

She was very good at her job. Now in her mid-forties, the daughter of a Stockton police officer had worked her way through Princeton while competing as a nationally ranked figure skater. After a knee injury sidelined her Olympic dreams, she graduated at the top of her class at Johns-Hopkins Medical School and completed her residency, two fellowships, and a Ph.D. at UCSF. A couple of years earlier, she had taken over as Chief Medical Examiner from the legendary Dr. Roderick Beckert, who finally retired after four decades of distinguished service. Her early reviews were stellar.

Erickson's tone was deferential. "Over the course of the past twenty years, how many autopsies have you performed?"

"Hundreds."

She flew around the world to provide advice on difficult cases. Though diminutive in physical stature, she spoke in precise sentences with an air of authority. We had nothing to gain by letting her talk, and I wanted to get her off the stand as quickly as possible.

"Your Honor," I said, "we will stipulate that Dr. Siu is an internationally recognized expert in the field of autopsy pathology."

"Thank you, Mr. Daley."

Erickson was disappointed. He wanted to spend a few more minutes letting Dr. Siu build rapport with the jury. He introduced her autopsy report into evidence and handed it to her. "When did you conduct the autopsy on Duc Tho?"

"The morning after he died."

"You were working on a Sunday?"

"I happened to be in the office."

It was not unusual to find her there on weekends.

"Did you pronounce Mr. Tho?"

"No. He was pronounced at the scene."

"Time of death?"

"Officially, ten-fifty-five p.m. on Saturday, December fourteenth. Based upon the security video, I determined that he was shot at ten-forty-seven p.m. From this visual evidence and the nature of the wounds, I concluded that he died instantly."

"Cause of death?"

"Multiple gunshot wounds. Massive injuries to the heart, lungs, spleen, trachea, and esophagus which led to internal bleeding and the stoppage of function of all major organs."

"No further questions."

The judge looked my way. "Your witness, Mr. Daley."

"Thank you, Your Honor. My colleague, Ms. Fernandez, will be handling cross." It was time for Rolanda to get her feet wet.

Rolanda stood and buttoned her jacket. "May we approach the witness, Your Honor?"

"You may."

As she walked across the courtroom, I flashed back to the shy eleven-year-old who liked to hang out in her aunt's office. Out of the corner of my eye, I could see Rosie sitting in the back row, eyes beaming.

Rolanda stood tall in front of the witness box. Her tone was a pitch-perfect mix of authority and empathy. "Nice to see you again, Dr. Siu."

"Nice to see you, too, Ms. Fernandez."

"You said that you conducted the autopsy the morning after Duc Tho died."

"Correct."

"Were you called to the scene on Saturday night?"

"No."

"So you were not present when he died."

"Correct. However, I visited Alcatraz Liquors the following day. I always like to visit the scene if I can."

Rolanda pointed at the diagram of the store, which was still on the easel next to the witness box. "The security video and the eyewitness accounts indicate that Duc Tho entered the store, then turned to his right to face the counter, right?"

"Yes."

"Whereupon he was shot six times in the chest."

"Correct."

"And he fell backward into a rack of potato chips and slumped to the floor."

"Yes."

"Did you find any bullet wounds on Mr. Tho's arms?"

"There were no defensive wounds."

Rolanda took a step forward and turned ninety degrees to her right. "So Mr. Tho walked into the store, turned to his right, and was hit by six bullets."

"Correct."

"Could you tell which bullet hit him first?"

"No. The bullets hit his chest in rapid succession and fragmented upon entry and lodged inside the body. The entrance wounds were very close together which created a single contiguous wound."

"Were you able to determine the angle through which the bullets passed into his chest?"

"No."

"But it's clear that the shots came from somewhere over by

the counter, right?"

"Correct."

"Based upon the wounds, can you describe the exact trajectory of the bullets?"

"The owner of the store admitted that he shot from directly behind the cash register."

"I understand." Rolanda smiled respectfully. "But I'm asking whether you can verify the precise trajectory of the bullets based solely upon the entrance wounds."

"No."

Rolanda was still smiling. "Depending upon the precise angle of Mr. Tho's body when he was hit, it's possible that the shots were fired from somewhere other than directly behind the register, right?"

"Objection. Speculation."

"Sustained."

Rolanda tried again. "It's possible that the shots were fired from somewhere between the deli counter and the front window, right?"

"Objection. Speculation."

"Sustained."

"No further questions."

"Redirect, Mr. Erickson?"

"No, Your Honor."

Rolanda's face was flush with adrenaline as she returned to the defense table. As she walked by me, I whispered, "Nice work."

"We're just getting started."

The war was on. I decided that Rolanda would play a larger role in this trial.

40

"MY CALCULATIONS WERE VERY PRECISE"

The silver-haired sage pulled at the Windsor knot of his Turnbull & Asser tie. "Based upon my analysis of the security video and the entrance wounds, I believe that the bullets that killed Duc Tho were fired from behind the cash register."

Erickson nodded at the woman from the Verizon store, who nodded back.

Captain Jack Goldthorpe was a studious sixty-eight-year-old white coat who had been SFPD's ballistics guru for three decades. His friends called him "Captain Jack." Around the Hall of Justice, the one-time Navy Seal was known as the "Gun Guy." When he wasn't in court, he was hunkered down in a windowless office in the basement of the Hall, where he matched bullets to weapons, calculated distances from muzzles to bodies, and analyzed trajectories of bullets. Meticulous in appearance, manner, and speech, he embodied a genial competence. Juries loved him.

Erickson handed him the AR-15, wrapped in plastic. "Do you recognize this weapon?"

"Yes. It's a Bushmaster AR-15 found at the scene. Ortega Cruz is the registered owner. He admitted that he used this weapon in self-defense to fire the shots that killed Duc Tho."

Erickson handed Goldthorpe a sandwich-sized evidence bag. "Do you recognize the contents?"

"I do. These are six bullet casings found on the floor of Alcatraz Liquors on the night of Saturday, December fourteenth."

"Does that mean that six shots were fired that night?"

"It does. I suppose that it is theoretically possible that these casings could have found their way to the floor on another occasion, but that seems highly unlikely."

"Were you able to determine the type of weapon from which those bullets were fired?"

"Yes. The casings were consistent with bullets fired from an AR-15 rifle."

Thomas turned to me, eyes pleading. I responded with a subtle gesture for him to stay calm. There was no question that the bullets had been fired from the AR-15.

Erickson was taking his time. "Captain Goldthorpe, were you able to determine whether the indentations on the casings matched the firing pin on the AR-15?"

"They did. I therefore concluded that the casings were from bullets fired from that weapon."

"No further questions."

"Cross exam, Mr. Daley?"

"Just a couple of questions." I had little interest in prolonging this discussion, but I wanted to give the Google guy something to think about. "Captain Goldthorpe, you said that you were able to determine the precise location from which the shots were fired."

"Within a very small range from behind the cash register."

"But you can't see the shooter in the video."

"That's true. However, the video clearly showed where Mr. Tho was standing when he was shot."

"But you couldn't possibly have slowed down the video enough to have seen the trajectory of the bullets."

"That's also true. Even super slow-motion cameras used in sporting events aren't calibrated to show the precise path of a bullet fired at close range."

"So your computations couldn't have been that precise."

"Yes, they were. From the security video, I created a three-dimensional computer model showing Mr. Tho's position when the shots were fired. I determined that the shots hit Mr. Tho head-on, which means that they were fired from the area behind the cash register."

Now for some smoke and mirrors. "You said that Mr. Tho was standing right in front of the register—just like I'm standing in front of you."

"Yes."

Keeping my feet planted, I rotated my torso slightly to the left. "If Mr. Tho was still turning a little bit as he was shot—like this—might your analysis have changed?"

"Possibly."

"If Mr. Tho had been turning as little as an inch or two at the time he was struck by the bullets, is it possible that the shots could have been fired from somewhere to the left of the register? Perhaps from the area over by the deli counter?"

"That's not what happened, Mr. Daley."

"But you were looking at a blurry video of an event that took three seconds."

"My calculations were very precise."

"But it's possible that Mr. Tho was moving a little as he was shot, right?"

"Objection," Erickson said. "Speculation."

"Sustained."

I was surprised that he hadn't interrupted sooner. "Let me ask you about one more thing, Captain. You can't see the shooter in the video, right?"

"Right."

"So you have no evidence that Ortega Cruz shot Mr. Tho."

"He admitted it."

"He could have been lying. You have no physical evidence other than his word that he pulled the trigger, right?"

Goldthorpe invoked a grudging tone. "That much is true."

"No further questions."

It was a small victory.

"Please call your next witness, Mr. Erickson."

"The People call Sergeant Kathleen Jacobsen."

Right on cue. Jacobsen was their fingerprint expert.

41

"HIS FINGERPRINTS WERE
ON THE GUN"

"My name is Sergeant Kathleen Jacobsen. I have been an SFPD evidence technician for twenty-eight years."

Erickson was at the lectern. "Do you have a particular area of expertise?"

"Fingerprints, blood spatter, and chemical and physical evidence."

Jacobsen was an unflappable pro with a commanding demeanor. One of the first lesbians to move up the SFPD ranks, she had completed her undergrad degree at USC and her master's and Ph.D. at Cal. I quickly stipulated to her expertise. Her credentials were not in question.

Erickson remained a respectful distance from the stand. "Are you the lead evidence technician in the investigation of the death of Duc Tho?"

"I am."

"Were you called to the scene on the night of December fourteenth?"

"I was."

"Did you supervise the collection of the evidence?"

"I did."

Erickson walked to the evidence cart, picked up the AR-15, paraded it in front of the jury, and handed it to Jacobsen. "Can you identify this rifle?"

"It's the AR-15 that Ortega Cruz used to shoot Duc Tho."

"Move to strike," I said. "Assumes facts not in evidence. We have heard testimony that the bullets that killed Mr. Tho were fired from that weapon. However, no proof has been entered into evidence that Mr. Cruz pulled the trigger."

Erickson shot me a look of disdain. "He admitted it."

Yes, he did. "We've heard uncorroborated testimony from people other than Mr. Cruz."

"He will testify later today."

And he will admit it again. "Then we should have this conversation after he does."

"Your Honor, we have, in fact, heard testimony that Mr. Cruz shot Duc Tho."

"Agreed. The objection is overruled."

As it should have been. I was just trying to muddy the water.

Erickson moved in front of Jacobsen. "Did you find any fingerprints on this weapon?"

"I did. Ortega Cruz's."

"Anybody else?"

"No."

Erickson picked up a shirt wrapped in clear plastic. He introduced it into evidence and handed it to Jacobsen. "Could you please identify this item?"

She touched her wire-rimmed bifocals. "It's the shirt that Ortega Cruz was wearing on the night of December fourteenth."

"Did you find traces of gunpowder?"

"I did."

"Were they consistent with the gunpowder found in the bullets that killed Mr. Tho?"

"They were."

"Were you able to draw any conclusions?"

"I was. Mr. Cruz had fired a weapon causing gunpowder traces to embed in this shirt."

Erickson took the shirt from Jacobsen and returned it to the cart. He picked up the Kel-Tec and gave it to Jacobsen. "Do you recognize this firearm?"

"I do. It's a Kel-Tec P-3AT found at the scene under the victim's body."

"Did you find any fingerprints on this weapon?"

"Yes. Duc Tho's."

"Anybody else's?"

"Ortega Cruz's."

"Do you know how Mr. Cruz's fingerprints found their way to this weapon?"

"He informed us that he disarmed this weapon for the safety of himself and others present in his store."

"No further questions."

Our turn. "May we approach the witness?" I said.

Judge McDaniel nodded.

I addressed Jacobsen in a respectful tone. "Nice to see you again, Sergeant."

"Nice to see you, Mr. Daley."

I handed her the AR-15. "Who is the registered owner of this weapon?"

"Ortega Cruz."

"Is it legal to possess this firearm in California?"

"Objection," Erickson said. "Relevance."

"Overruled."

Jacobsen shook her head. "It's illegal in California."

"Was Mr. Cruz arrested for possessing an illegal weapon?"

"Objection. Relevance."

"Overruled."

"Mr. Cruz was issued a warning and the weapon was confiscated."

"I trust that you aren't planning to give it back?"

"Correct."

On to business. "Where on this weapon did you find Mr. Cruz's fingerprints?"

"On the handle and the barrel."

"What about the trigger?"

"We found a smudged print that we could not identify."

"You have no physical evidence that Ortega Cruz pulled the trigger on the night that Duc Tho was killed, do you?"

"He admitted it. We also found gunpowder residue on his shirt."

"Which proves that the shirt was in the vicinity of gunpowder at some point. But it's impossible to know precisely when the traces landed on his shirt, isn't it?"

Erickson was on his feet. "Objection, speculation."

Not so fast. "Your Honor, Mr. Erickson introduced Sergeant Jacobsen as an expert on evidentiary issues. If he's allowed to ask for her expert opinion, I should be able to do so, too."

"Overruled."

Jacobsen eyed me with a bemused look. "In my *expert* opinion, it is theoretically possible—albeit very unlikely—that the gunpowder became attached to Mr. Cruz's shirt at some time other than the night of December fourteenth."

"It could have happened at the shooting range, right?"

"Right."

"Or somebody else could have been wearing his shirt and fired a weapon, right?"

"Sure."

"And it's also possible that the gunpowder residue landed on his shirt because he was standing next to somebody who fired a weapon, right?"

"It's possible."

"You testified that you found a smudged print on the trigger. It's possible that somebody other than Mr. Cruz fired this weapon, right?"

Erickson was up again. "Objection. This is pure speculation."

Yes, it was.

"Sustained. Please move along, Mr. Daley."

"Sergeant Jacobsen, in addition to testing somebody's clothing for gunpowder residue, you can also test their skin, right?"

"Right."

"Did you test Mr. Cruz's hands?"

"Yes. We found gunpowder residue on his hands."

"There were several other people in the store that night. Did you test their hands and clothing for gunshot residue?"

A hesitation. "No."

"Why not?"

"Because Mr. Cruz admitted that he fired the shots that killed Duc Tho."

"You didn't consider the possibility that somebody else fired the shots?"

"Objection. Argumentative."

"Sustained."

I took the AR-15 from Jacobsen and handed her the Kel-Tec. "Sergeant, you testified that Ortega Cruz told the police that he found this weapon under the victim's body and he disarmed it, right?"

"Correct."

"And you found Mr. Cruz's fingerprints on this weapon?"

"Yes."

"Where?"

"On the handle."

"That means that Mr. Cruz must have touched this weapon, right?"

"Yes. We also found Duc Tho's fingerprints."

"How do you know that Ortega Cruz didn't plant this weapon under Mr. Tho's body?"

"Objection. Speculation."

"Overruled."

"I don't know, Mr. Daley."

"You would therefore acknowledge that Mr. Cruz could

have placed this weapon under Mr. Tho's body, right?"

"Objection. Speculation."

"Sustained."

I took the Kel-Tec back from her and held it up. "You don't know for sure how this weapon made it to the floor underneath Duc Tho's body, do you?"

"Mr. Cruz told us that it probably fell out of Mr. Tho's pocket when he was shot."

"*If* it was inside his pocket at the time."

"Mr. Cruz said it was. His son and nephew corroborated his story."

We would get to that later. "You testified earlier that you found Duc Tho's fingerprints on this weapon."

"Correct."

"Which hand?"

"Right. Thumb, index finger and palm."

I couldn't dispute this. "Sergeant Jacobsen, is there any physical evidence proving that Duc Tho had this weapon in his possession when he walked into the store?"

"His fingerprints were on it."

"But you found it after he was killed. Is there any physical evidence proving that this weapon was inside his pocket when he walked inside the store?"

"Ortega Cruz said so."

"His statement isn't physical evidence. Isn't it possible that somebody wrapped Mr. Tho's hand around this weapon to produce fingerprints, and planted it under his body?"

"Objection. Calls for speculation."

"Your Honor, I'm not asking Sergeant Jacobsen to speculate." *Yes, I am.* "I'm asking her for her expert opinion."

"I'll allow the witness to answer."

Jacobsen shook her head. "Yes, Mr. Daley. It's theoretically possible." She looked at the jury. "It's also theoretically possible that I will be the starting point guard for the Golden State Warriors when the season opens next month."

The tension was broken by uncomfortable laughter. I glanced at the juror who worked at the Verizon store. Her expression indicated that she wasn't convinced.

I walked to the front of the witness box. "You said that the fingerprints on the Kel-Tec were from Duc Tho's right hand."

"Correct."

"Were you aware of the fact that Duc Tho was left handed?"

"Yes."

"Doesn't it seem odd that he would have been holding the gun in his right hand?"

"Not really. According to his mother, while Duc Tho used his left hand to throw baseballs, he also did many things with his right hand, including writing."

I should have let it go. "No further questions."

42

"SOMETHING IS COMING DOWN"

Thomas was frustrated. "You should have known that Duc did stuff with his right hand."

I tried not to sound defensive. "His mother told us that he was left-handed."

"And I could have told you that he wrote right-handed. You should have asked."

I probably should have. Rolanda, Thomas, Melinda, and I were sitting around a table in a closet-like meeting room during the mid-afternoon break. The ninety-degree heat was making my headache worse. "We're going to take some lumps during the prosecution's case."

Melinda had been glaring at the ceiling. She lowered her eyes and spoke in a muted tone. "You need to slow them down."

"It isn't always possible."

"Then make it possible."

"You need to be realistic."

"You need to be more assertive."

"We are going to continue to challenge every piece of evidence. For now, it's the best that we can do."

"Then what?"

"We'll go after them during our defense."

* * *

"How bad was it?" I asked.

Rosie shrugged. "Not so bad. You don't have much to work with."

I felt worse. Rosie never sugarcoated anything. We were standing outside the courtroom. The trial was going to resume in five minutes.

She read my expression. "You're doing everything you can, Mike."

"Can you stick around?"

"I have a conference call. I'll try to stop by at the end of the day."

"Any advice before you go?"

She smiled. "Let Rolanda do most of the talking."

* * *

My iPhone vibrated as we were about to re-enter the courtroom. Pete's name appeared on the display. "How's the battle, Mick?" he asked.

"Not great. Got anything we can use?"

"Inspector Lee went down to San Bruno after he testified."

"It might not have anything to do with our case."

"He was in a big hurry to talk to somebody. He got a police escort."

"What do you think it means?"

"Something's coming down. Who's their next witness?"

"Ortega Cruz."

43

"I THOUGHT HE WAS GOING TO KILL ME"

"My name is Ortega Cruz. I am the owner of Alcatraz Liquors on Eddy Street."

Erickson was at the lectern, arms at his sides. "How long have you owned that business?"

"Twenty-six years."

Clean-shaven and sporting a going-to-church suit, Cruz looked more like a banker than the proprietor of a liquor store in the Tenderloin.

Erickson moved in closer. "Mr. Cruz, were you at work at ten-forty-seven p.m. on December fourteenth of last year?"

"Yes."

"Who else was there?"

"My son, Tony, my daughter, Isabel, my nephew, Hector, a deliveryman named Odell Jones, and a customer named Eugene Pham." Cruz confirmed that Tony was behind the deli counter, Isabel was at the desk in the alcove, Hector was next to the window, Jones was filling the refrigerator, and Pham was looking at wine in the back of the store.

"Where were you?"

"Behind the register."

Cruz was following Erickson's lead and keeping his answers short.

"Did someone come into the store at ten-forty-seven that night?"

"Yes. A man named Duc Tho."

"Had you ever seen him before?"

"Once or twice."

"What happened next?"

"He reached inside his pocket and started to pull out a gun."

"You're sure he had a gun?"

"Yes."

"Anything else?"

"He demanded money."

"How close to you was Mr. Tho?"

"About five feet."

"And you saw him reach for a gun?"

"Objection," I said. "Asked and answered."

"Sustained.

"Your store is in the Tenderloin, isn't it?"

"Yes."

"That's a rough neighborhood, isn't it?"

"One of the most dangerous in San Francisco."

"Why?"

"Crime. Drugs. Violence. Prostitution. Poverty. Unemployment."

"Has your store ever been robbed?"

"Dozens of times."

"How do you protect yourself?"

"I keep a gun under the register."

"Did you have a gun behind the counter that night?"

"Yes."

Erickson showed him the AR-15. "Is this the gun that you had behind the counter?"

"Yes."

"You purchased it legally?"

"In Nevada. I completed all of the necessary paperwork."

Erickson lowered his voice. "How did you feel when Duc Tho walked inside your store?"

"I thought he was going to kill me." He took a deep breath. "Or my son or my daughter or my nephew."

"How much time did you have to react?"

"A second or two."

"What did you do?"

"What I had to do. I shot him in self-defense. I was protecting my kids and my nephew."

"How did you feel after you shot him?"

"Terrible."

"Given the circumstances, would you do it again?"

"Objection," I said. "Calls for speculation."

"Overruled."

"Yes," Cruz said. "I would do it again."

Erickson stepped back from the box. "What did you do after you shot Mr. Tho?"

"I checked on him to make sure that he couldn't fire his gun. Then I called the police."

"Was he dead?"

"Objection. Mr. Cruz isn't a doctor."

"Sustained."

Erickson didn't hesitate. "Did it appear to you that he was dead?"

"Yes."

"Did you touch the body?"

"Yes. To check for a pulse. There was none."

"Did you move the body?"

"No."

Erickson held up the Kel-Tec. "Do you recognize this weapon?"

"Yes. It's a Kel-Tec P-3AT handgun that I found under Duc Tho."

"How could you see it if it was under the body?"

"It wasn't completely covered up."

"Did you touch this weapon?"

"Yes. I removed the bullets to protect myself, my children, and my nephew. I left the gun on the floor and showed it to the police when they arrived."

"You were familiar enough with this weapon that you were comfortable disarming it?"

"I was in the military. I own several firearms and I go to the range every weekend."

Erickson was satisfied. "How long before you called the police?"

"Less than a minute. I checked on my kids and my nephew first."

"Were you cooperative when the police arrived?"

"Of course."

"Do you recall who was the first officer at the scene?"

"Sergeant Ignacio Navarro from Tenderloin Station."

"Did you inform him that you had shot Duc Tho?"

"Yes. In self-defense."

Erickson repeated, "In self-defense. You also told him that you disarmed the Kel-Tec?"

"Yes."

"No further questions."

"Cross exam, Mr. Daley?"

"Yes, Your Honor." *Game on.* As I buttoned my jacket, I saw the note that Rolanda had scribbled on the legal pad. It read, "No surrender."

I walked to the front of the box, and I wasn't going to move. "Mr. Cruz, how long was Duc Tho inside your store before you say that you shot him?"

He took a sip of water. "A couple of seconds."

"You were scared because he threatened you with a gun and demanded money?"

"Yes."

"So scared that you had to shoot him?"

"Objection. Asked and answered."

"Sustained."

I took a step back and acted out Tho's movements. "Mr.

Tho walked inside your store, turned to face you at the register, demanded money, and pulled a gun, whereupon you shot him?"

"In self-defense."

"In self-defense," I repeated. "I just want to be sure that I understand the exact sequence. Did he pull the gun or demand money first?"

"He demanded money."

"Before or after he turned?"

Cruz hesitated. "As he was turning."

"What did he say to you?"

"'Gimme the money.'"

"You're absolutely sure that he said those words?"

He waited a beat. "Yes."

"And then he threatened you with a gun?"

"Yes."

"Before or after he demanded money?"

"Right after."

"Did he point the gun at you?"

"No. I shot him before he had the chance."

"But he drew the gun, right?"

"He was about to."

"But you shot him first?"

'Objection. Asked and answered."

"Sustained."

"Mr. Cruz, did you see the gun before you shot Mr. Tho?"

A pause. "No. It was still inside his pocket."

"If it was still inside his pocket, how did you know that he had a gun?"

Cruz spoke deliberately. "He had a gun. I found it underneath his body after I shot him."

"In self-defense."

"Right."

"But you just said that you couldn't see the gun."

"I could tell."

"But you said that his right hand was still inside his pocket when you shot him, right?"

His tone was more adamant. "He had a gun."

I gave him a perplexed look. "Let the record show that Mr. Cruz just confirmed that he could not see a gun because Mr. Tho's hand was still inside his pocket when Mr. Cruz shot him."

Erickson was on his feet. "Move to strike. Mr. Daley is testifying."

Yes, I am.

"The jury will disregard Mr. Daley's interpretation of Mr. Cruz's testimony."

As if they'll be able to un-ring the bell. "No further questions, Your Honor."

"Redirect, Mr. Erickson?"

"Yes, Your Honor." He spoke from the prosecution table. "Mr. Cruz, did you honestly believe that there was a gun in Mr. Tho's possession when he walked inside your store?"

"Yes."

"Did you fear for your life and the lives of your children and nephew?"

"Yes."

"And based upon that fear, did you shoot and kill Mr. Tho in self-defense?"

"Yes."

"And did you find a loaded Kel-Tec handgun underneath his body after you shot him in self-defense?"

"Yes."

"No further questions."

"Redirect, Mr. Daley?"

"No, Your Honor."

"Please call your next witness, Mr. Erickson."

"The People call Antonio Cruz."

44
"I THOUGHT WE WERE GOING TO DIE"

Erickson was standing in front of the witness box in the silent courtroom. "Where were you when Mr. Tho entered your father's store?"

Tony Cruz was wearing an ill-fitting navy blazer. He poured himself a cup of water and looked for moral support from the gallery, but his parents were not allowed in court because they were on our witness list. "Behind the deli counter."

Erickson pointed at the diagram. "That's over here?"

Tony nodded.

"You'll need to answer out loud for the record."

"Yes."

Rolanda and I figured that Tony's role would be brief. Erickson would have him corroborate his father's story and get him off the stand.

"Did you see Duc Tho enter your father's store?"

"Yes."

"What happened next?"

"He asked for money and threatened my father."

"How did you feel about it?"

"I thought we were going to die."

"What did your father do?"

"He yelled at us to duck and he shot Tho in self-defense."

"You saw everything?"

"Yes. It was really bad. There was lots of blood."

"You must have been relieved when it was over."

"I was."

"No further questions."

I nodded to Rolanda, who walked over to the witness box. Her tone was gentle. "Was it busy when Duc Tho came inside your father's store?"

"No."

"What were you doing?"

"Watching TV."

"What were you watching?"

"ESPN. SportsCenter, I think."

Erickson stood up. "Your Honor, could you please instruct Ms. Fernandez to get to the point?"

"Please, Ms. Fernandez."

Rolanda smiled. "I'm getting there, Your Honor." She turned back to Tony. "Did you have your iPhone with you?"

"Yeah."

"Were you talking to somebody on your phone when Duc Tho came inside?"

"No."

"Watching a video?"

"No."

"Listening to music?"

"Maybe."

"Did you have your earbuds in?"

"I might have."

"And you saw Mr. Tho come inside the store?"

"Objection. Asked and answered."

"Sustained."

Rolanda inched closer. "It was a scary experience, wasn't it?"

"Yeah."

"And it happened very fast."

"Right."

"Have you ever been at the store when it was robbed?"

"I've seen shoplifters."

"What about armed robbers?"

"No."

"Have you ever used a gun?"

"Just at the range. My dad takes us."

"So you must have been really scared when Duc Tho pulled the gun, right?"

A hesitation. "Uh, yeah."

Rolanda gave him an inquisitive look. "You saw him pull the gun, right?"

Tony swallowed. "Well, not exactly."

"What do you mean?"

"It was inside his pocket. My father yelled at me and my sister and my cousin to get down."

"And then your father shot him?"

"Yes."

"So you didn't see the gun until your father found it under Mr. Tho's body?"

He nodded as if to reassure himself. "Yeah."

"You said that Mr. Tho demanded money when he came inside."

"He did."

"What exactly did he say? 'Gimme the money'?"

"I think he just said the word 'money.'"

"You're sure about that?"

"Pretty sure."

"And you're pretty sure that he said the word 'money' even though you had your earbuds in?"

"Yeah."

"You were very brave, Tony."

"I was lucky that my dad knew how to protect us."

"No further questions."

The judge glanced at Erickson. "Redirect?"

"No, Your Honor. The People call Hector Cruz."

45

"HE DID WHAT HE HAD TO DO"

Hector's direct exam was shorter than Tony's. Following Erickson's lead, he confirmed that he was standing near the window when Tho walked in. Tho threatened Ortega with a gun and demanded money. His uncle shot him in self-defense. His testimony was over in less than a minute.

I sent our not-so-secret weapon to handle cross exam. Rolanda gave Hector a comforting smile as she approached him. "May I call you Hector?"

"Okay." He gulped water as he tugged at the lapel of his hand-me-down gray suit. I was surprised that his uncle hadn't insisted that he wear a tie.

Rolanda put a hand on the edge of the witness box. "You were working as the security guard at your uncle's store when Duc Tho entered, right?"

Hector nodded a little too emphatically. "Right."

"You were carrying a gun that night, right?"

"Right."

"You knew how to use it, right?"

"Right." Hector sat up taller. "I'd shot it at the range with my uncle."

"But you didn't use it that night, did you?"

"By the time I realized what was happening, my uncle had already shot Duc Tho."

"Makes sense." Rolanda pointed at the diagram. "You were over here between the window and the register when Duc Tho came inside, right?"

"Right."

"You saw him come in through the front door, right?"

"No."

Rolanda gave him a perplexed look. "How is that possible? You were right there."

"I was looking out the window."

"But you saw him pull a gun, right?"

"Uh, no." He started talking faster. "It happened fast. My uncle yelled at us to get down. Then he shot him in self-defense."

"You didn't see him pull a gun?"

"No."

"But you heard him ask for money, right?"

"Right."

"Did he say, 'Gimme the money'?"

"Something like that." Rolanda let the answer hang, and Hector felt compelled to fill the void. "He definitely said the word 'money.' I'm not exactly sure what else."

Rolanda responded with a reassuring smile. "Hector, you were talking on your cell phone when Duc Tho entered the store?"

His eyes darted at Erickson for an instant. "Yeah."

"With whom?"

"My ex-girlfriend."

"What were you talking about?"

"Nothing in particular."

"You must have been discussing something."

"We were talking about maybe getting together."

"Did you?"

"Objection. Relevance."

"Sustained."

Rolanda was still smiling. "Hector, when you talk on your cell, do you hold the phone up to your ear, or do you use a microphone with earbuds?"

"Depends."

"Were you using buds that night?"

"I don't think so."

"So when Duc Tho walked into the store, you were holding the phone up to your ear and talking to your ex-girlfriend?"

"I think so."

Rolanda held up a hand. "How did you hear Duc Tho ask for money if you were talking on your phone?"

His tone turned adamant. "I heard him say the word 'money.'"

"Out of your other ear?"

"Yeah."

Rolanda finally took a step back. "Hector, are you absolutely sure that Duc Tho said the word 'money' when he walked into your uncle's store?"

"Objection. Asked and answered."

"Sustained."

"And are you absolutely sure that Duc Tho had a gun when he walked into the store?"

"Objection. Asked and answered."

Rolanda finally turned to the judge. "He hasn't answered that one, Your Honor."

"Overruled. Please answer the question, Mr. Cruz."

"Yeah, he was carrying a gun."

"But you didn't actually see it, did you?"

"My uncle found it under his body."

"But *you* didn't see it until after Mr. Tho was dead, right?"

"My uncle shot him in self-defense. He did what he had to do."

"So he says."

"Objection."

"Withdrawn. Are you still working at the store?"

"No."

"Why not?"

"My uncle decided that he didn't need a security guard."

"Or maybe he decided that he didn't need *you*."

"Objection. There wasn't a question there."

No, there wasn't.

"Withdrawn." Rolanda folded her arms. "Your uncle is intimidating, isn't he?"

"Sometimes."

"You're afraid of him, aren't you, Hector?"

"No."

"He told you to say that Duc Tho demanded money and flashed a gun, didn't he?"

"No."

"And he told you to say that he acted in self-defense, didn't he?"

"No."

"You're under oath, Hector."

Erickson stood up. "Objection, Your Honor. There wasn't a question there."

"Sustained."

Rolanda was within two feet of Hector. "Your uncle didn't shoot Duc Tho in self-defense, did he?"

"Yes, he did."

"He told you to lie to protect himself, didn't he?"

"No."

"Or is he protecting you?"

His voice went up. "No."

"You're lying, aren't you, Hector?"

"Objection," Erickson said. "Argumentative."

"Sustained."

Rolanda hadn't taken her eyes off Hector. "Where do you live, Hector?"

"Daly City."

"Were you at home on Thursday night?"

Erickson was up again. "Objection. Relevance."

"Overruled."

Hector acknowledged that he hadn't been at home on

Thursday night.

"Where were you?" Rolanda asked.

"San Bruno."

"At San Francisco County Jail?"

"Yes."

"On what charge?"

Erickson tried again. "Objection. This line of questioning is irrelevant."

"Your Honor," Rolanda said, "we are entitled to question Mr. Cruz's credibility."

"Overruled."

Rolanda cleared her throat. "Why were you in San Francisco County Jail?"

"They're saying that I bought crystal meth, but they're wrong."

"It's a set-up?"

"Yeah."

"Are you out on bail?"

"Yeah."

"Who paid your bail, Hector?"

"My uncle."

"You owe him big time, don't you?"

"Objection. Argumentative."

"Sustained."

Rolanda didn't stop. "You'd do anything your uncle told you to do, wouldn't you?"

"Objection. Argumentative."

"Sustained."

"You'd even lie for him, wouldn't you?"

"Objection. This line of questioning is inappropriate."

Yes, it is.

"Sustained."

"No further questions, Your Honor."

"Redirect, Mr. Erickson?"

"No, Your Honor."

"Any other witnesses?"

"No, Your Honor. The People rest."

The judge turned to me. "Mr. Daley, do you wish to make a motion?"

"Yes, Your Honor. Based upon the evidence presented thus far, we believe that as a matter of law, the prosecution has not shown that Duc Tho engaged in a provocative act when he entered Alcatraz Liquors. We further believe that Mr. Erickson has not introduced sufficient evidence that Ortega Cruz acted in self-defense when he allegedly shot and killed Duc Tho. As a result, pursuant to Section 1118.1 of the California Penal Code, a jury cannot find guilt beyond a reasonable doubt based upon the evidence presented. We therefore move that all charges against our client be dropped as a matter of law."

Erickson didn't bother to stand. "Objection, Your Honor."

"Noted." The judge turned back to me. "Your motion is denied, Mr. Daley. Please call your first witness."

I was tempted ask for a recess and start fresh in the morning, but I didn't want the jury to go home without hearing from us. "The defense calls Anita Tho."

46
"HE WAS A GOOD BOY"

"My name is Anita Tho." Her voice was barely a whisper. "I am Duc Tho's mother."

The gallery was almost empty at five minutes to four on Wednesday afternoon. Rosie had returned and was sitting in the back row. Anita sat in the witness box, hands clasped. It looked as if she wanted to make herself disappear.

Rolanda's tone was subdued. "We're very sorry for your loss, Ms. Tho."

"Thank you, Ms. Fernandez. He was a good boy."

"Where were you living on the night of December fourteenth of last year?"

"In a single room hotel on Larkin."

"Were you employed at the time?"

"No."

"Did your son live with you?"

"Yes."

"Was he employed?"

"He did odd jobs when he could find them."

We had told her to use this euphemism for "selling drugs."

"When was the last time that you saw him?"

"Around nine o'clock that night. He was going to a party with Thomas Nguyen. He said that he wouldn't be out too late." She sighed. "He worried about me as much as I worried about him."

"When did you hear about the events at Alcatraz Liquors?"

"The police came to see me around midnight."

"It must have been awful."

Anita's lips quivered. "It was."

Rolanda inched closer. "Did they ask you to identify your son's body?"

"Yes."

"It must have been horrifying."

"It was."

"Did the police tell you what happened?"

"They said that Duc had tried to rob a liquor store."

"Had he ever attempted to rob anybody?"

"No."

"Did the police provide any other details?"

"They said that Duc had pulled a gun and the shopkeeper shot him in self-defense."

"Did you believe them?"

"No." Anita's eyes narrowed. "Duc didn't have a gun."

"How can you be so sure?"

"He didn't like guns. He was afraid of them."

"Can you tell us why?"

"Yes. When he was in second grade, the father of one of his friends was killed in a drive-by shooting across the street from where we lived. Duc saw it."

"I take it that this made an impression on him?"

"Absolutely. He was terrified of guns from the time he was a little boy. He always told me that he would never own one."

"Thank you, Ms. Tho. No further questions."

Erickson approached the witness box cautiously. "I'm also very sorry for your loss, Ms. Tho. I'd like to ask you just a few questions about your son."

He was about to engage in a delicate dance. He needed to try to rebut her testimony without appearing to attack her or her deceased son.

"Ms. Tho, you said that you and your son shared a one-room apartment."

"We did."

"It must have been very tight quarters."

"It was."

"And you and your son must have been very close."

"We were."

"Your son dropped out of high school, didn't he?"

"Objection," I said. "Relevance."

"Sustained."

Erickson tried again. "Your son got into some trouble, didn't he?"

"Objection. All kids get into trouble."

Judge McDaniel's chin rested in her hand. "Please be more specific, Mr. Erickson."

"Yes, Your Honor. Ms. Tho, your son was arrested several times, wasn't he?"

"Objection. Relevance. Ms. Tho's son is not on trial here."

"Overruled."

Anita didn't flinch. "Yes, Mr. Erickson. My son was arrested twice. In each case, the charges were dropped."

"What were the charges?"

"Objection. Relevance."

"Overruled."

Anita showed a hint of irritation. "Possession of drugs."

"Did you know that your son was in possession of drugs?"

"I had suspicions."

"Did your son keep all of his belongings in your apartment?"

"Yes."

"What about his car? Or a storage locker? Or a friend's house?"

"Objection," I said. "Calls for speculation."

"Sustained."

Erickson held up a hand. "Did he stay in your room every night?"

"Most nights."

"But some nights he stayed with friends?"

"Yes."

"And when he did, he must have brought some clothes to wear the next day, right? And maybe some toiletries and perhaps other belongings?"

"Probably."

"It's possible that he may have left some of his belongings at a friend's house, right?"

"Objection. Calls for speculation. In fact, this line of questioning is pure speculation."

"Sustained."

Erickson backed away from the witness box. "Ms. Tho, you couldn't watch your son twenty-four hours a day, could you?"

"Of course not."

"You had no way of knowing everything that he purchased, right?"

"Obviously."

"You didn't know about everything that he kept in his drawers in your apartment, right?"

"Right."

"Isn't it possible that your son had a gun that you didn't know about?"

"Objection, Your Honor. Calls for speculation."

"Sustained."

Erickson had made his point. "No further questions, Your Honor."

The judge looked at me "Redirect?"

I nodded to Rolanda, who stood at the defense table. "Ms. Tho, just so we're clear, do you have any knowledge that your son had a gun?"

"No, he did not."

"No further questions."

Judge McDaniel put on her reading glasses. "It's after four o'clock. We're adjourned until ten a.m."

* * *

Rosie stopped us as we were leaving the courtroom. "Good move to put Anita on at the end of the day. At least it gave the jury some doubt about whether Tho had a gun."

I shrugged. "Maybe."

Rolanda wasn't satisfied. "We're going to need more."

"You busy tonight?" I asked Rosie.

"No. I'm taking the night off from politics."

"Do you have time to help two of your favorite lawyers prepare for trial?"

Her eyes lit up. "I'll meet you at the office."

47

"SOMETHING HAS COME UP"

The overtaxed ceiling fan was doing its best to recirculate the air in my office at eight o'clock on Wednesday night. "What's the plan?" Rosie asked.

I pointed at the names of the witnesses printed on my white board. "Our ballistics expert will testify that the bullets could have been fired from anywhere behind the counter. It opens up the possibility that Tony or Hector shot Tho."

"You think the jury will buy into a claim that somebody other than Ortega shot Tho?"

"Probably not."

Pete took a bite of cold pizza. "Then what, Mick?"

"Odell Jones will testify that he didn't hear Tho ask for money."

"He said that he didn't hear anything."

"I didn't say it was a slam-dunk winner."

"You planning to put Eugene Pham up to say the same thing?"

"No. He has no credibility. They might arrest him right there in court."

"Good call, Mick."

"Then we'll get our lipreading expert to testify that Tho never said the word 'money.' Next we'll get the Lion of the Loin to say that he didn't see a gun when Tho walked into the store that night."

"You're planning to put a homeless guy on the stand?"

"He's very articulate. Finally, we'll put Ortega Cruz on the stand again and get him to say that he never saw Tho pull the gun."

"He already did. Besides, he'll say that he *thought* that Tho was going to pull a gun. That's enough to get you to self-defense."

"The jury may doubt that Tho had a gun."

"Except for the one they found on the floor with his prints."

"And Ortega's prints."

"Good luck with that, Mick."

"I'll lean on him. I'll try to show that he's a hothead who made up the story about the threatened robbery."

"What's Plan B?"

There is none.

Pete lowered his voice. "Got anything else?"

I looked at Rolanda. "Any suggestions?"

"We can put Tony and Hector back on the stand."

"You think you can get one of them to confess?"

"I can be very persuasive."

"That sort of thing only happens on Perry Mason."

"You never know." Rolanda gave me a thoughtful look. "We talked about putting Thomas on the stand."

"You think it will help?"

"Yes. He can testify that Tho wasn't going to rob the store. He can corroborate Anita's testimony that Tho didn't have a gun. He can argue that there was no reason for Cruz to shoot Tho because he wasn't going to rob the store. And he can remind the jury that he didn't go inside."

"It goes against the conventional wisdom to put the defendant on the stand."

"This isn't a conventional case. We already know that Thomas didn't shoot Tho, so we don't have to worry about a confession."

Rosie added her two cents. "There isn't much downside and it will humanize him with the jury."

"It could blow up on us," I observed.

"That's always a risk." Rosie turned to Rolanda. "Anything

else?'

My niece smiled with confidence. "If all else fails, we'll improvise."

* * *

"It isn't enough," Rosie said.

"I know."

We were sitting in her office at nine-forty on Wednesday night. The door was closed.

"Thanks for helping us tonight," I said. "Rolanda appreciated it. So did I."

"You're welcome." She got a faraway look in her eyes. "It felt like old times. Remember when we were idealistic young lawyers fighting the good fight?"

"I do."

"Do you miss being in court every day?"

"Yes. Mostly, I miss being young."

She smiled. "You're the one who told me that we aren't that old."

"We aren't. I just *feel* old."

"Still glad you decided to represent Thomas?"

"I never ask myself those questions when I'm in the middle of a trial."

"Fair enough."

I smiled. "The answer, by the way, is yes."

"Why?"

"It's who we are and what we do. He needed a lawyer."

"You're in a philosophical mood tonight."

"It happens when I'm tired. Besides, he isn't a bad kid. He just ended up in the wrong place at the wrong time."

She turned serious. "You got anything else?"

"If you're asking if we have any hard evidence that might get us an easy acquittal, the answer is no."

"Is there a 'but'?"

"Just a hunch. It seems like a thoughtful jury. We've cast

doubt on whether Tho had a gun. Our lipreader will testify that Tho didn't ask for money. That might be enough to keep them from convicting Thomas." I added, with a smile, "It helps that Rolanda is a very good lawyer."

Rosie beamed. "Are you going to let her take a couple of witnesses tomorrow?"

"I'm going to let her take the lead. She's connecting with the jury. They like her."

"I was thinking the same thing."

"You should come and watch her work her magic."

"I'll be there."

* * *

Pete knocked on the open door to my office. "Got a sec?"

"Yeah."

He took a seat on the corner of my desk. "I need to show you something." He pulled out his iPhone and showed me a photo of a weedy field surrounded by bamboo trees. "My guy in Vietnam just sent it over. It was taken in an old cemetery near a village called Cib Tran Quang."

I looked at my brother. "Is this where Tommy is buried?"

"Could be. They can't tell for sure. The cemetery hasn't been used in years. Most of the markers are gone. The few that are left are almost impossible to read."

"How many graves were there?"

"Maybe a hundred. There is a chance that there are some remnants of decomposing bones—if they can find the right grave. They might be able to do DNA testing."

"What are the odds?"

His lips turned down. "I'd say about one in a thousand."

Not great. "Tommy had a couple of gold fillings that wouldn't have decomposed. I still have his dental records."

"You kept them all these years?"

"You never know."

"My guy in Vietnam has connections with the government.

They said they'd let him take a look."

"That's all we can ask."

He smiled. "He just needs to find a couple of gold fillings smaller than a baby aspirin in the middle of a graveyard that was abandoned thirty years ago."

"I didn't say this was going to be easy."

My cell phone rang. Erickson's name appeared on the display "Hi, Andy," I said.

His voice was tense. "I need to see you right away. Something has come up."

48
"WE FOUND ANOTHER WITNESS"

Erickson's tone was subdued. "We found another witness."

I was sitting in the chair opposite his desk. "It's too late to add a witness. You've finished putting on your case."

"We'll talk to the judge."

"She's a stickler. She won't let you do it."

"I think she will." He handed me a copy of a draft motion, which I shared with Rolanda. "In the spirit of fair play, I wanted to let you know that we're filing papers tomorrow."

Rolanda answered him. "We'll oppose it."

"If I were in your shoes, I would do the same thing."

"Who is the witness?"

"His name is Tran Vu."

"And who is Tran Vu?"

"The guy who sold the Kel-Tec to Duc Tho."

Not good. "The judge won't allow it. We haven't had an opportunity to question him."

"That's why I called you." Erickson pointed at the door. "Vu is sitting down the hall."

* * *

Tran Vu tugged the sleeve of his orange jumpsuit. "Who the hell are you?"

"Michael Daley. I'm representing Thomas Nguyen."

"I got nothing to say to you."

Vu was sitting between Erickson and his lawyer in a steamy conference room. The only illumination came from a flickering light. Vu's attorney was a small-timer who worked out of an office that he sublet from one of the bail bond shops across the street from the Hall. A burly sheriff's deputy stood guard at the door.

Vu's lawyer spoke to his client in an even tone. "We talked about this, Tran."

"I didn't agree to an interview with Nguyen's lawyers."

"If you don't help Mr. Erickson, I can't help you. Tell Mr. Daley what you told us."

Vu frowned. He was a muscular young man with a shaved head and a world of attitude who had condensed a lifetime of criminal activity into the past five years. According to the rap sheet that Erickson had graciously provided, Vu started stealing cars before he was old enough to drive. He soon graduated to drug dealing, armed robbery, and extortion. He'd worked his way up the criminal ladder in the Tenderloin on an expedited basis—sort of like the kids who get their MBAs in a year and a half by going to summer school—except the curriculum is different.

Vu's lips turned down. "I sold a gun to Duc Tho."

"When?" I asked.

"A couple of weeks before he died."

"What kind?"

"A Kel-Tec P-3AT."

"You remember the exact make and model?"

"I know guns."

I believed him. "How much did he pay you?"

Vu's eyes narrowed. "Two hundred dollars."

"Had you ever done business before?"

"No."

"Where did you get the gun?"

He smirked. "I found it in a Dumpster."

He was lying, of course. "I take it that you didn't turn it in to the police?"

Vu's lawyer fingered the stud in his ear. "You don't need to answer him, Tran."

Erickson interjected. "Yes, you do."

"No, I didn't turn in the gun."

"Which means that your possession of it was illegal."

His smirk widened. "I didn't have time."

Right. "Because you sold it to Tho."

"Yeah."

"And it just so happens that the gun you sold to Tho was the same one that they found at the liquor store where he was killed?"

"I don't know. All I know is that I sold him a Kel-Tec a couple of weeks before he died."

"Did you remove the serial number and all of the identifying information on the gun?"

"I don't know anything about that. I sold it as-is."

Sure. "Where do you live, Tran?"

"Sixth Street."

It was the skid row area near Moscone Center. "What do you do there?"

"I'm an entrepreneur."

"Really? What do you sell?"

"Stuff that I scavenge on the street. Household goods. Watches. Cell phones. iPads. You'd be amazed what people throw away."

I'm never amazed at the lies that people tell. "Why were you arrested this time?"

He shot another glance at his lawyer, who nodded. "The police believe that I was dealing in stolen goods. They're wrong."

Hard to imagine. "Are you charged with a felony?"

"Yeah."

"Your first?"

"No."

"So you're looking at some substantial jail time."

"Yeah."

"I take it that Mr. Erickson might be willing to reduce the

charges if you cooperate?"

"I'm a concerned citizen who decided to come forward with information."

"And you just happened to come forward today?"

"Seemed like the right thing to do."

"You're prepared to testify that you provided this gun to Duc Tho?"

"I *sold* it to him." His expression turned smug. "It happens to be the truth."

And I happen to be the Easter Bunny. He was getting more self-confident as his story became more preposterous. I looked over at Erickson. "I take it that you aren't planning to charge him for selling the gun to Tho?"

"No."

"What deal did you offer him on his current charge?"

"Nothing out of the ordinary."

"Let me guess. His case is a 'wobbler.'" It was the euphemism for charges that fell somewhere in the gray area between a misdemeanor and a felony. "You were going to charge him with a felony. If he testifies, you're going to knock it down to a misdemeanor."

"It could go either way."

"Or maybe you'll just give him immunity and dismiss the charges."

"Possibly."

"Bad form, Andy."

"You know how things work, Mike. We make judgments every day. Mr. Vu has agreed to provide testimony that's relevant to your client's case. How we deal with his situation doesn't concern you."

"Judge McDaniel isn't going to let him testify."

"I think she will."

Vu's attorney stood up. "I think we're done."

49
"HE CAN'T BE SERIOUS"

"That was a crock," Rolanda said. "He can't be serious."

I scanned Erickson's motion to add Vu to his witness list. "Evidently, he is."

We were sitting in my office at a quarter to twelve on Wednesday night. Rolanda was tired and frustrated. I was just tired.

She wasn't finished venting. "You said that we could trust him. Why did he wait until the last minute to spring this?"

"Maybe he just found Vu. Or maybe this is coming from Ward."

"Or maybe he isn't as trustworthy as you think." She flipped open her laptop. "I'll put together our opposition motion. It won't take long."

"Thanks."

She glanced at her computer. "Did Pete find out anything about Vu?"

"He's a small-time fence in the Tenderloin. He sells anything he can get his hands on. Mostly cell phones. Some iPads and laptops."

"Guns?"

"Not as far as we know."

"Seems he's branching into new markets." Rolanda grimaced.

"You okay?" I asked.

"Fine."

"Is your stomach bothering you again?"

"Too much pizza and Diet Coke."

"I don't want you to get an ulcer, Rolanda."

"I'm fine, Mike."

I recognized Rosie's "Don't even think about questioning me" tone. "I'll stick around and take a look at your filing."

"That would be great."

"You think we can keep Vu from testifying?"

"Yeah, but we might not want to."

"How do you figure?"

"We'll make it clear to the jury that Vu is testifying only because he cut a deal with the prosecutors. It brings his credibility into question. More important, if Erickson is willing to put a witness like Vu on the stand, it looks like he isn't confident about his case."

"Do you think we should agree to let him testify?"

"No, we should fight it. Even though we should be able to destroy Vu's credibility, we don't want to have testimony on the record that puts a Kel-Tec in Tho's hands."

"I think that's the right call."

"Besides, it will be fun to wipe that smug grin off Vu's face on the stand."

Rosie would have said the same thing. "Would you like to do the honors in the morning?"

"Love to."

* * *

"I didn't expect you so late," Rosie said.

We were sitting at her kitchen table at one o'clock on Thursday morning. Tommy was asleep. Sylvia was watching TV in the living room.

"We had a little unexpected news after you left tonight," I said. I told her about Erickson's motion to call a new witness.

Rosie shook her head. "Betsy won't go for it."

"She might. Vu has relevant information. Andy will argue that we've had a chance to question him."

"Maybe you shouldn't have gone over to meet him."

"Hindsight is twenty-twenty. We'll fight it in the morning.

If the judge lets him testify, Rolanda will destroy his credibility on cross."

"She's a pit bull when she needs to be."

"Just like her aunt."

Rosie reached over and slapped my hand. "How are you holding up?"

"I'm fine."

"And Rolanda?"

"She's okay, but she's having stomach trouble again."

"It's been going on for a couple of weeks. She doesn't like to talk about it."

"She reminds me of your mother." I waited a beat. "Is she pregnant?"

"I don't think so."

"I hope it isn't anything serious." I took Rosie's hand. "Would you talk to her about going to the doctor? She might be more receptive if it comes from you."

"I will."

"Thanks. Do you have time to watch the trial in the morning?"

"I'll see you there."

50
"HE CHANGED HIS MIND"

An irritated Judge McDaniel templed her fingers in front of her face. "You can't be serious, Mr. Erickson."

"We are, Your Honor."

We had convened in the judge's chambers at ten o'clock on Thursday morning. She was annoyed by Erickson's last-minute motion to add Vu to his witness list. She was furious that she had to put a sitting jury on ice while we argued about it.

She speed-read Erickson's motion. "Why wasn't this witness added earlier?"

"He came forward on Sunday."

"Why didn't I hear about this on Sunday?"

"We wanted to interview him and verify his story."

I interjected. "They've spent four days trying to cut a deal in exchange for his testimony."

"Is this true, Mr. Erickson?"

"We've been discussing various scenarios with his attorney."

I spoke up again. "All of which involve granting him immunity on certain charges and reducing other charges if he agrees to testify in our case."

Erickson kept his tone measured. "His testimony is relevant to Thomas Nguyen's case. It has substantial probative value."

"What kind?"

"He sold the Kel-Tec to Duc Tho."

Rolanda corrected him. "He claims that he sold *a* Kel-Tec to Tho. He admitted that he didn't know if it's the same gun that they found under Tho's body."

The judge took off her reading glasses. "Is that true, Mr.

Erickson?"

"Yes."

Rolanda tried again. "We learned of this at ten o'clock last night. We haven't had time to check out his story or prepare for his testimony."

Erickson disagreed. "Ms. Fernandez and Mr. Daley met with Mr. Vu last night."

"For ten minutes," Rolanda snapped. "Then Vu's lawyer pulled the plug."

This was a slight misrepresentation of how we concluded the interview, but I had no intention of pointing it out to the judge. We went back and forth for another ten minutes. Erickson kept repeating his point—which was legitimate—that Vu would provide relevant testimony. Rolanda and I countered with an equally valid argument that Vu was unreliable. We played to the judge's sense of order by claiming—justifiably— that it was too late to include a new witness after the prosecution had concluded its case.

Judge McDaniel listened patiently. Finally, she spoke to Erickson. "I am very disappointed in you, Andy. You know that it is inappropriate to add a witness at this point."

"But Your Honor—,"

"I'm not finished. While I believe that your behavior has been less than exemplary, you have persuaded me that this witness does, in fact, have information with probative value."

Rolanda interrupted her. "But Your Honor—,"

"Let me finish, Ms. Fernandez. I have decided that I will allow this witness to testify."

Erickson nodded. "Thank you, Your Honor."

"But I have some conditions. First, I am going to call a recess for the rest of the day to let Ms. Fernandez and Mr. Daley interview Mr. Vu at length and otherwise conduct whatever additional due diligence they need to prepare. In particular, I am ordering you to provide Mr. Vu's arrest record and the police reports for the crime for which he is accused. I will also expect you to make the arresting officer available for Ms. Fernandez and Mr. Daley to interview."

"Yes, Your Honor."

"Second, given the circumstances, I am going to give Ms. Fernandez and Mr. Daley great leeway in conducting their cross examination of this witness. I am also going to let them add the arresting officer to their witness list."

"Yes, Your Honor."

She was going to let us ask Vu anything that we wanted.

"Finally, I want to make it clear that any attempts to add another witness will not be well received. Understood?"

"Yes."

The judge started to gather her papers when there was a knock at the door. Her clerk came inside. "Excuse me, Your Honor. One of Mr. Erickson's colleagues is here. She needs to talk to him. She says it's urgent."

Now what?

Erickson looked relieved to have an excuse to exit the room. "Pardon me."

Rolanda, Judge McDaniel and I sat in silence for five minutes as we waited. The judge stared at her computer and pretended that we weren't there.

Erickson returned a few minutes later and spoke to us in a muted tone. "Your Honor, we will be withdrawing our motion to include Mr. Vu on our witness list."

Though she tried to hide it, I could see the hint of a smile on Judge McDaniel's face. "Really? May I ask why?"

"He changed his mind. He's decided not to testify."

Their deal fell apart.

"So we'll pretend that this conversation never happened?"

"Yes, Your Honor."

"Fine." She pushed back her chair and stood up. "Let me give you a little friendly advice, Andy. If something like this happens again, I would encourage you not to waste this court's time by trying to introduce new witnesses or making other frivolous motions."

"Yes, Your Honor."

"Let's get back to work. The jury is waiting for us."

* * *

"Do you think Erickson was really planning to call Vu as a witness?" Rolanda asked.

"Probably," I said. We were walking down the corridor toward Judge McDaniel's courtroom. "Andy isn't the type to sandbag."

"Maybe he was trying to distract us."

"I don't think so, Rolanda. He's already introduced evidence that Tho had a gun. Vu's testimony would have been helpful, but not essential. Besides, his credibility would have been questionable and it's a bad idea to irritate the judge." I opened the heavy door to the courtroom. "Ready to roll?"

"Absolutely."

51

"IT IS IMPOSSIBLE TO DETERMINE THE PRECISE SPOT"

Rolanda stood at the lectern. "Please state your name for the record."

"Dr. Robert Stumpf." He spoke in a commanding baritone.

"Are you a medical doctor?"

"No. I earned my Ph.D. at UC-Berkeley. I also received my bachelor's and master's degrees there."

Go Bears!

"What is your specialty?"

"Forensic ballistics."

From his full head of meticulously coiffed hair to his custom Brioni suit, everything about Bob Stumpf was in muted shades of gray. Forty years earlier, the lanky Modesto native went to Cal on a basketball scholarship, where he was Tommy's fraternity brother. A torn ACL had cut short his athletic career, so he focused on his studies in criminal justice. He was now a world-class authority on firearms. When I explained the circumstances of our case, he graciously agreed to testify for free, which was helpful, because we couldn't have afforded him otherwise.

Rolanda edged closer to him. "Dr. Stumpf, what is your current occupation?"

"I'm a full professor of forensic ballistics at the University of California at Berkeley. I've held that position for thirty-three years."

"Could you please explain what you mean by 'forensic ballistics'?"

"It's the study of evidence relating to firearms at a crime

scene. It includes matching ammunition to weapons, analyzing bullet fragments, and investigating projectiles."

"Would it include determinations of the path of bullets?"

"Absolutely."

He was smoother than the bottle of Glenfiddich that I would present to him as a thank-you for his testimony.

Rolanda was standing perfectly still. "You're familiar with the facts surrounding the death of Mr. Duc Tho at Alcatraz Liquors on December fourteenth of last year?"

"I am."

"You have had an opportunity to review the police reports, the security video, the autopsy report, and the ballistics report prepared by Sergeant Kathleen Jacobsen?"

"I have."

"Do you agree with the conclusions of Sergeant Jacobsen's report?"

"For the most part." Stumpf cleared his throat. "As you know, I have great respect for Sergeant Jacobsen."

Even when you're prepared to testify that you think she's wrong.

"Could you please tell us the portions of the report that you agreed with?"

"The six bullets that killed Mr. Tho were fired from the AR-15 found in the store."

"Is there something that you didn't agree with?"

"Yes." Stumpf lowered his voice. "I disagree with Sergeant Jacobsen's conclusion regarding the location of the shooter."

"Could you be more specific?"

"Certainly." Stumpf took off his aviator-style glasses. "Actually, I think it would be more accurate to say that I think her conclusion was a little too specific."

He was getting a little too cute.

"How so?" Rolanda asked.

Stumpf glanced at the jury. "The ballistics and autopsy

reports concluded that Mr. Tho was struck in the chest by six bullets." He used his right index finger to make a circle in the middle of his chest. "The bullets entered Mr. Tho's body within a one-inch radius which created a single contiguous wound. This indicated that the shooter was an experienced marksman and an excellent shot."

"How long did it take to fire the six shots?"

"Based on my review of the security video, my calculations indicate that it was approximately 2.4 seconds."

"That seems like a lot of shots in such a short time."

"It's about average for someone who is familiar with an AR-15. It's a semi-automatic firearm, which means that you need to pull the trigger each and every time you fire a shot. That distinguishes it from a fully automatic weapon, such as a machine gun, where you can fire multiple rounds with just one tug of the trigger."

"How many shots can a person fire in one second with an AR-15?"

"It varies. If you've never shot the weapon, you would be lucky to fire more than one round per second. However, if you're experienced with the AR-15, it isn't uncommon to fire three, four or even five rounds per second with reasonable accuracy. I've heard claims that people have fired eight rounds a second, but I have never personally seen anyone do so."

He was a natural teacher. The jury was dialed in.

Rolanda got down to business. "The fact that Mr. Tho was hit by six bullets fired in less than three seconds wasn't extraordinary, was it?"

"Not at all—especially if the shots were fired by somebody familiar with an AR-15."

"Are you sure that all six shots were fired by the same person?"

"It is theoretically possible that someone could have fired one or more of the shots and handed the weapon to someone else who fired the rest, but it would have been virtually impossible given the timing."

"Is all of this consistent with the results of Sergeant Jacobsen's report?"

"So far."

"But you mentioned that there was at least one element that you disagreed with."

"There is. Sergeant Jacobsen concluded that the shots were fired from directly behind the cash register. I am not sure that this was the case."

"Would you explain why?"

"Of course. Would you mind if I step out of the witness box for the moment?"

Erickson offered no objection.

Stumpf left the stand and took up a spot in front of the jury. He acted out Tho's actions as he spoke. "When Mr. Tho entered the store, he turned to his right to face the counter. As he was turning, he was hit by six bullets, all of which entered his chest while he was still on his feet. My review of the video indicated that Mr. Tho was still turning when the first bullet struck. He was still rotating slightly as the second and third and fourth bullets struck."

"How did that impact your analysis?"

"If the victim is stationary, we can determine the precise angle from which the shots were fired with great certainty. If the victim is moving, it becomes more difficult."

"Could you have been more precise if the bullets had passed through Mr. Tho's body?"

"Possibly. However, Mr. Tho's wounds were so close together that neither we nor the Medical Examiner could make a definitive determination of angle of entry. In addition, the bullets were designed to fragment upon entry, so there were no exit wounds. Our analysis is exacerbated by the fact that it is possible that the shooter was also moving."

"What did you conclude?"

"Based upon the forensic ballistics and video, it is my professional opinion that it is impossible to determine the precise spot from which the shots were fired."

Ta-da!

Rolanda was pleased. "Could you please give us your best estimate of the range of locations from which the shots were fired?"

"Objection," Erickson said. "Speculation."

"I'm asking for his expert opinion," Rolanda said.

"Overruled."

Stumpf returned to his seat in the witness box. "The shots could have come from almost any location from the deli counter over to the window."

"No further questions."

She did well.

"Cross exam, Mr. Erickson?"

"Just a couple of questions." Erickson stood at the prosecution table. "Dr. Stumpf, the report indicated that Ortega Cruz admitted that he fired the shots that killed Duc Tho, didn't it?"

"Yes."

"Did you find any definitive forensic evidence that someone other than Mr. Cruz fired those shots?"

"No."

"No further questions."

Judge McDaniel gestured at Rolanda. "Please call your next witness."

"The defense calls Odell Jones."

52
"I DIDN'T HEAR ANYTHING"

"My name is Odell Jones. I'm a deliveryman for Budweiser."

"How long have you held that position?" I asked.

"Thirty-two years."

Rolanda's stomach was bothering her again, so we decided that I would handle Jones's direct exam.

Jones had swapped his Budweiser polo shirt for a sport jacket and an oxford shirt. Big John was in the back of the gallery to provide moral support. Rosie was sitting next to him. Barring something unexpected, Jones would be on the stand for just a few minutes.

"Did you make a delivery to Alcatraz Liquors on the night of December fourteenth of last year?" I asked.

"Yes."

"What time did you arrive?"

"Ten-forty-five p.m."

"How long were you there?"

"About five minutes."

"Did you see a young man named Duc Tho enter the store at ten-forty-seven p.m.?"

"No. I was in the back loading a refrigerator."

"Did you hear him say anything?"

"No."

"Did you see anyone shoot Mr. Tho?"

"No."

Good. "Mr. Jones, were you aware that the owner of the store, Mr. Ortega Cruz, kept an AR-15 rifle behind the counter?"

"Yes."

"Do you know if he still keeps a weapon in the store?"

"Yes. A Glock."

"How do you know?"

"He's shown it to me on several occasions."

"Did he ever threaten you?"

Jones paused. "Not really."

"Could you please be more specific?"

"One time, he was angry because I had arrived late. He told me that if it happened again, he would use the gun on me."

"No further questions."

Erickson addressed Jones from the prosecution table. "When Mr. Cruz said that he would use the gun on you if you were late again, was it your belief that he was serious?"

"No."

"You also said that you didn't hear Mr. Tho say anything when he entered the store."

"Correct."

"Is it possible that Mr. Tho said something to Mr. Cruz without you having heard it?"

"Objection. Speculation."

"Sustained."

"In fact, he might have threatened Mr. Cruz, right?"

"Objection. Speculation."

"Sustained."

"No further questions."

Judge McDaniel looked at me. "We're in recess for lunch, Mr. Daley. We'll resume at two o'clock."

"Yes, Your Honor."

We were scoring points and perhaps giving the jury some evidence of reasonable doubt, but we hadn't come up with a silver bullet that would get us an acquittal. Trial work was an all-or-nothing deal. In the grand scheme of things, we were getting killed.

53
"WE'RE DONE"

Thomas stared at his uneaten turkey sandwich. "We're done, aren't we?"

"We're still in the game," I said.

Thomas, his mother, Rolanda, Rosie, and I were sitting inside a consultation room down the hall from Judge McDaniel's courtroom. Our lunches were untouched.

I kept my tone even. "The jury is listening. We're scoring points."

"Not enough."

"We aren't finished."

His voice filled with frustration. "We need more than a hired gun to testify that it's theoretically possible that somebody other than Ortega Cruz fired the shots."

"We've cast doubt on whether Cruz killed Tho."

"He admitted it."

"We're showing that he might have been trying to protect somebody."

"It doesn't prove anything."

"We don't need to prove it. We just need to provide enough evidence to convince one juror to vote for acquittal."

"They aren't buying it."

"I disagree." I wasn't sure if I was trying to convince my great-nephew or myself.

"What makes you think that the testimony from Jones did any good? You just got him to say that he didn't hear anything."

"It mitigates the self-defense claim."

"He was in the back of the store. The fact that he didn't

hear anything doesn't prove that Tho didn't threaten Cruz."

"It's hard to prove a negative—especially since we have two corroborating witnesses."

Melinda spoke up in her son's defense. "You need to prove that somebody else shot Tho."

"That's going to be very hard."

"Then you have to show that Tho didn't threaten Cruz. That's our defense, right?"

"We're putting the lipreading expert on later this afternoon. She'll testify that Tho never threatened Cruz. We're also going to show that Cruz is trigger happy and has a bad temper. If we can convince the jury that he acted unilaterally, then he had the necessary criminal intent to be charged with murder or voluntary manslaughter. If Cruz had criminal intent on his own, it can't be imputed to Thomas."

"You're saying that we need to prove that Cruz is guilty of murder?"

"We don't need to prove it beyond a reasonable doubt. We just need to convince one juror that it's a reasonable possibility."

"Anything else?"

"We're going to put up Brian Holton."

"The homeless guy? What on earth for?"

"He'll testify that Cruz threatened him several times."

"You realize that he isn't the most credible witness in the world."

"We do."

"Then what?"

"We'll put Cruz on the stand and see if we can shake him."

* * *

"This isn't going well," Rosie observed.

"No, it isn't," I said.

We were standing in the otherwise-empty corridor outside Judge McDaniel's courtroom.

"Thomas and his mother are scared," she said.

"Can't blame them."

"You got anything left?"

"We've got a couple of rabbits left in our hat."

"Really?"

I answered her honestly. "No."

"Are you really going to have the homeless guy testify?"

"Yes."

"Then what?"

"I'll go after Ortega Cruz."

Rosie was about to respond when a red-faced Jerry Edwards came strolling up the hallway, unlit cigarette in his hand. "Care to comment on your trial?"

"Nope."

"From where I've been sitting, it doesn't look like things are going so well for your side."

"No comment, Jerry."

"You got anything besides smoke and mirrors?"

Not really. "We have a couple more witnesses."

"You think it will make any difference?"

Probably not. "Yes."

He pulled the sleeve of his thread-bare suit jacket. "Still glad you took this case?"

"Yes. Still think we're giving my great-nephew special treatment?"

"No."

* * *

Pete's tone was hushed. "Where are you, Mick?"

"My auxiliary office."

"The men's room?"

"Yeah."

"Which stall?"

"Pete, I need to get back to court."

"Which stall, Mick?"

"Number three."

"Good. You've always done your best work in stall number three."

"I don't have time for this."

His tone turned serious. "Who's up next?"

"Our lipreading expert followed by the Lion of the Loin."

"Anybody else?"

"Ortega Cruz."

"See if you can slow-walk them through their testimony."

My pulse started to race. "You got something that we can use?"

"I don't know yet."

54
"WATCH HIS MOUTH"

The willowy African-American woman with the hoop-style earrings and Hillary Clinton pantsuit leaned forward in the witness box and spoke with understated authority. "My name is Dr. Candace Greene."

Rolanda nodded. "What is your area of expertise, Dr. Greene?"

"Children with hearing disabilities."

"Would that include knowledge in the science of lipreading?"

"Yes."

Rosie's college classmate had grown up in the projects at Hunters Point. She was the youngest of four daughters of a single mother.

"Where did you go to college?" Rolanda asked.

"San Francisco State. My undergraduate degree was in psychology. I also earned my teaching credential there."

"You have several advanced degrees, don't you?"

"I have a master's and a Ph.D. in special education from UCLA."

Erickson got to his feet. "Your Honor, we will stipulate that Dr. Greene is an expert in the field of lipreading."

Rolanda wasn't satisfied. "Are you also prepared to stipulate that Dr. Greene is a nationally recognized authority in her field?"

"Yes."

"Thank you." She turned to the judge. "Your Honor, we respectfully request permission for Dr. Greene to leave the witness box so that she can point out certain items in the security video."

"That's fine."

As Greene left the stand and took her place in front of the TV monitor, I opened my laptop and cued the security video.

"Dr. Greene," Rolanda said, "are you familiar with the security video taken at Alcatraz Liquors at ten-forty-seven on the night of December fourteenth of last year?"

"Yes."

"Would you mind if we showed you that film one more time to refresh your memory?"

"Certainly."

Actually, Rolanda wanted to refresh the jury's memory.

Rolanda pointed at me and I played the video. Tho walked into the store and turned to his right. His mouth opened for an instant. His eyes opened wide. His chest exploded. I stopped the video. At Rolanda's request, I re-ran it in super-slow-motion.

Rolanda turned back to Greene. "You've had a chance to review this film in detail?"

"I have."

"And you've had an opportunity to study Mr. Tho's movements?"

"Yes."

"In particular, you were able to study the movements of his mouth in both real time and slow-motion?"

"Yes."

"Does it appear to you that Mr. Tho said something?"

"Possibly."

"Based upon your expert knowledge as a lipreader, what did he say?"

"I don't know."

"I beg your pardon?"

Greene shot a conspiratorial glance at the jury. "I don't know," she repeated.

Rolanda pretended that she hadn't anticipated the answer. "I don't understand. You're a nationally recognized expert at lipreading."

"It's much more of an art than an exact science."

"How so?"

"A lot depends upon context and environment. It helps if you're in a well-lit room and you can see the speaker head-on. It becomes much more difficult if the speaker is moving. Good lipreaders also study body language. In addition, many words and letters look similar. For example, without context, it is almost impossible to distinguish the letter 'B' from the letter 'P.'"

"How much can a competent lipreader discern?"

"Between thirty and forty percent of what's being said. A highly trained lipreader can distinguish between forty and fifty percent."

"What about an expert?"

"There is some evidence that a small percentage of lipreaders can identify as much as ninety percent."

"You're an expert. What percentage can you identify by sight alone?"

"Under ideal conditions, between fifty and sixty percent."

Rolanda feigned disappointment. "Let's look at this video once more in slow motion."

Greene stood in front of the TV. "Would it be possible for me to control the video this time? It will make it easier for me to point out certain things."

"No objection," Erickson said.

I handed Greene the remote. She pressed the start button, then stopped the video almost immediately. "This is where Mr. Tho walked into the store. Notice that his mouth is closed. He hasn't said anything yet."

She advanced the video a little further and stopped it again. "This is where Mr. Tho turns toward the counter. Since the camera is above the register, we have a good view of his mouth, although his face is somewhat in the shadows." She ran it a little more and used her hand to circle Tho's mouth. "Here Mr. Tho has opened his mouth. It almost looks as if he's smiling." She advanced it a little more. "You can see that his mouth was still open when the shooting started."

"What did he say?"

"I don't know. His mouth was in a position where he could have said 'Hi.' Or he might have said 'Ah.' Or he might have said nothing."

"Can you tell whether he said more than one word?"

"No."

"Is it possible to determine whether he uttered more than one syllable?"

"Based upon the shape of his mouth and the positions of his lips and tongue, no."

"Based upon your experience as an expert lipreader, what do you think he said?"

"I don't know."

"Would you care to hazard an educated guess?"

"I'm afraid that's impossible."

Rolanda glanced at the jury. No discernable reaction. She turned back to Greene. "Have you reviewed the police reports relating to the events at Alcatraz Liquors on the night of December fourteenth of last year?"

"Yes."

"Are you aware that the owner of the store, Mr. Ortega Cruz, told the police that Mr. Tho entered his store and demanded money?"

"Yes."

"Are you also aware that Mr. Cruz's son and nephew also told the police that Mr. Tho demanded money?"

"Yes."

"Based upon the video evidence, do you think that Mr. Tho

did so?"

Greene's tone was emphatic. "No."

"How do you know?"

"Watch his mouth." Greene restarted the video and played it until the end. "Now watch my mouth when I say the word 'money.'" She faced the jury and enunciated each syllable. "When I said the word 'money,' I pressed my lips together. It's the only way that you can make the sound of the letter 'M.' When Mr. Tho walked into the store, he opened his mouth, but he didn't press his lips together."

"Is it therefore your expert opinion that Mr. Tho did not say the word 'money' when he entered the store?"

"Yes. I would go further to say that he didn't say any word containing the letters 'M,' 'B,' or 'P.'"

"No further questions, Your Honor."

"Cross exam, Mr. Erickson?"

"Yes." He approached Greene. "You said that even an expert lipreader can only discern forty to fifty percent of what's been spoken."

"Correct."

"That means that your ability to determine what Mr. Tho said has about a fifty-fifty proposition, right?"

"Yes, but —,"

Erickson stopped her. "No further questions."

Rolanda was up immediately. "Mr. Erickson didn't allow Dr. Greene to finish her answer."

The judge nodded. "Did you wish to add something, Dr. Greene?"

"Yes. Your Honor. While it is true that I can distinguish only about half of the words spoken, I can distinguish certain sounds with almost one hundred percent certainty. I was able to determine that Mr. Tho did not say any words containing the letter 'M.'"

"Thank you, Dr. Greene. Anything else, Mr. Erickson?"

Erickson scowled. "Just one more question. Dr. Greene, isn't it possible that Mr. Tho's manner of speaking and diction habits might have made it more difficult for you to discern not only the words that he was saying, but certain sounds that he might have made?"

"Yes."

"Including the question of whether he said any words containing the letter 'M'?"

"Yes. It's also possible that Mr. Tho was a professional ventriloquist, in which case he would have had special training to say many words without moving his lips or mouth. In such circumstances, I wouldn't have been able to read his lips."

Erickson had the good judgment to leave it there. "No further questions, Your Honor."

Judge McDaniel looked at her watch. "I think we have time for one more witness this afternoon, Ms. Fernandez."

"The defense calls Brian Holton."

The Lion of the Loin was going to get his moment in the sun.

55
"HE WANTED TO SEND A MESSAGE"

The Lion of the Loin unbuttoned the jacket of the double-breasted suit that he had chosen from the donated clothing closet at the P.D.'s Office. I had lobbied for something more subdued, but he had insisted on a flashier look with pinstripes and wide lapels. He spoke in a measured tone. "My name is Brian Holton."

Rolanda stood in front of the witness box. "What is your occupation?"

"I'm retired."

Don't get cute.

Cleanly shaved with a fresh haircut, Holton looked more like a mid-level government bureaucrat than a homeless guy. He was also reasonably well rested. We had rented him a room at the Holiday Inn on Tenth Street near City Hall, where we had assigned one of Pete's operatives to babysit him. Holton had tried to escape only once. The shopping cart with his belongings was parked safely inside Pete's garage in Marin. We had also provided him with ten crisp twenty-dollar bills. He would receive an additional installment at the end of his testimony if he followed Rolanda's lead.

Rolanda was all business. "Were you standing outside Alcatraz Liquors at ten-forty-seven p.m. on the evening of December fourteenth of last year?"

"Yes."

"Did you see a man named Duc Tho enter the store?"

"Yes."

"Had you ever seen him before?"

"A couple of times."

"Had you ever seen him carry a weapon?"

"No."

"Was he carrying a weapon that night?"

"I didn't see a gun."

Rolanda nodded with satisfaction. "Mr. Holton, what happened when he went inside?"

"He turned to face the counter. Then he was shot."

"Did you see who shot him?"

"No."

"Did Mr. Tho draw a gun?"

"Not that I saw."

"Did he say anything when he went inside the store?"

"Not that I heard."

So far, so good.

"Mr. Holton, are you acquainted with Mr. Ortega Cruz?"

"Yes. He's the owner of Alcatraz Liquors."

"Do you know him well?"

"Pretty well. He used to pay me a little cash to keep the troublemakers away from his store."

"Does he still pay you to watch his store?"

"No."

"Do you know that he keeps a gun under the counter by the cash register?"

"Yes. He's shown it to me."

"How many times?"

"Several."

"Once? Twice? Three times?"

"I'd say at least a dozen times."

"Why did he show it to you so many times?"

"Objection," Erickson said. "Speculation."

"Sustained."

Rolanda smiled. "I'll rephrase. Mr. Holton, did Mr. Cruz ever tell you why he showed you his weapon?"

"Objection. Hearsay."

"Overruled."

Holton sat up taller. "He said he wanted to send a message to the people in the neighborhood that he had a gun and he wasn't afraid to use it."

"Did you ever see him pull out the gun and threaten other people?"

"Several times."

"Anyone in particular?"

"He had a lot of trouble with the Vietnamese gangs."

"Did you ever him see lose his temper?"

"Many times."

"What did he do when he lost his temper?"

"He yelled."

"No further questions."

Erickson walked to the front of the witness box. "Mr. Holton, you said that Mr. Cruz showed you his weapon on several occasions, right?"

"Right."

"Did he ever threaten to shoot you?"

"No."

"Did you ever see him shoot anybody else?"

"No."

"So, it's possible that he may have been joking, right?"

"Objection," Rolanda said. "Calls for speculation."

"Sustained."

"And it's also possible that Mr. Cruz may have been showing off or simply blowing off steam, right?"

"Objection. Speculation."

"Sustained."

"Mr. Holton, where do you live?"

"In the Tenderloin."

"Where?"

"Here and there."

"You live on the street, don't you?"

"Yes."

"Who provided you with the suit that you're wearing today?"

"Mr. Daley."

"Who paid for your haircut?"

"Mr. Daley."

"Did Mr. Daley pay for you to stay in a hotel last night?"

"Yes."

"I'll bet that you're very appreciative."

"I am."

"Are you so appreciative that you'd say anything that Mr. Daley asked you to say?"

"Objection. Relevance."

"Overruled."

The Lion folded his arms. "No, Mr. Erickson. When you live on the street, you get by on your wits and your reputation. If you're an idiot or a liar, you'll be dead within weeks. I won't lie for anybody—even if they give me a suit or pay for a haircut or put me up at the Holiday Inn. At the end of the day, it just isn't worth it."

Erickson stood there for a moment, flustered. "No further questions, Your Honor."

"Redirect, Ms. Fernandez?"

"No, Your Honor."

Sometimes you get a little help from unexpected sources.

"Please call your next witness, Ms. Fernandez."

"The defense calls Ortega Cruz."

56
"I SHOT HIM IN SELF-DEFENSE"

"I trust that I don't need to remind you that you're still under oath?" I said.

A confident Ortega Cruz sat ramrod straight in the witness box. "No, Mr. Daley."

Rolanda and I had agreed that I would handle Cruz's direct exam. She was building a nice rapport with the jury, and I wanted her to do our closing argument. This was likely to get chippy, so I was taking the role of the bad cop.

The gallery had a few more spectators than earlier in the day. Edwards was parked in his usual spot behind the prosecution. Rosie was sitting in the back on the defense side. Melinda was behind the defense table. Nick "the Dick" Hanson was making an unexpected cameo. He was sitting next to Big John.

Maria Cruz was sitting by herself in the back row on the prosecution's side. It was her first appearance at the trial. Since she was on our witness list, we had to approve her appearance in court, which we did. It would have made no sense to antagonize her. We hadn't seen Tony since he finished his testimony the previous day. We hadn't seen Isabel at all.

The door opened and Pete came inside. He nodded at me and took a seat next to Rosie.

I turned back to Cruz. "I'm going to show you the security video when Duc Tho entered your store."

"Fine."

The courtroom was silent as I rolled the video twice: first at normal speed, then in super slow-motion. Each time, I stopped it right before Tho was shot.

"Mr. Cruz, would you please confirm that this is, in fact, the security video taken at your store on the night of December fourteenth of last year at ten-forty-seven p.m.?"

"Yes."

"That's Mr. Tho in the video?"

"Correct."

Erickson got to his feet and sounded bored. "Your Honor, we've covered this territory. We would appreciate it if you would ask Mr. Daley to get to the point."

"Please, Mr. Daley."

"Yes, Your Honor." My eyes were still on Cruz. "You testified earlier that Mr. Tho came into your store."

"Right."

"He demanded money."

"Yes."

"And threatened you with a gun."

"Correct."

"I'm going to run the video once more in slow motion. I want you to tell me to stop the tape at the point where you saw Mr. Tho threaten you with the gun."

I ran the video again in super slow motion. Cruz remained silent.

"Mr. Cruz?"

"Yes?"

"You didn't stop me."

"We've been through this, Mr. Daley. The gun was inside Mr. Tho's pocket."

"Then how did he threaten you?"

"I could see it."

"But you just admitted that it was inside his pocket."

"I could see an object in his pocket in the shape of a gun."

I ran the video again. This time I stopped it just after Tho had turned. "Is this when you claim you saw a gun?" I emphasized the word "claim."

"Yes."

"I don't see anything that looks like a gun."

"It was in his hand inside his pocket. I knew it was there."

It's your story and you're sticking to it. "Mr. Cruz, you testified that Mr. Tho demanded money."

"He did."

"You're absolutely sure he said the word 'money.'"

"Yes."

"When?"

"When he came inside the store."

"But exactly when did he demand money? On his way inside?"

"No."

"After he turned to face the register?"

"Maybe."

"While he reached inside his pocket?"

"I don't recall exactly."

I cued the video again. "I want you to tell me to stop the video where Mr. Tho demanded money."

I ran it in super slow-motion. Cruz stopped me immediately after Tho turned to face the register. "There," he said.

"You're absolutely sure?"

"Yes."

"And he said the word 'money'?"

"Objection," Erickson said. "Asked and answered.

"Sustained."

I darted a glance at the jury. No reaction. "Mr. Cruz, I want you to watch my mouth when I say the word, 'money.'" I said the word slowly while exaggerating each syllable. "Did you notice anything?"

"No."

"Did you notice that I pressed my lips together?"

"Yes."

"I'm going to roll the video again. Could you please tell me to stop it when you see Mr. Tho press his lips together?"

"Okay."

I ran the video again. Cruz remained silent. "Mr. Cruz?"

"Yes?"

"You didn't stop me."

"It happened too fast."

"Mr. Tho never said the word 'money,' did he?"

"Yes, he did."

"But he never put his lips together."

"I know what I heard. My son heard the same thing. So did my nephew."

"A deliveryman who was inside the store at the time didn't hear Mr. Tho say anything."

"He was in the back of the store."

"Neither did your daughter."

Cruz glared at me. "She was doing her homework. She wasn't paying attention."

"She heard you tell her to duck."

"I shouted to get her attention."

"Do you know a man named Brian Holton?"

"Yes. He's a homeless man who used to spend time in front of my store."

"You used to pay him to keep troublemakers away, didn't you?"

"I gave him a few dollars."

"And free beer?"

"Sometimes."

"He testified earlier that he was in front of your store on the night that Mr. Tho was killed. He also said that he didn't see Mr. Tho pull a gun or hear him ask for money."

"Objection," Erickson said. "There wasn't a question there."

No, there wasn't. "I'll rephrase. Mr. Cruz, would it surprise you to hear that Mr. Holton testified that he didn't see a gun in

Mr. Tho's pocket?"

"No."

"Would it also surprise you that he didn't hear Mr. Tho ask for money?"

"No."

"Can you explain the discrepancies between your account and his?"

"Mr. Holton was outside. He was also frequently drunk or high. The fact that he didn't notice that Mr. Tho had a gun should come as no surprise. The fact that he didn't hear anything isn't a surprise either since Mr. Holton was outside and Mr. Tho was inside."

"You're saying that he was lying?"

"Maybe he was mistaken."

"Did you ever show him the weapon that you kept behind the counter?"

"I might have."

"Would it surprise you to hear that he testified that you showed it to him on several occasions?"

"Not really."

"Are you in the habit of flashing your weapon?"

"It's a deterrent."

"And from time to time, you have, in fact, used it, right?"

"Only when necessary. And only in self-defense."

"And it's your story that after you heard Tho ask for money, you shot him?"

"I *did* hear him. I shot him in self-defense."

"Just like you shot another man a couple of years ago in self-defense?"

"He tried to rob me."

"You said the same thing about Duc Tho."

"It's the truth."

"And this time, Duc was the only witness other than your children and your nephew, right?"

"Right."

"And they'll say whatever you tell them to say, won't they?"

"Objection. Argumentative."

"Sustained."

I pointed an accusatory finger at Cruz. "You're lying to protect your children or your nephew, aren't you?"

"No."

"You're under oath, Mr. Cruz."

"I'm telling the truth."

I turned off the TV and walked back to the defense table. Before I took my seat, I turned around to face Cruz. "You have a lot of Vietnamese customers, don't you?"

"A lot of Vietnamese live in the neighborhood."

"Mr. Holton testified that you don't like them."

"Not true."

"In fact, he testified that you told him on several occasions that the Vietnamese gangs were always trying to rob your store."

"I don't recall."

"Duc Tho came into your store frequently, didn't he?"

"No."

"And he gave you trouble, didn't he?"

"No."

"And you didn't like him because he was Vietnamese, right?"

"No."

"And you made up this whole story about killing him in self-defense, didn't you?"

"No."

"You wanted to send another message to the people in the neighborhood that the Vietnamese gangs should find somebody else to rob, didn't you?"

"No."

"Mr. Tho never asked for money."

"Yes, he did."

"And he never threatened you or your children or your nephew."

"Yes, he did."

"You shot and killed him because he was Vietnamese, didn't you?"

"No."

"Do you think anybody in this courtroom believes you?"

"Objection. Argumentative."

"Sustained."

"No further questions, Your Honor."

Judge McDaniel looked over at Erickson. "Cross exam?"

"No, Your Honor."

The judge flicked off her computer. "We'll resume at ten o'clock tomorrow morning."

57
"IT ISN'T ENOUGH"

"How is Thomas holding up?" Rosie asked me.

"He's discouraged. So is his mother."

The mood was subdued in Rolanda's office at ten-thirty on Thursday night. The aroma of Thai food filled the room. Rosie was working with Rolanda on her closing.

Rosie's eyes twinkled. "Remember when you told me that we still have plenty of juice to try cases on short notice?"

"Yes."

"You were wrong."

Beautiful Rosie.

Rolanda tried to lift my spirits. "You did a good job on Cruz's direct."

"It isn't enough."

"You didn't have much to work with."

"Then we should have found more."

"We got this case a week ago, Mike."

I willed myself not to snap at her out of frustration. "I told Thomas that we want him to testify tomorrow. He's willing."

"Do you think it will help?"

"I don't see how it can hurt. It will give the jury a human face to take into deliberations. He'll confirm that he was outside in the car. He'll say that Tho wasn't going to rob the store. And he'll say that Tho didn't have a gun."

"Erickson might go after him on cross."

"It will make Thomas look more sympathetic."

Rosie stroked her chin. "I think it's probably worth putting him on the stand."

I trusted her instincts. "Then it's agreed." I looked over at my niece. "I think it would probably be good if you handle his direct exam."

"Sure."

"Heard anything from Pete?"

"He's on his way."

"Does he have anything that we can use tomorrow?"

"We'll find out when he gets here."

I was hoping for more. "Rolanda?"

"Yes?"

"You've done a terrific job."

"This case isn't over."

"I wanted to mention it before we get into the chaos tomorrow."

"Thanks, Mike."

Rosie's expression didn't change, but I knew that she was filled with pride. "Let's go through your closing one more time," she said.

Rolanda nodded. "Sure."

* * *

"You look like hell, Mick."

"Thanks, Pete."

My brother, Rosie, and I were sitting in my office at eleven-fifteen on Thursday night. Pete was drinking a Coke. I was tempted to break out the bottle of Jack Daniel's that I kept in my bottom drawer, but I opted for a Diet Dr Pepper. We were due in court in less than eleven hours.

I spoke to Rosie. "Thanks for helping Rolanda with her closing."

"She'll do fine."

"She's very good."

"I know. She's learning from the best."

"Did she go home?"

"Not yet. I'm going to give her a ride in a few minutes. Anything else I can do?"

"Not tonight."

She looked at Pete. "Did you find anything?"

My brother scowled. "Not really."

"Is there a 'but' coming?"

"I talked to a couple of Isabel's friends and got onto her Facebook and Instagram again."

I didn't feel compelled to ask him how he managed to do it. "And?"

"Seems her father doesn't like her boyfriend. For that matter, he didn't like her past couple of boyfriends."

Rosie and I exchanged a knowing look. We hadn't always been ecstatic about Grace's boyfriends, either. "Any idea why?" she asked.

"Among other things, they were all Vietnamese."

"So?"

"Ortega has a problem with Vietnamese."

"Do you know why?"

"No. Maybe it has something to do with the time he spent in Vietnam. Maybe he doesn't like the Vietnamese gangs who give him grief at the store. Or maybe he doesn't like the fact that his daughter is dating a Vietnamese guy."

"How does this relate to our case?"

"Duc Tho was Vietnamese."

"You think it's more than coincidence?"

"Just saying."

Rosie turned to me. "Is Isabel on our witness list?"

"Yes, but we weren't planning to have her testify."

She looked at Pete. "Can you have one of your people serve her with papers to appear in court tomorrow?"

"At this hour?"

"First thing in the morning."

"Sure. Are you going to call her?"

"I don't know."

"What's the point?"

"Maybe it will rattle her father."

Pete smiled. "If one of my operatives shows up with a summons for her, you can bet that it will get his attention."

* * *

Rosie returned to my office a few minutes later. "I need your help, Mike."

"Are you okay?"

"I'm fine, but Rolanda just threw up. She's in a lot of pain. I think we'd better take her to the emergency room."

Crap. I glanced at Pete. "You help Rosie and Rolanda. I'll get the car."

58
"IT'S THE RIGHT THING TO DO"

"She's going to be fine," Rosie said, relieved.

"Did her appendix rupture?" I asked.

"No. They caught it just in time."

Rosie, Pete, and I were standing in an otherwise empty waiting room at St. Francis Hospital at three-thirty on Friday morning. The TV was showing a replay of the Giants game, the sound off. Rosie's brother was staying with Rolanda. The emergency appendectomy had gone well. Rosie reported that Rolanda would probably go home tomorrow. The miracles of modern medicine.

"How's she feeling?" I asked.

"Tired."

"And your brother?"

"Relieved. Rolanda is disappointed that she won't be able to do her closing today."

"That's the last thing I'm worried about. We'll get an extension."

"Judge McDaniel hasn't given you any breaks."

"She'll understand."

"I have another suggestion." She flashed an impish smile. "Let me do it."

"Are you serious?"

"Yes."

"I can't let you."

"I want to."

"You aren't prepared."

"Yes, I am. I've heard most of the testimony. I prepped Rolanda for her closing."

"I'll deal with it, Rosie."

"I can do it better, Mike."

Probably true. "I'm Thomas's great-uncle."

"And I'm his great-aunt—well, sort of."

"This isn't about nepotism."

"It's *all* about nepotism. You wouldn't have taken this case if Thomas wasn't your great-nephew. And I wouldn't be suggesting this if I wasn't Rolanda's aunt. It's the right thing to do. I'm more prepared than you are."

"We'll get an extension and let Rolanda handle it."

"I'm not letting her near a courtroom for at least a month." She held up a finger. "That part is also nepotism. She's my niece before she's my employee. Besides, it makes sense from a strategic standpoint to let me do this."

"How do you figure?"

"If we win, I'll take credit. If we lose, we'll argue on appeal that Thomas wasn't represented by competent counsel."

"You're competent."

"But I'm unprepared."

"You just said that you're more prepared than I am."

"I am, but we won't mention it on appeal."

Rosie. I lowered my voice. "You miss being in court, don't you?"

"Maybe a little."

"You really want to do this?"

"Yes."

"Fine with me."

"Great."

"You realize that Jerry Edwards will try to nail you."

"Politics is a contact sport. I can handle him."

"It may cost you some votes on election day."

She gave me a dismissive wave. "The election is more than a month from now. People have short memories." She waited a beat. "You should probably let me handle Thomas's direct exam, too."

"I love you, Rosita."

"Let's not get sentimental, Mike. We need to prepare for trial."

Pete smiled at Rosie. "First you say that we shouldn't take the case. Then you say that you won't help. Now you want to do the direct exam of the defendant and the closing. You lawyers will take any side of any argument, won't you?"

Rosie grinned. "Any lawyer can take any side. Exceptional lawyers win no matter what side they take."

"I stand corrected."

I glanced at my watch. "Maybe we should go home and get some sleep."

Rosie's eyes gleamed. "Sleep is overrated. I'm not leaving until Rolanda wakes up. We can prepare here."

"We're due back in court in six hours. You're the one who told me that we aren't as young as we used to be."

"We aren't *that* old, Mike."

59
"I'M GOING TO PLAY A HUNCH"

Thomas tugged at the necktie that I had helped him put on a few minutes earlier. His voice was tentative as he sat in the witness box at ten o'clock on Friday morning. "I was just sitting in the car."

Rosie stood directly in front of him. Her perfect makeup, stylish hair, and flawless attire provided no hint that she had arrived from St. Francis Hospital fifteen minutes earlier. It was a reminder that trials are theatrical productions where casting, costumes, and script are critically important. It also helps to have a superstar playing the lead.

Rosie worked without notes. "Thomas, you and Duc were friends, weren't you?"

"Yes."

"You were going to a party on the night of December fourteenth of last year?"

"Yes."

Ideally, Rosie would have been asking open-ended questions to elicit thoughtful and sympathetic answers that would have built empathy with the jury. Unfortunately, that wasn't going to work for Thomas, so we told him to follow Rosie's lead and keep his answers short. True to form, he had quickly reverted to his habit of staring down as he spoke.

Rosie's tone was patient. "You drove that night?"

"No, Duc did."

"And you decided to stop at Alcatraz Liquors?"

"Yes. Duc was going to buy beer for the party."

"That's the only reason he went inside the store?"

"Objection," Erickson said. "Calls for speculation as to Mr.

Tho's state of mind."

"I'll rephrase," Rosie said. "Did you and Duc discuss what he would buy at Alcatraz Liquors?"

Thomas finally looked up. "Yes. Beer."

"Did he mention anything about robbing the store?"

"No."

"You knew Duc pretty well, didn't you?"

"Yes."

"You also knew that he was expelled from Galileo for selling drugs, didn't you?"

"Yes."

There was no reason for Thomas to lie to protect his friend's reputation.

"Thomas, did Duc own a gun?"

"Yes."

"Do you know what kind?"

"A handgun. I don't know the model."

"Do you know where he got it?"

"A guy on the street."

"Do you know where he kept it?"

"No."

"Did he have it with him that night?"

"No."

"Are you sure?"

"Yeah."

"How can you be so sure?"

"You don't bring a gun to a party."

"You were sitting right next to him in the car when you went to Alcatraz Liquors, right?"

"Yes."

"Did you see a gun?"

"No."

"Did you go inside the store?"

"No. I was just sitting in the car."

His delivery was a little wooden, but fine in the circumstances.

Rosie glanced my way and I closed my eyes. "No further questions," she said."

"Cross exam, Mr. Erickson?"

"Just a couple of questions."

Stay the course, Thomas.

Erickson remained seated. "Mr. Nguyen, in addition to being expelled from high school, you knew that Duc Tho had been arrested several times, right?"

"Yes."

"And you knew that he owned a gun, right?"

"Right."

"And you were sitting right next to him in the car that night, weren't you?"

"Yes."

"Yet he never mentioned robbing the store?"

"No."

"And he never mentioned his gun?"

"No."

"And you claim that you didn't see a gun even though you were less than a foot away from him?"

"Yes."

"You're absolutely sure?"

"Objection," Rosie said. "Asked and answered."

"Sustained."

Erickson stood up and took a couple of steps toward Thomas. "You know that the police found a handgun under Mr. Tho's body, right?"

"Yes."

"Was it the same one that you mentioned a moment ago?"

"I don't know."

Erickson's tone turned strident. "Come on, Mr. Nguyen. Your friend was a drug dealer who owned a gun. You knew that he was going to rob the store that night, didn't you?"

"No."

"And you knew that he had a gun, didn't you?"

"No."

"Do you expect anybody in this courtroom to believe you?"

"Objection. Argumentative."

"Sustained."

"No further questions."

Thomas had held his own. His grandpa would have been proud.

Judge McDaniel spoke to Rosie. "Any more witnesses, Ms. Fernandez?"

"Just one, Your Honor. The defense calls Isabel Cruz."

The judge's expression indicated that we had caught her by surprise.

I whispered to Rosie, "What are you doing?"

"I'm going to play a hunch."

60
"HE SMILED"

The bailiff's tone was subdued. "Please state your name for the record."

"Isabel Cruz." Her voice was quiet, but steady.

"What is your occupation?"

She touched the sleeve of her school uniform and glanced at her parents, who were sitting behind the prosecution table. We had agreed to let them watch Isabel's testimony even though they were on our witness list. "I'm a junior at Mercy High School."

The judge invoked a maternal voice. "Isabel, I'm Judge Betsy McDaniel. I expect people in my courtroom to treat everyone with respect—especially our witnesses. If you're wondering if you have to answer a question or if you'd like to take a break, I want you to let me know and I will stop the proceedings. Does that sound okay to you?"

"Yes."

The judge shifted her gaze from Erickson to Rosie and me. "You understand my ground rules?"

We answered in unison. "Yes, Your Honor."

"Good." She turned to Isabel. "Ms. Fernandez is representing Thomas Nguyen. She's going to ask you some questions. She has assured me that you'll be back in school by lunch. Okay?"

"Okay."

"And you understand that you're under oath, which means that you must tell the truth?"

"Yes."

"Please proceed, Ms. Fernandez."

"Thank you, Your Honor. May I approach the witness?"

"Yes."

The courtroom was silent as Rosie walked to the front of the witness box. Out of the corner of my eye, I could see Ortega Cruz and his ex-wife in the gallery. Maria's hands were clasped, eyes looking reassuringly at her daughter. Ortega was seething.

Rosie put her hand on the rail. "I'm Rosie Fernandez."

Isabel nodded. "I know. I've seen you on TV."

Rosie smiled. "May I call you Isabel?"

"Sure."

"Isabel, I need to ask you a few questions about what happened at your father's store on the night of December fourteenth of last year. I know this may be hard, so I want you to take your time and do the best you can."

"I didn't see anything."

"Okay." Rosie didn't move. "You were at the store when Duc Tho came inside, right?"

"Yes."

"How long had you been there when he entered?"

"About an hour." Isabel explained that she had gone to a movie with a friend, who had dropped her off at the store. "My dad was going to drive me home."

"Where were you when Mr. Tho entered the store?"

"Sitting at my father's desk."

"That's in the alcove behind the deli case?"

"Yes."

"What were you doing?"

"Chemistry homework."

"Are you planning to go to college after you graduate?"

"Yes."

"Good." Rosie held up a reassuring hand. "I understand that your father, your brother, and your cousin were also in the store."

"They were."

"Had you ever seen Duc Tho before?"

"I don't think so."

"Did you see him enter the store?"

"No."

"Because you were looking at your chemistry book, right?"

"Right."

"Your father told us that Duc Tho entered the store, turned to face the counter, flashed a gun, and demanded money. Did you see any of it?"

"Not really."

"Maybe a little?"

Isabel looked at her father, who frowned. "No," she decided.

"Would you like some water?"

"Yes, please."

Rosie poured a cup of water and handed it to her. "More?"

"No, thank you."

Rosie placed the pitcher on the table next to the stand. "So, you didn't see Duc Tho come inside the store?"

"No."

"But you might have seen him when he turned to face the cash register, right?"

Another glance at Ortega. "No, I didn't."

"Maybe out of the corner of your eye?"

"Maybe."

"Did he say anything?"

"Not to me."

"To your dad?"

"I don't remember."

"He didn't say 'Gimme the money' or 'This is a robbery'?"

"I didn't hear anything."

"Did he look at you?"

"He might have."

"What did he do when he looked at you?"

"He smiled." She quickly corrected herself. "At least I think he did."

"Were you afraid?"

"Not really."

"Did you see him reach for a gun?"

"No."

"Did you hear him ask for money?"

"No."

Rosie's tone remained even. "What happened next?"

"My father yelled for us to get down."

"Then what?"

"I got under the desk."

"Then what?"

"He shot him."

"That must have been scary."

"It was."

Rosie pushed out a sigh. "Did you see him shoot Duc Tho?"

"No. I was under the desk."

"Did you hear the shots?"

"Yes."

"How long did you stay under the desk?"

"Until my dad said it was okay to come out."

Rosie paused to let Isabel gather herself.

Judge McDaniel quickly filled the void. "Any further questions, Ms. Fernandez?"

Rosie looked in my direction as if to ask whether it was enough. I scratched my nose. It was the signal to wrap up. I saw the look in her eyes indicating that she wasn't quite finished. Then she crossed her fingers. It was the sign we had used since we were rookie public defenders. She was going to follow her instincts.

Rosie scanned the courtroom for a long moment. Finally,

she turned to Isabel and spoke softly. "Did you know that I have a daughter about your age?"

"No." Isabel didn't know where Rosie was heading.

"You remind me of her. She's in college at USC."

Isabel didn't know what to do, so she shrugged.

Erickson spoke from his seat. "Your Honor, I fail to see any relevance here."

Neither did I.

He added, "As far as I can tell, Ms. Fernandez didn't ask Ms. Cruz a question."

She hadn't.

Rosie addressed the judge in a tone that she might have used while they were having coffee at Peet's after Pilates class. "I'm getting to my point."

"Make it fast, Ms. Fernandez."

"Yes, Your Honor." She turned back to Isabel. "Do you have a boyfriend?"

Erickson was on his feet again. "Objection. Relevance."

Rosie's tone turned lawyerly. "I will show relevance in just a moment."

"I'll give you a little leeway, Ms. Fernandez, but you'd better get there very soon."

"Yes, Your Honor." Rosie smiled at Isabel and repeated her question. "Do you have a boyfriend?"

"Yes."

"What's his name?"

"Henry Minh."

"How long have you been together?"

"About six months."

Erickson was still standing. "I must object, Your Honor. There isn't a shred of relevance."

Rosie held up a hand. "There will be in a moment."

"Get to the point now, Ms. Fernandez."

"Yes, Your Honor." She inched closer to the witness box.

"Isabel, my daughter has a boyfriend, too."

No, she doesn't.

"Grace's boyfriend is a good guy. I like him a lot." In response to my inquisitive look, Rosie gave me a glance that said, "Trust me." "Does your father like your boyfriend?"

Isabel darted another glance at Ortega. "Yes."

"That's great. Because we haven't always been ecstatic about all of Grace's boyfriends. I'll bet maybe your dad hasn't always been so happy about some of your boyfriends, either, right?"

"Maybe a little."

"But he was always polite around them, right? Even if he didn't like them?"

"Right."

"And even if their background was a little different from yours, right?"

"Right."

"Because your dad's store is in a neighborhood where there are people of a lot of different nationalities, right?"

"Right."

"So he must be pretty understanding if, say, you brought home a boyfriend of another nationality or religion, right?"

"For the most part."

It was a more equivocal answer than I expected. Kids are lousy liars.

Rosie was standing right in front of Isabel where she was blocking her father's view. "You probably don't know this, but Grace's father—my ex-husband—used to be a priest. He didn't like it when she dated boys who weren't Catholic. You know what I mean?"

"Sort of."

"But your father didn't have a problem with Henry just because he is Vietnamese, right?"

"Right."

Rosie responded with a puzzled look. "Maybe a little?"

A hesitation. "Maybe."

"But he got over it when he got to know Henry, right?"

"It took him a little while."

"But he came around, right?"

"For the most part." She reconsidered. "Yes, he did."

I saw where Rosie was going.

Rosie's tone turned serious. "Parents are very protective—especially fathers, right?"

"Right."

"Isabel, did your father dislike Henry because he's Vietnamese?"

A hesitation. "Kind of."

"Does your father have a problem with Vietnamese people?"

Another pause. "Maybe a little."

"Maybe it's because he works in a neighborhood where there are a lot of Vietnamese people, right? And when he has problems at his store—like somebody trying to rob him—it's probably a Vietnamese person who has given him trouble, right?"

"Right."

"Maybe that's why your father wasn't so happy when you started going out with Henry."

"Maybe."

"Maybe your father was unhappy when a young Vietnamese man came into his store and smiled at you, right?"

"I don't know."

"Did he tell you not to date Vietnamese boys?"

Isabel was starting to cry. "Yes."

"I think your father was unhappy because you were going out with a Vietnamese boy. In fact, it's the third Vietnamese boy that you've dated in the past two years, isn't it?"

"Yes, but—,"

"I think your father shot Duc Tho because he didn't like the way that he looked at you."

"Not really. I mean no."

"He was already angry because you were dating a Vietnamese boy, wasn't he?"

"Sort of. I mean no."

"Did he ever threaten one of your boyfriends?"

"No."

"But he made it clear where he stood, right?"

"Yes."

Erickson finally stopped them. "Objection, Your Honor. This is outrageous. Ms. Fernandez's line of questioning is pure speculation."

Yes, it was.

"Furthermore, Thomas Nguyen is on trial here, not Ortega Cruz."

"Maybe he should be," Rosie said. Her eyes locked onto mine for an instant, then she turned back to the judge. "Your Honor, we would like to request a meeting in chambers."

"For what purpose?"

"To make a motion."

61
"INSTINCT"

Judge McDaniel drummed her fingers on her desk. "What's this about, Ms. Fernandez?"

Rosie's tone was respectful. "I think you know, Your Honor."

"It needs to come from you."

"Based up on the testimony that we just heard from Isabel Cruz, we now have evidence that her father was predisposed to dislike young Vietnamese men—especially if they showed any interest in his daughter. It proves that Ortega Cruz had independent criminal intent to shoot Duc Tho when he came inside his store."

Erickson's tone was incredulous. "You're saying that Ortega murdered Tho?"

"It's up to you to decide on the charge."

"He acted in self-defense."

"No, he didn't. We have introduced evidence that Tho did not, in fact, demand money. We have cast substantial doubt upon Ortega's claim that Tho was carrying a gun when he entered the store. We already know from the video that Tho never pulled a gun—if he was carrying."

"His fingerprints were on the gun."

"Which could have been planted." Rosie turned and spoke to the judge. "There was no provocative act when Tho came inside the store. As a result, under California law *as written*, Thomas Nguyen cannot be guilty of felony murder."

"Do you wish to make a motion, Ms. Fernandez?"

"We do, Your Honor." She pointed at me.

"Your Honor," I said, "the defense moves that all charges

against our client be dropped as a matter of law."

"Do you wish to say anything, Mr. Erickson?"

"Ortega Cruz admitted that he shot Duc Tho in self-defense. He testified that Tho came into the store, demanded money, and threatened him with a gun—even if he didn't take it out of his pocket. A gun was found under Tho's body—with his fingerprints. That's more than enough evidence to conclude that Tho engaged in a provocative act. At the very least, it's an issue of fact that should be left to the jury to decide."

Judge McDaniel pushed out a sigh. "I find Ms. Fernandez's arguments more persuasive than yours, Mr. Erickson. I don't know if there is sufficient evidence to bring charges against Ortega Cruz for murder or even manslaughter. That's up to you. On the other hand, I believe that the defense has now provided sufficient evidence to question Mr. Cruz's motives. Moreover, there is substantial doubt that Mr. Tho engaged in a provocative act under California law. I am therefore ruling that as a matter of law, the felony murder rule does not apply to the actions—or, more precisely, the inactions—of Thomas Nguyen. As a result, the defense motion is granted and the charges are dismissed."

My heart beat faster. "Thank you, Your Honor."

"We're done. I'm going to dismiss our jury."

* * *

"I don't think Erickson is going to invite me to a ballgame anytime soon," I said.

Rosie chuckled. "He'll get over it. I don't think he was crazy about the felony murder charge in the first place. It was probably Ward's idea. There will be other cases. We'll all need to work together constructively."

"Spoken like a diplomat."

She arched an eyebrow. "Or a politician."

We were sitting at the defense table in the otherwise empty courtroom. Thomas and Melinda had gone home to celebrate.

Rosie was in a philosophical mood. I was dead tired.

"Were you able to reach Rolanda?" I asked.

"Briefly. She's doing fine and going home tomorrow. I told her that we would come over and see her this afternoon. She was pleased with the result."

"She's going to be an excellent lawyer."

"She's *already* an excellent lawyer." Rosie closed her briefcase. "Were you able to talk to any of the jurors before they left?"

"A couple. They were happy to go home and relieved that they didn't have to make a decision."

"Any hint on which way they were leaning?"

"The woman from Verizon said she would have been hard-pressed to vote for a conviction. The Google guy was leaning our way."

"At the very least, it sounds like we would have ended up with a hung jury." She smiled. "Of course, if I had been given an opportunity to do my closing, I would have convinced them to vote for an acquittal."

"Quite right. Do you think Ortega shot Tho because he smiled at his daughter?"

"Don't know. Don't care. Doesn't matter."

"You didn't answer my question."

"Could be. We didn't need to prove it. We just had to argue it." She took a deep breath. "I feel bad for Isabel. It's hard being a teenager. It was bad enough that she was there when her father shot Tho. She didn't want any part of this."

"You think Ortega shot Tho?"

"Yes. Do you?"

I nodded. "Yes. Do you think they'll press charges?"

"I doubt it." Rosie looked over at the empty seat where Ortega had been sitting. "Ortega left court without a police escort. Nobody was in a hurry to arrest him. If they do, it will be tough to prove murder or even manslaughter beyond a reasonable doubt. He'll say he acted in self-defense."

"He'll probably win that argument. His son and nephew will corroborate his self-defense story."

She arched an eyebrow. "Is there any doubt in your mind that Tho walked in with a gun?"

"Nope."

"Me neither." She stood up. "We'll let Ward and Erickson decide if they're going to press charges. For now, our work is done."

"I was surprised that Judge McDaniel ruled in our favor."

"I wasn't. Betsy thinks the felony murder rule is a joke."

"Why did she keep ruling against us?"

"Because she's a good judge. She put aside her personal views and applied the law as it's written. That's what judges are supposed to do. This morning, we finally gave her a legitimate legal basis to rule for us."

"She could have let the jury decide."

"Juries are unpredictable. She wanted to resolve the case herself."

"How do you know?"

"I don't. I'll ask her about it at Pilates next week."

Rosie. "How did you know that Isabel would say that her father didn't like her Vietnamese boyfriend?"

"Instinct. Fathers never like their daughters' boyfriends. And it wasn't *my* instinct. It was Rolanda's."

I wasn't surprised. "Let's go see her."

"I just texted her that we're on our way."

"Do you have time for a celebratory drink afterward?"

"I'll have to take a raincheck, Mike. I have a fundraiser tonight."

62
"HAPPY BIRTHDAY, TOMMY"

The newly elected Public Defender of the City and County of San Francisco squeezed my hand. "Are you okay?" Rosie asked.

My white dress shirt was sticking to my body in the stifling heat. "I'll be fine."

"It's okay to cry."

"The first thing they teach you at the seminary is that a priest can't cry at a funeral."

I inhaled the tropical air as I looked up at the mature trees forming a canopy over us. Six weeks had passed since Thomas's trial had ended. At noon on November 25th, a dozen of us were standing in a semi-circle near the stump of a bamboo tree outside a village called Cib Tran Quang, fifty miles southeast of Haiphong. The old dirt road was now paved. The huts had been replaced by cabins with indoor plumbing and electricity. A gate marked the entrance to the cemetery. The soil around the stump had been freshly raked and was cordoned off by metal stakes adorned in red ribbons.

I turned to Melinda. "It's just the way you described it."

"It's just the way that I remembered it."

"Today would have been your father's sixtieth birthday."

"I know." My niece was stoic as she turned to Thomas, who was wearing a gray suit. "That's where we buried your grandparents. I'm sorry that you never got to meet them."

Grace, Pete, Tommy, Big John, and I were standing to Rosie's left. Tommy looked stylish in a navy suit. Grace wore a white blouse and a black skirt. Her eyes were filled with tears. Pete was wearing a suit for the first time since our mother had died almost ten years earlier. Big John stood with his arms folded, sunglasses covering his eyes.

I motioned at a razor-thin man standing at attention next to the stump. He was wearing a Vietnamese Army dress uniform. His breast was covered with medals. On either side of him stood two soldiers of lesser rank, also in dress uniforms. Each of them held a white urn.

The three soldiers stepped forward and marched over in unison and stopped in front of us. The ranking soldier spoke to me in American English.

"Mr. Daley, I am General Hoang. On behalf of the Vietnamese government, we wish to express our deepest condolences to you and your family. We are very sorry for your loss."

"Thank you, General." My eyes filled with tears. "We are very grateful for your efforts in helping us resolve this matter after so many years."

"The war ended a long time ago, Mr. Daley."

And after forty long years, it was finally over for our family.

"Mr. Daley," he continued, "as in most cultures, it is contrary to our customs to disturb the remains of the deceased. However, in this instance, and at the request of the families, we made an exception." He motioned toward his two subordinates, who stepped forward. "We are honored to present these remains to you. Our scientists were able to uncover some bone fragments with the DNA of Sergeant Thomas James Charles Daley, Jr. and Ms. Lily Ho. We also found a gold filling that matched the dental records of your brother."

"Thank you."

"We wanted to inform you that we have examined the records of this village, and we have determined that Sergeant Daley and Ms. Ho were married here on August twenty-third, nineteen seventy-five. Their daughter, Xuan, was born on July fourteenth, nineteen seventy-six. We will try to provide additional details in due course."

One of the soldiers handed me an urn holding Tommy's remains. The other soldier handed the second urn to Melinda. Tears streamed down her face as she thanked them.

General Hoang stepped back and saluted us. Then he and his subordinates marched over to the area near the gravesite and stood at attention.

A procession walked toward us from the opposite side of the gravesite. The senior senator of the State of California was flanked by her husband and a U.S. Marine colonel in her dress uniform. The colonel held an American flag, folded in the traditional triangle shape. The senator and her husband shook hands with each of us. The soldier presented the flag to me and saluted.

The senator spoke in a somber tone. "On behalf of the United States of America, we are very grateful for your brother's service to our country and his sacrifice. We are also very sorry for your family's loss."

"Thank you."

"When we return to San Francisco, we have made arrangements for your brother's burial with full military honors."

"He would have liked that."

The senator lowered her voice. "I remember your brother, Mr. Daley. I saw him play at St. Ignatius and Cal. He was an outstanding football player and a fine young man. I'm sure you have wonderful memories."

"We do."

The senator shook my hand. So did her husband. The Marine saluted me. I struggled to maintain my composure as the memories came flooding back in the middle of the Vietnamese jungle.

Pete came over and put a hand on my shoulder. "You're the

ex-priest, Mick. You should say something."

I thought about Tommy throwing the football in our backyard. I remembered the celebration at our house after St. Ignatius won the city championship. I recalled the pride in my father's eyes when he signed the letter of intent to play at Cal. I remembered my mother's anguish when he boarded the plane to Vietnam. And the horrible night when the Marines appeared on our doorstep to report that he had gone missing. In my search for answers, I decided to become a priest. A few years later, I didn't find those answers and decided to go to law school. After almost four decades, I was finally getting an opportunity to give Tommy the goodbye that he had always deserved.

"Gather around," I said. "I want everybody to hold hands. I'm going to keep this short because it's hot. And because that's what Tommy would have wanted."

We formed a semi-circle in front of the stump. I placed the urn holding Tommy's remains along with the flag on the small table in front of us. Melinda put the urn holding her mother's remains next to Tommy's. I closed my eyes and took a deep breath. Then I struggled to find the right words.

"We have gathered here today after too many years to celebrate the lives and pay our respects to Tommy Daley and Lily Ho. Tommy was a wonderful son and brother. We now know that he was also a beloved husband, father, and grandfather. Lily was a cherished daughter, wife, mother, and grandmother. I never had the privilege of meeting her, but I now know that she and her mother saved Tommy's life. That makes her a hero. I am profoundly grateful that she was a member of our family. And that she and Tommy blessed us with Melinda and Thomas."

I spent a moment talking about Tommy's all-too-short life. The son. The brother. The football hero. The war hero. "He was also my hero. And my best friend."

Tears were running down Big John's cheeks. Pete's eyes were closed as he rocked back and forth.

I let go of Rosie's hand and put my arm around her. She hugged me and held me close.

I looked at the table with the two urns and the American flag. "Tommy and Lily, we know that you are in heaven with our Mom and Dad. We're sorry that it took us so long to give you a proper sendoff, but we hope that we've done right by you today. We love both of you and we miss you terribly. We can't bring you back, but now we can bring you home. In the name of the Father, the Son and the Holy Spirit, may God bless you and look after you and all of those who love you. And may you rest in eternal peace."

I looked over at Big John, who responded with an approving nod.

As we started to walk away, I turned back and looked at the stump of the old bamboo tree where my brother had been buried almost four decades earlier. I felt the lump in my throat when I whispered, "Happy birthday, Tommy."

* * *

"What are you listening to?" Rosie asked.

I took off my earbuds and heard the roar of the 777. "Leonard Cohen's 'Hallelujah.'"

"Seems fitting."

"I thought so. Where are we?"

"Somewhere between Guam and Hawaii."

"How much longer?"

"Another six hours." She reached over and took my hand. "You spoke beautifully."

"Thank you." I squeezed her hand. "The kids were good."

"They're good kids."

"It was a long way to go for a memorial service for an uncle they'd never met."

"They've heard a lot about your brother. And our Tommy

wanted to know more about the guy he was named after." She glanced at Big John, who was dozing in the seat across the aisle. "Is he okay?"

"Yeah."

"He took it hard."

"Tommy was his first nephew—and his favorite. My mom was his only sister. And my dad was his best friend."

"I wish I had met your brother."

"You would have liked him."

"You miss him, don't you?"

"Every day."

"I wish your parents could have been here."

"So do I."

We sat in silence for a moment. Then Rosie—beautiful Rosie—smiled at me. "What's the first thing you want to do when we get home?"

"I'd like to get a cheeseburger and a chocolate shake at Bill's Place. It was Tommy's favorite restaurant when we were kids."

"Done. Anything else?"

I touched her cheek. "I'd like to spend more time with you."

"Now that you're working for me, that's inevitable."

"Sounds good to me."

"We'll need to be careful of our anti-nepotism rules."

"We'll work around them. Still glad you decided to become a politician?"

"So far. Ask me again in five years."

"I will."

"Do you think you can handle being head of the Felony Division without me?"

"Absolutely. And if I need your help, I know where to find you in your fancy new office down the hall." I lowered my voice. "Thanks for helping with Thomas's case. We couldn't have done it without you."

"You're welcome."

"It was fun to be back in court, wasn't it?"

"Yes."

"Are you going to be able to try any cases now that you're a big-shot politician?"

"Maybe once or twice a year." She touched my cheek. "What did you have in mind when you said that you wanted to spend more time with me?"

"Instead of staying at your place twice a week, I'd like to stay three times a week. If all goes well, we can think about increasing it to four days a week."

She grinned. "You think that's a good idea?"

"It's a great idea." I held her hand tightly. "I love you, Rosie."

"I love you, too, Mike."

ACKNOWLEDGMENTS

Writing stories is a collaborative process. I would like to thank many kind people who have been very generous with their time.

Thanks to my beautiful wife, Linda, who still reads all of my manuscripts and keeps me going when I'm stuck. You are a kind and generous soul and I am very grateful.

Thanks to our twin sons, Alan and Stephen, for your support and encouragement for so many books. I am more proud of you than you can imagine.

Thanks to my teachers, Katherine Forrest and Michael Nava, who told me that I should try to finish my first book. Thanks to the Every Other Thursday Night Writers Group: Bonnie DeClark, Meg Stiefvater, Anne Maczulak, Liz Hartka, Janet Wallace and Priscilla Royal. Thanks to Bill and Elaine Petrocelli, Kathryn Petrocelli, and Karen West at Book Passage.

Thanks to my friends and colleagues at Sheppard, Mullin, Richter & Hampton (and your spouses and significant others). I can't mention everybody, but I'd like to note those of you with whom I've worked the longest: Randy and Mary Short, Cheryl Holmes, Chris and Debbie Niels, Bob Thompson, Joan Story and Robert Kidd, Donna Andrews, Phil and Wendy Atkins-Pattenson, Julie and Jim Ebert, Geri Freeman and David Nickerson, Ed and Valerie Lozowicki, Bill and Barbara Manierre, Betsy McDaniel, Tom Nevins, Ron and Rita Ryland, Bob Stumpf, Mike Wilmar, Mathilde Kapuano, Guy Halgren, Aline Pearl, Jack Connolly, Ed Graziani, Julie Penney, and Larry Braun. A big thanks to Jane Gorsi for your incomparable editing skills.

A huge thanks to Vilaska Nguyen of the San Francisco

Public Defender's Office. If I ever get in trouble, I will call you first.

Thanks to Jerry and Dena Wald, Gary and Marla Goldstein, Ron and Betsy Rooth, Debbie and Seth Tanenbaum, Joan Lubamersky, Tom Bearrows and Holly Hirst, Julie Hart, Burt Rosenberg, Ted George, Phil Dito, Sister Karen Marie Franks, Brother Stan Sobczyk, Jim Schock, George Fong, Chuck and Nora Koslosky, Jack Goldthorpe, Christa Carter, Scott Pratt, Bob Dugoni, and John Lescroart. Thanks to Lauren, Gary and Debbie Fields.

Thanks to Tim and Kandi Durst, Bob and Cheryl Easter, and Larry DeBrock at the University of Illinois. Thanks to Kathleen Vanden Heuvel, Bob and Leslie Berring, and Jesse Choper at Boalt Law School.

Thanks as always to Ben, Michelle, Margie and Andy Siegel, Joe, Jan and Julia Garber, Roger and Sharon Fineberg, Jan Harris Sandler, Scott, Michelle, Kim and Sophie Harris, Stephanie and Stanley Coventry, Cathy, Richard and Matthew Falco, and Julie Harris and Matthew, Aiden and Ari Stewart.

ABOUT THE AUTHOR

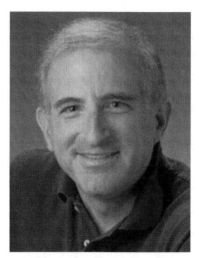

Photo by Sean Casey

Sheldon Siegel is the New York Times and USA Today Bestselling Author of the Mike Daley/Rosie Fernandez series of critically acclaimed courtroom dramas featuring San Francisco criminal defense attorneys Mike Daley and Rosie Fernandez. He is also the author of the thriller novel The Terrorist Next Door featuring Chicago homicide detectives David Gold and A.C. Battle. His books have sold millions of copies worldwide and been translated into a dozen languages. A native of Chicago, Sheldon earned his undergraduate degree from the University of Illinois in Champaign in 1980 and his law degree from Boalt Hall School of Law at UC-Berkeley in 1983. He has been an attorney for more than thirty years, and he specializes in corporate and securities law with the San Francisco office of the international law firm of Sheppard Mullin Richter & Hampton LLP.

Sheldon began writing his first novel, SPECIAL

CIRCUMSTANCES, on a laptop computer during his daily commute on the ferry from Marin County to San Francisco. Sheldon is a San Francisco Library Laureate, a former president of the Northern California chapter and member of the national board of directors of the Mystery Writers of America, and an active member of the International Thriller Writers and Sisters in Crime. His work has been displayed at the Bancroft Library at UC-Berkeley and he has been recognized as a distinguished alumnus of the University of Illinois and a Northern California Super Lawyer.

Sheldon lives in the San Francisco area with his wife, Linda, and their twin sons, Alan and Stephen. He is currently working on his next novel.

Made in the USA
Lexington, KY
30 November 2018